Alpha Song

Books by Maik Nwosu

Novels
Invisible Chapters
Alpha Song
A Gecko's Farewell
The Book of Everything

Poetry
Suns of Kush
Stanzas from the Underground

Short Stories
Return to Algadez

Drama
A Quintet for Dawn

Alpha Song
by
Maik Nwosu

CROSSROADS
New York, 2025

Published by
CROSSROADS
1178 Broadway
3rd Floor, #1333
New York, NY 10001

First paperback edition, Beacon, 2001.
Printed in the United States of America

This is a work of fiction. All names, characters, places, and incidents are products of the author's imagination or are used fictitiously.

ISBN 979-8-9904712-3-8

Library of Congress Control Number: 2024905055

Taneba

Some relationships follow us to our graves. That is the burden of being and memory. It has been so from generation to generation.

After you have read this, my secrets will overtake me. But what does it matter? I am already bound for the world beyond. What more precious legacy can I leave to you, my son, than my most prized possession – my secrets: my memory? At forty-five and "a dead man walking," according to the doctors, secrets are dangerous.

Most probably, you will ask: why this legacy? Apart from the fact that I do not have much else to bequeath to you, you are still too young for me to do much else than leave this record for you. I also hope that my secrets will deepen for you perhaps the greatest lesson I have learned from living: the sun always rises. Sounds simple enough? Yes, it does, but there are many people pampering their lives away because they choose to believe there can ever be a night without daybreak. Always, nature teaches us the truest lessons, and the more man contrives to forsake nature the more he contrives against himself. Even though I loved the night with a single-minded passion, I never forgot that it was a passage into daylight. And vice versa. Everything passes, except perhaps the essence of things.

Do not misunderstand me. I am not about to apologize for my life. I don't even think anyone should, unless he has violated another life. I cannot spit upon myself. I lived my life according to my lights and, in a fashion, according to my night...and day. Life is something we go through searching for a meaning. In the end, we all die from living anyway because life is a terminal disease.

There were some who concluded that because I loved the night very much there must be some evil in me. Often, people rail against that which they dread, that which they do not understand. Not that all things can be understood, but to live with mysteries as revelations certainly is some sort of comprehension. I loved the night because it was in my blood, I preferred to believe, because it uplifted me above the tedium and the treachery of daylight, because I was in love with the love of the night, because I could roar with it. And a roaring decade it was. Every life without a roaring decade seems wasted to me. Tut, I would not want it.

Sometimes, I am amazed at where life has taken me. Ten years of living abroad, two of them in prison. Those two years, tut! But it was in prison that I fell in love with your mother. She was a great woman, and a part of me died with her. I first gave my heart to her before I gave it to the church. You can even say that I gave it to the church because I gave it to her. In the years that we were together, I was a chanting presence in that church. After she died, however, and after I visited home, everything changed. When I returned, I kept my heart to myself. Perhaps, I was full of answers then.

These days, I am full of questions. I have always believed that every man is entitled to three generations of existence: the age of tutelage, that of potency, and of mediation. I have lived only two. Is it then that I come from a lineage fated to die rather young from strange illnesses? My mother's mother, I am told, died in that manner. My mother died of a strange fever. Now, the doctors are gaming with hyphenations and tongue twisters trying to encode what the matter with me is. Whatever it is has already wrecked my immune system and I cannot have much longer to live. Is it the years of hard drinking, of wild partying, of horsing around with the women I have known? And there have been many, very many.

I used to praise God for keeping many of His secrets, the most important ones, to Himself. If man had the secret of air, who would breathe? If man had the secret of the sun, what would rise? If man had the secret of the stars, where would shine? Now, I am not so sure He should have kept so many of His secrets to Himself. It is certainly painful to see that medical science, for all its vaunted advancements, is still fatally imprecise. Perhaps it will always be so, especially as man overtakes the doctors in his ever-experimental lifestyle and his invention of new killers or deaths in the process. But I wander. Those are questions for you to answer. And after you have, there will be new ones. There always will be.

Now, all I can hope for – like my mother before me, like her mother before her – is to depart this world at night, in my bed. Perhaps then I will catch up with it. In that decade, there were three of me: Taneba the father who judged the mayhem of the night, Taneba the son who reveled in its 'vaganza, and Taneba the spirit who descanted its mysteries. Three of me in one person. My united desire was to catch up with the night. But always it was one step ahead. Perhaps now... If I could even choose the hour, I would say: at three o'clock. How they labored in school to teach us that the night ends at midnight! But that is just about half of its lifespan. All the hours between sundown and sunrise sum up the age of the night. I arrived this world at midnight, at the beginning of the high tide of the night, and I would want to leave it at three o'clock – at the beginning of its low tide.

I, Taneba Taneba, son of my mother, this is my last will and testament.

Tamuno

The story of that decade goes back to that New Year's Day when I turned twenty-five. The usually brimming streets of cosmopolitan Lagos had thinned out with people thronging to the countryside to celebrate the Christmas and New Year holidays. If you were not resident in Lagos, however, you might not be able to tell the difference. There were still many people on the streets hurrying to their various destinations or just lounging around. I had no particular place to go, so I belonged to the latter category. At the time, I had been living in Lagos fully for four years – working in the sorting department of the general post office and mainly passing the nights in my uncle's house – my maternal uncle.

Eleven years ago or thereabouts, I had conceived how I would celebrate my twenty-fifth birthday – a swanky party with plenty of food, wine, and women. I would be living in a posh area of Lagos and I would be the proud owner of expensive cars, an uplifting bank account, and a reassuring job or enterprise. At twenty-five, my reality was different.

I was an orphan. In reality, I had been for a long time – since the day, ten years ago, when my mother died. I was her only child. She had been an only child herself, almost. But my father was not. His family was rich in numbers. It was also rich in strife, but it was united in its opposition to the union between my father and my mother. The union was apparently an unwelcome deviation from the tradition of corporate marriages in which one business or political interest married into another and thus strengthened its base or widened its universe. The fact that I was an only child further stiffened the opposition. My father rode the waves, swearing that he would not be dictated to on the subject of whom he would spend his life with and restating severally that he was bound to my mother forever.

"I am tired of yessing along," he thundered. "You know, in my family you either become a rebel or a saint. I will not be a saint in this matter."

I will forever remember that outburst. He had always been fond of whistling, like a man searching for a musical key, so much so that he was known as "the whistler." It seemed to me that he whistled more afterward and ironically paid less attention to my mother. Would she have survived if it had not been so? After she died, he seemed to discover the serial monogamist in him. In five years, he went through two marriages. His family blamed my mother's ghost. Perhaps even his relatives were secretly worried that my mother had freshly been buried when my father remarried. But that did not stop him from traveling from marriage to marriage. At the time he died, he was said to be contemplating a fourth marriage. Cardiac arrest put an end to that, if that was indeed the case. Among his two other wives and his four other children, I was an outsider.

My refuge was my mother's only sibling, who was the postmaster at the general post office. He saw to my university education. But even with him, there were often reminders that I really belonged somewhere else. His wife was more understanding, maybe because of her own family history. So, I reckoned I would last a bit longer in that house. For the holidays, my uncle took his family to the countryside. I had opted to remain in Lagos. I preferred the anonymity of Lagos streets to the even stronger reminders in my maternal home that I should be somewhere else as my father's inheritor – locked in battle with his wives and other children.

Shortly after my father's death, his family had made its leaning on the matter clear through a front-page newspaper announcement: "The Brass family of Kaiama Creek has noted diverse claims, including those yet to be expressly stated, to the legacy of Chief Elias Brass. The Brass family recognizes only the claim of Madam Antonia Brass and her two male children, all of Kaiama Creek Incorporated. The Brass family spans a long period in history, right down to the source of the seas, and it is prepared to take any action to safeguard this noble lineage. All bogus claimants are therefore warned to channel their energy into more profitable ventures."

Even before the advertisement, I had taken the view that I lost the battle while my father was still alive. He had not stopped his first other wife from demonizing me. Besides, moving from one marriage to another, he had created merciless battlefronts. Why then fight for another man's inheritance when I could be my own inheritor? It was at this time that I flung my surname into the sea of sources and renamed myself Taneba Taneba – my first name echoed, for emphasis.

Enough about my father. He should have accounted for his own life. My story of that decade of the night goes back only as far as that New Year's Day when I turned twenty-five and was wandering the streets, all dressed up with nowhere to go. If I could obviously not manage a swanky party, I had contemplated other ways of celebrating this important birthday, which to me marked the beginning of my second generation of existence. After reviewing my options, however, I decided to trust to providence. I did not have any real talent for making friends. I loved people, especially observing them. In the university, where I studied Sociology, my acquaintances had named me Alien because they said I had a manner of self-detachment that worked against close relationships. Of course, they did not know my story – how I had battered my head on the door, wailing to be let into my father's world, but had been locked out. My father again!

Wandering the streets of my neighborhood was not new to me. In my maternal uncle's claustrophobic apartment, bursting from corner to corner with children and maids, I was more or less an absent resident. Usually, I preferred to come home only to sleep. Between the time I must leave the office and the time I must go home, I hung around the streets. I had my favorite spots. There was Isa, the *mai suya*, who had taken a fancy to me and usually had some grilled meat and stories of his exploits in the civil war to entertain me with. There was Silas Peter, who ran a sundown pepper soup joint. There was Yellow, who haunted the streets, especially the region of the public telephone booths.

But the place I was most often to be found was a restaurant by the main entrance to the neighborhood. Its owner was a Senegalese woman whom everyone called Mama Senegal. Although she had a matronly appearance, she was not that old – certainly not beyond her early fifties. Her restaurant was open every day of the week, including weekends when loneliness drove me with a whip like a merciless schoolmaster. When Mama was not there, one of her two beautiful daughters kept shop. Even without my expressly asking, she had adopted me. My credit there was beyond question. The restaurant had a good view of the road, which allowed me to indulge my fancy of people-watching. And it was almost opposite the most interesting house in the neighborhood, an architectural wonder that the owner had named January 15.

January 15 was a phenomenon that kept the neighborhood wagging. The date seemed to be a conjuration of the day the blood-feast known as the civil war officially came to an end. It was also that day in the year when the mangling Nigerian military, fleeing from the reality and the ghosts of the civil war, marked the Armed Forces Remembrance Day. Because not many could see a connection between these events and the marbled house, the less imaginative said the date marked the owner's birthday. The more imaginative insisted it signified a death wish: the owner would love to leave this world on a harmattan-swept morning in the middle of the first month of the year. January 15 did indeed keep the neighborhood wagging, especially because if it had an individual owner, no one appeared to know his identity. There were all manners of coming and going at all times of the day and night, in and out of the house, that made this knowledge a simple impossibility.

I concerned myself more with the going and coming than the arguments provoked by various unraveling of the inscrutable meaning of this January 15. When I pondered the name at all, it was to note the house owner's failure of imagination. If he had to name a house for the first month of the year, why not the very first day – the grand New Year's Day when most people walked the streets taller in spirit, elevated by new hopes? Because that was my situation, I presumed it was so with everyone else. And it was not difficult to notice the bounce in almost every step. Pondering how each year usually embodies the cycle of birth and death – dreams in the maternity at the beginning and dreams in the mortuary at the end – I made my way to Mama Senegal's. And then...the unusual happened.

A wide-bodied car exiting from January 15 stopped as I walked past. I paid no heed, not even when the motorized window on the driver's side slid down and a blast of pop music from the car stereo filled the immediate neighborhood. Not until the music was turned down and I heard a voice calling me by a name from another generation: "Alien!" Before I had even turned and focused properly, the tall, fleshy occupant was already out of the car. His smile gleamed against the background of his dark skin and black suit. I was engulfed in an ecstatic embrace and, although I was not skinny, the gusto of it nearly swept me off my feet. My birthday apparition was a presence, an absence to many, from my Sociology class in the university.

His name was Tamuno, and he had been the biggest truant in our class. He missed classes as if doing so was a requirement for obtaining a degree, often staying away from the campus for long periods. Whenever he returned, he had plenty of money to spend and a parade of girls at his beck and call. He was some sort of folk figure in the department. He was credited with the statement: "I'm not a stopwatch student" – in response to a lecturer's fury about his frequent absence. And the statement had spawned a relay of new campus slang expressions. His manner of dressing and general lifestyle aided his being associated with one inner society or the other. Tamuno graffiti, those extolling or mocking or denouncing him, grew into some sort of campus art. So too Tamuno rhymes.

That he had become some sort of campus sport appeared not to bother Tamuno at all. In fact, he seemed to enjoy the popularity or notoriety. He had been registered as a student four years before I was admitted into the university. He stayed long enough to become my classmate in my final year. At best, we were acquaintances – until we were assigned to the same thesis supervisor. From a casual meeting in the lecturer's office, I gradually became his thesis consultant and ended up writing the entire thesis for him. He got an A. I received only a B for my own thesis. I had worked harder for Tamuno than I had done for myself because I sorely needed the money we had agreed on as my fee. I was therefore pained when I received only a fraction of it. Unless you were around a matter of hours or a few days after Tamuno's return, when he threw money around like a pirate home from the seas, all he had to give was his gleam of a smile and his bonhomie. He asked for my address, promising to look me up and settle the debt. I reckoned it was only his good-natured posturing. I told him honestly that I did not know where I would be, because I was then considering not taking up my maternal uncle's invitation to work in the general post office.

"No problem, my brother," he told me easily. "I'll find you, wherever, and I'll pay you back big time." He kissed the gold pendant on his long necklace as some sort of oath, hugged me and bounced away.

All these had since paled in my memory, and I had almost forgotten about Tamuno. He had that sort of overwhelming charisma that is never forgotten entirely. In the sorting department at the post office, I had developed a fond pastime – reading postcards from all over the world. Given the pace of work, it was not an easy hunger to feed. But there were some startling discoveries in those postcards – words and phrases and sentences and whole cards that enlarged my world, flooding it with sunshine and visions of the far country in which I was no longer alone. And I had come across quite a number of postcards that reminded me of Tamuno.

Great news, brother. I've just got my degree from Cambridge. Finally. After doing a hundred spins, and another hundred more. I feel like a king.

All this while, Tamuno lived in that corner of my mind where I never willingly remembered him, but I never really forgot him. And now, like a dream, there we were in the middle of the street hugging each other. He was like a birthday present sent to me from the unlived chapters of my life. And he was dressed for the role. He wore a black suit, a white shirt, and a string tie that made him look like a rock star. The gold necklace was still there, despite the tie, only this time there were two pendants – each struggling to outdo the other in size. And Tamuno now had a ring on every finger, instead of on only one or two, each shining like a gold nugget. All that was missing was a wrap with my name on it: "Happy birthday, Taneba."

"Alien!" he exclaimed in his baritone voice once more. "I told you I would find you, remember? I told you I would find you wherever."

"Sure, but this is certainly a chance meeting."

"Whatever, the great thing is that I found you, brother. Happy New Year."

"Happy New Year to you too."

"So, what are you doing here?"

"Walking the streets. And you?"

"I went to see my friend. He came in last night."

"Your friend, there?"

"Sure, brother. Isn't it a beautiful house?"

"No doubt about it."

I invited him to Mama Senegal's to have a drink with me. Mama Senegal's did not seem like the place to invite the glowing Tamuno to. His appearance even made the place look embarrassingly shabby. But he came along with me easily and greeted everyone familiarly with toothy smiles before we clinked glasses.

"So, what are you up to these days?" he asked me.

"I work in the post office..."

"You what?"

"In the sorting department."

"Don't do it, brother. You should be a professor somewhere. You know what I did? I put up my thesis, the same one we worked on, in my club. People flip through it and tell me I'm a genius. That's what you are, brother, not some postage stamp superintendent or something."

"We are what we become. We are what happens to us." Reflexive quotations from my postcard memory bank.

"You see what I mean? You're a genius. You know what I've decided? I know I owe you, but we're going to forget that fee."

A frown creased my forehead. I still needed the money, and at that moment my excitement at seeing Tamuno was greatly dampened. He noticed.

"Come on, brother, how will that advance you? What I've decided to do is to give you a gold card. I run this nightclub called The Owl. You can come in any time you want – on the house. A genius like you can make some serious connections there. A deal?"

We shook hands on this new accord, because I reckoned that since I was obviously not going to get any money from Tamuno I had better hold on to this dubious offer. In any case, I had previously given up any hope of collecting my fee, of ever seeing him again.

"So, you run a nightclub now?"

"It's one of my departments. I manage the night."

Typical Tamuno extravaganza, I told myself. "What do you mean you manage the night?"

"Anything at all that goes on in the night, brother, anything good, I've got a little finger in it. Anything you want done in the night or anything you want the night to do for you, just whisper to me."

An alarm bell went off in my brain. "You're not in the extermination business?"

"It depends on what you mean, brother."

"You know," I lowered my voice, "murder...and robbery."

"No, that department doesn't exist in my business."

I relaxed. It was a good time to ask him the question the neighborhood had been answering with a hundred tongues.

"Your friend, there, why is his house called January 15?"

"Oh, that. That's the day he made his first big run."

"Meaning?"

I did not like what I was thinking – that the name was some kind of joke which everyone else had taken rather seriously, some sort of memorial to crime in which we had all labored to find nobility.

"Are you also into *runs*?" I asked Tamuno. There had been that rumor in the university.

He pondered me awhile before he answered. "That's not the sort of question I normally answer, brother. But you can say I'm into highs."

When he learned it was my twenty-fifth birthday, he offered to take me on a night tour of Lagos. Although I felt shabby beside him, I blessed him in my heart. And I stepped with him into the night brimming with dreams and renewed faith.

The night had long fascinated me. Although my mother had told me that many other children are also born at midnight and that more children are probably born at night than during the day, I held on to my belief that I had a special pact with the night and its mysteries. The night is like a spirit and usually it possesses different people in different ways, often freeing them from their daytime inhibitions. Growing up in the village world of moonlight tales and night masquerades deepened my perception of the night as the scenic bridge or time of flux between man and the spirits. In that village world, there was a particular night masquerade with a deep voice that appeared only during the full moon. Usually, as it jangled past, invisible to us crouching in our corners of the night, its footsteps sounded to me like a personal invocation: Ta-ne-ba! Ta-ne-ba! Ta-ne-ba! I responded to every invocation, voicelessly. Not surprisingly, my first longing was to join the masquerade cult – especially the cult of the night masquerade, with its heady songs and haunting voices and jangling invocations on the way to and from the heart of mysteries.

The night is also the time for deaths. My mother reckoned that just as many children come into the world at night, so do many people depart from it then. She reasoned that the fact that God *created* light supposed that He came out of the darkness of the night. "That's the only reason why He did not create darkness, because He did not have to." That was also her explanation for the soul travel that takes place through dreams. She prayed to die at night, heralded into heaven by the stars of God. She did. The darkness of the night also invokes its demons – the night marauders who care less for the mysteries of the night than its armory, the head-hunters lurking behind even molecules of the night, and their kindred spirits. Wherever there is a mystery, it seems, mayhem is not far away. I preferred to dwell on mysteries.

And it was that that drew me, and two other schoolmates, to the stream bank one unforgettable night. In the village high school that I attended, there was an evidently thinning stream that the villagers had named after their main market day, Eke. They claimed it filled up on the night before the Eke market day and thinned out afterward. The person that was in part responsible for this phenomenon was a stout, dark-skinned girl who was some sort of priestess or daughter of the stream. She was known as Ada Eke and was said to disappear into the depths of the stream on the night before Eke, thus causing the stream to rise; her reemergence caused it to begin to thin out. The promised spectacle was so inviting that we ignored all warnings and sneaked out of school one night to witness it. Hiding in the bush beside the stream was easy. What was disturbingly difficult was reasoning with our fears and controlling our heartbeats.

Our first jolt was that in the half-hour or so before midnight, Ada Eke – clad only in a wrapper – actually came along. Despite our desire for spectacle, we had half-hoped that she would not. She walked up and down the stream bank for a while, muttering to herself like someone unhinged. In my enlarging eyes, I thought I even noticed her foaming at the mouth. In the state I was in, it would not have taken much for me to see elephants coming out of her ears.

When she was through with her muttering, she removed her wrapper with one deft move. Then, she waded into the edge of the stream and began to bathe. It was the very first time, after puberty, that I would see a naked woman. I was afraid my eyes would pop out of their sockets, but there was a tingling, stiffening sensation in my being that kept me rooted to where I was. She was not beautiful, but she was quite voluptuous. And from where I was hiding, I could have pounced on her rippling buttocks with one leap.

Did we imagine it, or did it actually happen? Her bath appeared to consist of her scooping water into her private region with obvious pleasure. I do not know with any certainty where our imagination outpaced the reality. Did she actually make love to the water, or vice versa? When she finally tied her wrapper again and departed, after what seemed like a leave-taking swim, my fellow voyeurs were disappointed that she had not disappeared into the depths of the stream. I would have been disappointed if she had.

I left high school shortly after. Five years later when I visited my alma mater, I was jolted to see a roadside motel where the stream had been. Although it had not been part of my plan, I made a point of passing the night there, wondering what it must be like to sleep on top of a stream of mysteries. I dreamed of that night on the stream bank, only this time I was alone and I was not hiding. When Ada Eke removed her wrapper and waded into the water, she turned and beckoned to me. And I was propelled toward her breasts glowing like the full moon.

Not too long after our departure, according to the story in the village, Ada Eke had unaccountably disappeared and the stream had dried up. The villagers had made many sacrifices. Eventually, they learned to live without the stream. I wondered to myself if a small body of water such as the Eke stream had not been doomed to disappear anyway. Was the web of mystery around one maiden, probably trying to make meaning out of her life in one big city, not altogether illusionary? But nothing can erase the fact that there once was an Eke stream and that there once was an Ada Eke, and that one night several years ago her lobes of temptation conjoined with the mysteries of the night to confirm my manhood.

At the university, where I was admitted as a student at seventeen, I did not have to sneak out at all. In any case, the campus was a large community and catered for virtually all my daytime and nocturnal needs. That changed, however, when I discovered the night market not too far away. The piping music drew me there, but I ended up in the stall of the woman who bought dreams. I had always wondered where the piping music came from in the dead of night. Some said the nearby village was celebrating a quinquennial festival. Some others said there was a night market nearby but that it was open only to indigenes. I wondered what sort of quinquennial celebration just went on and on, or what sort of market would shut itself in in that manner. I decided to find out – by following the sound of the music.

It led me to a clearing not far away from the road where all sorts of items were on sale, illuminated chiefly by lanterns. The consequence was the existence of shadowy perimeters of unlit or dimly lit spaces wherein darkness dialogued with light. At the center of the market was a band of musicians playing mostly horns and drums. There were dancers too, mostly colorfully attired girls whirling rather dizzyingly around an inner cycle. And, of course, there were spectators. I hastened to swell their number, and that was when I noticed the old woman beckoning to me from a nearby stall.

Hers was perhaps the most dimly lit stall in the market, and she looked as if she had been around since the beginning of the world. I stopped halfway. I was really not of a mind to respond to her invitation.

"Come. I no eat you." If she still had teeth left, that fact was not very evident in her voice.

Her spoken invitation and the thought that I was afraid of her suddenly struck me as comical. What harm could she possibly do to me, especially in that lively atmosphere in which the dominant interest was obviously commerce? So, I went toward her.

"You dream dreams?"

"I do, sometimes." I was wondering where this sort of conversation would lead.

"You look like nice boy. I buy your dreams."

Of course, she had to be crazy, I told myself as I walked away. But my departure was short-lived. I learned from a number of the spectators that the woman, known as Mama Rekia, indeed paid small sums for other people's dreams.

"What does she do with the dreams?" I asked.

"She dreams them," I was told.

It did not make much sense to me, since I was certain she could get to hear other people's dreams without having to pay for them.

"She wants more, always more. The village does not have enough dreams for her." Really? And where does she get the money to pay for the dreams? And for what purpose?

The questions grew in leaps. Reckoning that she must be afflicted with sleeplessness and – more important – that I needed the money, I made my way back to Mama Rekia's stall.

"I know you come back. You nice boy," she told me.

I said nothing, merely followed her into the interior of the dim stall. She sat on a rocking chair behind a table on which there was a bowl of water and invited me to sit on the chair opposite her.

"What your dream?"

It struck me that she was not commencing the conversation from the beginning.

"How much?" I asked.

"You tell me dream; the water tell me how much."

Not a striking offer, in my estimation, but I did not see how I could lose. Whoever heard of anyone buying dreams? I narrated to her the dream I had at the Highway Motel, about Ada Eke inviting me into the water. She listened to me with intense concentration, and when I was through she transferred her concentration to the bowl of water. I could see nothing in the water, not even a ripple, and I wondered why she was wasting so much time before paying me. When she was through with pondering the water, or whatever it was she had been doing, she wanted to know the color of the wrapper Ada Eke had been wearing, whether there had been any tattoo on her breast or buttocks, at what point she had waded into the water, where the wrapper had fallen, what sort of noises the bush had resonated with, whether the moon had been full. In short, she turned a simple narration into an oral examination.

"You no dream this dream," she said afterward. "You see her. Oh, you bad boy, I buy only dreams, only dreams."

For a couple of nights afterward, her voice pursued me: "Only dreams, only dreams." It was not difficult to convince myself that she was more interested in dream-like experiences. I decided to return. Passing Mama Rekia's examination had become a personal challenge. I soon had my story well-rehearsed – how I was pursued by a night masquerade chanting my name backward with multiple voices: Ba-ne-ta! Ba-ne-ta! Ba-ne-ta! As I raced through empty streets caving in on me, the masquerade turned into a forest and blocked my path. I raced into the air. It turned into a sea of clouds and blocked my way. I dived into the water. It turned into an unidentifiable animal and began to drink up the water. As it tried to become a night masquerade once more, I was filled with voices and I chanted it to death. But then I was transformed into a night masquerade and I found myself falling through a hole on the river-floor toward a scent of smoke.

After I finished my narration, she began her water ritual but broke off midway and started cackling almost uncontrollably. I measured the distance between where I sat, upright, and the door like a sprinter on the starting block. But before I could escape, she flooded me with questions.

"You no dream this dream," she told me afterward. "You make it. Oh, you bad boy, I buy only dreams, only dreams."

Only dreams. Why not? I had been trying to sell stones in

a market for sand. I had dreams almost every other night, so why not go and narrate one of the recent ones without a stream or a night masquerade in it to Mama Rekia? But I never saw her again. At the night market, I was told she had bought a dream about her own death and had died accordingly. Was that it? Was that what she had been looking for all along – a "nice" death? I was told she had left a message for me: "You make dreams; your dreams make." I suppose she meant since I was a dream-maker I should also nurture my dreams to fruition, or that since I was also a dream-maker I would prosper.

That was my dream as I stepped with Tamuno into the night. I was not interested in any "runs." I was not inclined in that direction at all. And I could foretell that his was not the night of mysteries or even mayhem as such but that of 'vaganza. I reckoned any situation that could uplift my life from its drab valley must be an epiphany on the road from promise to its realization. Almost in the same manner as my mother had given up on the day and prayed to depart at night, I had since given up on the day and prayed to arrive – or at least to take off – at night. I had already made the prefatory dreams. It was time to claim them. I had been on the slow lane for too long and I was suddenly in a hurry to get on the fast track – the world of music and dance, neon lights and orgasms, and dreams taller than the gates of daylight.

I've been doing some serious thinking about my life, sister. You telling me about God again reminded me how long I have been seeking His revelation. I think the main problem with my life is that I have been on the snail lane for too long and look where it has taken me – from one small town without a past to another without a future. I'm getting out.

Our tour that night was like an initiation rite. Speeding like a race driver, Tamuno took me on a brief visit to the main nightclubs in Lagos, telling me what made each one unique. They hailed him wherever we went and ushered him in with flourish. I was more or less in accord with his claim to the ownership of the night of the streets when we arrived at an obviously exclusive Lagos

Island club, Sundown!, where even the bouncer appeared better dressed than I was. Tamuno's attempt to gain entrance was blocked by a thickset bouncer.

"Tickets, please," he demanded in a strange accent.

Tamuno's smile gleamed. "You don't know me, brother?"

"I ain't got no brothers. Tickets, please."

"Listen, I'm Don, okay? From The Owl."

"I ain't got no ears. Tickets, please."

"I think you need to check with your manager."

"I ain't got no mouth. Tickets, please."

Tamuno led me out. Outside the club, there were pricey cars stretching perhaps a mile in each direction. He brought out his mobile phone and spoke to someone about his predicament. Soon, a mustachioed fellow in a tailcoat came running out. He apologized profusely to Tamuno, explaining that the bouncer was a stand-in for the regular who had traveled to the countryside for the year-end holidays.

"You don't know Don?" he asked the bouncer.

"No, sir, I dunno him."

"Now you do. Don't ever trifle with him again."

"Yes sir. Sorry to the Don. It's only business."

"Sure, always business, only you have to reclaim your ears and your mouth, brother."

Like its exterior, the interior of Sundown! was an elaborate toast to opulence. What first impressed me was the chilled, superior atmosphere. There were rather overdressed waiters and waitresses, a vast bar that looked like a futuristic museum of alcoholic and non-alcoholic beverages, a revolving dance floor, and grand seats. A brilliant spectrum of lights lit up both the ground floor and the upper gallery like a surrealistic scene in an operatic anthem to the night. While the patrons on the upper gallery could be seen, those on the ground floor were enshrouded by cubicles of tinted glass, through which they could see but not be seen.

The dancing was however not so grand. Unlike some of the other places we had been to, there was an imported band – and imported dancers – playing an exotic medley that must have been meant to appeal to the predominantly white patrons. In my estimation, the drums were rather out of harmony with the vocals and the dancers seemed to regard themselves as contortionists. Even in that grand atmosphere, they reminded me of snake charmers.

We did not stay long because Tamuno had to get to his own club on the mainland. It was when he did, with me, that I realized what a sacrifice he had made for my sake that night. Although he had called to say he would arrive late, he had been eagerly awaited long before we arrived. It was New Year's Eve and all the clubs teemed with fun-seekers desiring to feast on the night before the coming year soured. He introduced me to his assistants and the bouncers, and then left me at the bar while he attended to the club's patrons.

After Sundown!, The Owl was in no danger of being described as grand. It was a very interesting place nevertheless. As far as I could tell, it must have been a jukebox bar before it was transformed into a nightclub. Besides the bar stools arranged around the semicircular bar, the jukebox in one corner and the disc jockey in another, every other space had been cleared for dancing – or standing. Outside, on the covered terrace, there were tables and chairs, a snooker table, and a kiosk for chicken and chips. The Owl was really a discotheque.

At the bar, where I sat drinking yet another beer, Tamuno had indeed mounted his thesis – now richly bound – on a small lectern. I inspected it once more. *The Ends of Popular Culture: A Case Study of the University Community.* There was now a prefatory page informing the reader that the thesis had been adjudged the best in the department that year. Another page informed me that, because of the scholarship evident in the thesis, Tamuno had been invited to give a lecture on subcultures at a university in Ghana last year.

"Ah, oga know book well well," the barman said to me when he noticed my interest. "Plenty people wey don look that im book say im for be professor."

I did not know how to react, so I simply nodded and smiled. Mercifully, the pitch of the music made conversation difficult. But I did begin to have the feeling that Tamuno was underpaying me, that he was getting much more from my work than myself. But then there was also a voice within that asked me whether that was not more because of the showman in Tamuno than my diligence. I certainly would never have had the sass to put my thesis, bound in loud colors, on a lectern in a nightclub. And what was I griping about when other people were trying to gorge themselves on nocturnal delicacies?

The Owl, I figured, must have some sort of admission code. Surveying the patrons, it was hard to believe that anyone with just enough money for the ticket was being let in. The men looked definitely prosperous and were all well-dressed. The girls...the girls! In their achieved radiance and compelling dress modes, they looked as if they had been selected from a pageant for sexiness. The different ways in which breasts and buttocks were highlighted as dress-scant invitations were fascinating. And I could not help asking myself: where did these girls learn to twitter like birds?

Then the dancing. The men put up brave shows. But the girls were the clear sensation. They danced mostly as if with a fluid foreknowledge of the rhythm of the music, like river nymphs in kinetic dream worlds, lending the songs an atmospheric surge, and the surge the power of an elliptical nirvana. The night became a fetching orgasm of the spirit. I was transported to an island of supernal bliss wherein I lived in the present-present like an immortal. All my worries paled, and only my emotions glowed.

I came to only when the music stopped. As if on cue, the whole house began the countdown to midnight: 12, 11, 10. I did not know what it was all about initially, but I was a throaty contributor all the same. 9, 8, 7. Ada Eke, did you leave the night of the stream for the night of the dance? 6, 5, 4. Mama Rekia, you that bought dreams, how did I ever live my life so far outside the 'vaganza of the night? 3, 2, 1! Amidst the eruption of joy, the disc jockey – legs apart – let loose a heady rumble of pop music. The house went wild. Everything that had happened before seemed like a prelude.

Tamuno appeared as if from nowhere, gave me a thumbs-up sign and invited me outside where conversation was possible. After our arrival, I had noticed him answering calls intermittently on his mobile phone. After each call, he would beckon to one of his assistants and whisper to him. I did not know what it was all about, but I supposed it had to do with his management of the night. It was a wonder how far he had come in a few years. It was an even greater wonder how appreciative he still was of the fact that I ghostwrote his thesis. Before I left the university, I had made a name of sorts for writing examinations, school certificate examinations, for other people. What had come out of those risky ventures? I had also written entrance examinations that got people admitted into the university – and received only miles of promises and a liter or two of beer. Yet Tamuno, the absence called Tamuno, had remembered. He had told his workers that I was to come and go as I pleased. He had veritably given me a gold card, even though there had been no gold or card.

We sat in a corner beside the snooker table obviously reserved for Tamuno. Despite interruptions by men coming to greet and chat with Tamuno and girls coming to hug and whisper to him, we managed a conversation.

"How're you doing, brother? What do you think?"

"I've got a great feeling."

"I told you you would, brother. It's a special show here tonight, in most clubs really. That's why we had to count down to midnight because ordinarily we begin to swing at midnight. Normally, our countdown is to two o'clock. I invented the countdown. It's part of the great subculture of The Owl."

We laughed together.

"You own this place?"

"My friend does. I've only got a management percentage."

"Your friend, January 15?"

"Right," he chuckled. "So, you just relax and have fun. I just wanted to make sure that you're okay. Once more, happy birthday."

"Thanks."

Then something stirred in my brain. "I have to be off," I told him. "It's a great pity, but I really have to go. Thanks for everything. You've been wonderful."

"What's the matter? You feel a bit upside down?"

"That, but that's not it. I have to go to work this morning. Besides, I live with my maternal uncle. He's gone to the village for the holidays, but I'm sure he must have called tonight. I want to be there when he calls this morning."

"Don't do it, brother. You're too young to settle down to the tedium of growing old. You actually make me feel old at thirty-one. The secret of life, brother, is to try and remain young forever."

"You're right, but I also don't want to remain young toting my bag around the streets of Lagos."

"So, get a house."

"A house?"

"So, get a room, even a small room in a crowded house. The day you pay for that room is the day you pay for your freedom. That's why I always insisted on having a place of my own in school."

"Different people, different circumstances."

"Don't even think it, brother. I'll tell you my story someday, then we'll compare notes. So, you get a room of your own, okay?"

"Certainly, I can't do that tonight. So, I still have to be on my way."

"If you have to go, then you have to go. But I won't let you go just like that. It's your birthday, brother, and I'm going to give you a birthday present. Her name is Love. At least, she's got a promising name."

"Come on, Tamuno. You're going to give me a girl – just like that?"

Something stirred powerfully in my brain. "Thanks, but...where would I take her?"

His smile gleamed. "Why don't you let me manage the night for you – tonight, at least? Alonzo will take care of you."

He turned and beckoned to one of his assistants, whispered to him, and sent him off. My feelings were very mixed. I had neither Tamuno's easy tongue nor January 15's easy money, so I had practically been living in Lagos like a celibate. I was excited at the prospect of such a gift from Tamuno, but my mind was in turmoil.

The ebullient Alonzo soon returned with a girl whose gown clung to her as if it would come off only with vengeful measures of flesh. The result was very striking, but she was not really my kind of girl. Her height was a prayer for height, her size an invocation to space, and although she had a pretty face she lacked what I considered the most important feature of a pretty face – an easy smile. I have always been fascinated by tall, lithe girls who understood the chemistry of smiles.

"Love, meet my friend, Taneba," Tamuno made the introductions. "It's his birthday and I want you to take care of him for me."

She attempted a smile as we shook hands. "How are you, Taneba?"

"I'm fine, thank you. And you?"

"Fine. Happy birthday."

"Thanks."

When I later told Tamuno what transpired afterward, he almost expired from laughter. Alonzo had taken us, in another of Tamuno's cars, to a nondescript guesthouse where rooms could be had by the hour. After holding separate consultations with the man in charge and with Love, he had slipped a packet of condoms in my hands and departed. I had earlier refused Tamuno's offer of my fare, so there was no talk about my transportation home. As for Love, Tamuno had assured me that she would find her way home.

The guesthouse bar was still open, so I bought beer for two of us and we disappeared into the room.

"As soon as we entered, she lit a cigarette and sat on the bed. I locked the door and sat beside her. There was no hint of romance, so I began some sort of pillow talk. I doubt if she even heard half a word. She just kept staring at the wall as if lost in a fog. Then, with an 'excuse me,' she removed her shoes and went into the toilet. She tarried there for some time. When she reappeared, the cigarette was gone – and the gown too. She draped it on the only chair in the room, lay on the bed, and shrugged off her underwear. As simple as that. Almost like a zombie.

"She has great breasts, and a well-trimmed triangle. So, I should have been excited. But between her navel and that triangle was the tattoo of a clock. A clock, for God's sake! That was it. Even after I had pulled off my clothes and lay beside her, I just couldn't function. Every time I tried to, that tattoo would set off all the clocks in my brain.

"She did come out of her fog on a rescue mission, to be fair to her, but just as it looked as if we would get somewhere, the room attendant began a racket outside the door. 'E never do? Make una come out-o, other people dey wait!' Between that racket and that clock, nothing was possible.

"By the time I quieted the room attendant – just a brief respite, it turned out – she was already getting into her clothes. While I was scrambling into mine, she bid me a curt farewell and vanished into the night. It couldn't have been worse. And you know what? I was stiff all the way home."

"Are you sure you don't need an aphrodisiac, brother?" Tamuno asked playfully.

"Certainly not."

"It's the damnedest thing I ever heard, or something close. Sounds like an initiation to me. Alonzo must have taken you to the wrong place."

"It's not his fault. There are times when everything just goes wrong."

"You still want her? She's in the university, you know, studying law or something."

"I'd rather not. Sometimes when you nibble at something and it doesn't go down your throat, it's better to take care of your hunger with something else."

"Right, brother. Welcome to the night. You'll make it. I see myself in your eyes, and it's a better picture. I should know. I used to tell fortunes by looking into other people's eyes."

Really?

The night invited me with a lullaby. It welcomed me with a litany – of its barons and its angels, its glitter and its gloom, its romance and its hustle, its Missa Solemnis. You're my brother, and I can't deceive you, not after all the forests we crossed together in those antediluvian dawns. Beneath and beyond all the rollicking scenarios I'm sure you've heard about countless times, each repetition outdoing the previous ones in ambition, there was an abiding aura of starkness sensing into all things, into daylight. Show me the starkness of the night, brother, and I'll tell you what is hidden beneath the costumes of the day.

Bantu

I became a regular presence at The Owl. It was really a weekend club. That was when the heavens came down. On weekdays, Mondays to Thursdays in this case, it was only a jukebox bar with a snooker table on the terrace. Still, even on such days, it was an interesting place to be in. And I did not have to pay. So, I easily transferred my custom from Mama Senegal's and my previous haunts. The Owl became my private palace.

I soon got to know the main personnel fairly well – Sam, the barman, who thought the world of Tamuno; his attractive colleague, Esther, who was so friendly with the club girls and the regular male patrons that I suspected she had a secret desire to join in the flesh market; and Iron, the head bouncer, who was as silent and forceful as eternity. I also became close, sort of, to Tamuno's assistants – the wiry Lucas, who managed the figures; the ebullient Alonzo, who managed the "runs"; and the shadowy André. I was also on friendly terms with both Oscar, the disc jockey who operated on a contract basis, and Osas, who ran the chicken and chips kiosk. It appeared The Owl had made me less of an alien.

I was not an insider in Tamuno's management of the night, and I preferred it that way. I knew he took all sorts of calls on his mobile phone and would sometimes beckon to one of his assistants, whisper to him, and send him off. I knew he managed The Owl, which it was said provided him a base for the drug trade on the streets. That was all I knew. In his circles, he was some kind of god, a king of the streets.

He lived in a hotel suite not far from the club.

"You must be burning quite some money here," I told him the first time I visited him there. "It's a fine place, no doubt, but it must be burning holes in your pocket."

"Better holes in my pocket than in my heart, brother."

"You consider your life dangerous?"

"What do you think? This is show business, brother.

Beyond a point, it's no longer a game; it's breakneck hustling with everything you've got."

"Don't you think perhaps you should slow down?"

"And do what? I was born for the fast lane, for this life. Without it, I'm nothing.
So, I'll just do what I can, brother. Death is personal."

His gleam of a smile shone like stars. It was then that I noticed that some of his fingers were not glinting.

"What happened? Your fingers – your rings, I mean."

"Tomorrow, robins will sing. It really is no big deal."

They were words from his favorite song – the story of his life, he told me. It was a story and a song I would hear often. Tamuno was also an inveterate gambler. And he gambled with everything that he had, apart from his business – his money and his prized gold rings. That New Year's Day when I met him was one of the few times I would ever see them complete, a gold ring on every finger.

That first visit was the only time I would ever meet him alone in that hotel suite. Usually, there was a girl or two with him. Sometimes, the room would be brimming with girls, or a few men and plenty of girls, with some smoking either cigarettes or marijuana. How did he manage to get away with having marijuana smoked in that suite? That place usually gave me a heady feeling.

Tamuno often slept through the day and hardly ever left his suite until sundown. He had his operations well organized. Besides the sedan and the station wagon, he had a bus at his service. On weekends, Alonzo would take that bus to the university to convey campus girls hungry for fun and money. Those were the regulars at The Owl. I began to understand why these girls seemed different from my notion of what they should be.

There was, indeed, an admission code. Most of the girls that hung out on the streets were barred entrance. Unaccompanied girls were let in based on their adjudged elegance. The men were admitted based on a visual examination by the head bouncer, sometimes in consultation with Lucas or Alonzo. Because the price of everything in the club was three or four times its normal value, the men that usually presented themselves were those who required no secondary inspection. These were men with different sorts of intoxication on their mind, and it seemed to me that Tamuno's talk about making "serious connections" there had only been hype. Or was it because I was an opportunity prospector who neither knew how to go about it nor even what he was after?

I saw Love in the club a number of times, but we ignored each other as if it had been so since creation. I misjudged the situation, thinking she was waiting for me to make an advance. I would not, I promised myself. I had enough clocks in my brain terrorizing me. But one night I had one drink too many and I was feeling exceedingly kind to the world at large – especially the girls at The Owl, especially Love. My approach was rebuffed with a curt "Excuse me," spoken in an accented tone, before she vanished into the toilet. I consoled myself with an interior monologue on why the toilet was usually the first place the girls disappeared into on entering the club and often the place they disappeared into intermittently until they departed.

It appeared Love had told a tale about me. I just could not seem to have any success with any of the girls. Could they all be in an anti-Taneba cult? Not likely.

"No worry," Sam consoled me. "When you don catch one, others go begin rush."

Good old Sam. His theory of one into infinitude gave me little consolation, nonetheless. Every weekend at The Owl was such a determined arousal that I required more than philosophy. Usually, I could not afford to pay these girls, so there was that early to mid-month restraint when the music and the dancing sufficed for me. Because they had to. Even on month-ends when I was made brave and optimistic by my pay packet, I could as well have been whistling to myself. It became another personal challenge.

At the university, I had been a failure with women. Of course, there were the imports – girls from high schools – that we, other failures like me, arranged to bring into the campus. But I assured myself that even God Himself would judge me severely if I should spend four years in a university with a predominant female population and fail to date even one. So, I decided I had had enough of squandering my energy on girls sculpted for campus pageants. I went to a dance and, blessing the night, chose an ugly girl with a limp. After that, I had a couple of other successes before I graduated. One: infinitude.

It probably would have been the work of a lifetime finding a decidedly ugly girl in The Owl then. But I noticed that the girls bonded in clusters. There were those who regarded themselves as being in an upper cluster and looked down on the others. There was the cluster that was like a bridge. And there was the cluster that was looked down on – mostly, the girls who had not arrived with Alonzo on the bus. It was from this lattermost category that I managed my first success. But it was as if, having lowered my view, I would not be allowed to raise it again. The girls in the upper cluster would have nothing to do with me. I was branded. I began to work my way up carefully. It was something I felt I had to do without running to Tamuno, so I did not seek his help.

Meanwhile, the coming and going around him appeared to have increased. It was especially so on the nights his friend, January 15, came to the club. He was known there by a name that was strange to me – St Notorious, JP. He was probably a Catholic who had perhaps gone on pilgrimage because his JP meant Jerusalem Pilgrim. A fat young man, he moved about with a siren-blaring convoy and gun-toting policemen who acted as his bodyguards. On his arrival, the gate would be flung open, and he would be escorted to a reserved table on the terrace. He never came alone. He was usually accompanied by some friends and sometimes as many as twelve girls in platform shoes and miniskirts or body-mapping trousers. He had a predilection for suits garlanded with a surfeit of buttons. I never saw him dressed in anything else.

Once, Tamuno invited me over and introduced me.

"My friend, Taneba. He lives in your neighborhood."

"You do? Feel free to come in anytime."

Then the phone rang. One of his companions answered it, identified the caller, and then held the phone to his ear. I never ever saw January 15...St Notorious touch that phone.

"Zanda, you've staged the bull? Keep circling, south. Listen: no anthems this time. Yes, some post-runs, maybe. The hit I'll send in for the take. What? Singles...or doubles? More money. Yes, I feel the feel."

I never hung around them much. Not only did their language make me feel illiterate in a sense, it also made me uneasy. Besides, they were certainly notorious with respect to their consumption of liqueur. They drank whisky and brandy almost like beer and expected everyone else to do the same. While many of the girls and the other men were chain-smokers, St Notorious himself never smoked. Sometimes, he would fool around with a cigar, but that was all. Tamuno himself sat there drinking and smoking easily. There was no manager and master atmosphere around that table. They were like two kings from the ends of the earth meeting each other, one hosting the other.

What offended my sense of proportion most, especially in my situation, was that one fat young man should command such a galaxy of luscious young girls. Those girls had eyes for no one else – at least, not while St Notorious was there. What did he do with them? Even if he had a bed the size of an Olympic swimming pool, surely he could not be of much use to all of them. He was too fat for that, and it showed in his wheezing voice.

I did not understand them much, so I did not keep their company much. What often brought me or kept me at the table was the presence of Bantu. While Tamuno had the 'vaganza of carriage, conducting himself like the owner of all the spheres around him, Bantu had the 'vaganza of stories. An opportunity prospector like me, he was far better at it because he lived by his wits. He was a linguist by profession and had been educated abroad, in New York.

In his faded jeans, which he wore like his skin, Bantu – average height, average build, average everything – did not look like much. But he appeared to have traveled to every corner of the world and, according to him, was waiting for new corners to be mapped out. At thirty-four, he had been everything – teacher, sailor, tour guide, librarian, whatever. He was so dark-skinned and made so much of his days as a sailor that they called him Captain Black. Even his curious way of walking came from years of walking on the decks of ships braving the waves, according to him.

With St Notorious, he was mostly Captain Black, talking mainly about his trips around the world. "Man, the great thing about sailing is the open sea. When people talk about seasickness, I'm kind of lost. Where else would you feel the raw power of the world and its limitless frontiers? Then, there are the beckoning ports promising great dates. Man, I remember everywhere I've been – well, almost. After a hundred cities, them images kind of blur. But I remember Montego Bay and them girls peeling away the night knocking on my door."

St Notorious made a sign to one of his companions. He made a note in a pocketbook. Right there and then, he had decided that he would visit Montego Bay.

"I remember Santa Isabel and the great songs we danced to in them combos, man. Wow! We had fish bazaars for breakfast in Santa Isabel."

St Notorious made another sign to his companion. I began to wonder if Bantu was not leading him on so that he would be more generous to him that night.

"But all these pale when I remember Tahiti. Man, Tahiti! I remember that first sailing. Our captain stood on the deck a long time, reciting his favorite lines to the open sea: 'I would rather be ash than dust...' But even he had to stop when we set our eyes on Tahiti. You know what Tahiti does, man? It restores your soul. Tahiti. The island of the blessed. I've been traveling the world over, whistling from ship decks and recomposing the world, and I tell you: sailing from Tokyo to Tahiti is tops."

All eyes around that table were fastened on him.

"But even Tahiti, regardless of its splendor, pales when my mind goes to Zanzibar. Double Z. I have to die in Zanzibar, man, otherwise I'll rather live forever. It's got so much overwhelming beauty that it takes away all pain. Zanzibar is beyond restoration; it reinvents your soul. I remember them beaches, mesmerizing, like answers from God Himself. And them women! Man, don't even tell me about Montego Bay. Zanzibar must have been one of the last places God created, after He had learned from His errors."

St Notorious and his note-taking companion held whispered consultations. I suspected that one or two destinations would be struck off to comfortably accommodate Zanzibar and Tahiti. Apparently, they set store by Bantu's accounts. Tamuno was the only one who was unmoved. He had once told me: "Don't mind Black. His problem is he's been all over the world and now he has nowhere else to go. Must be a terrible state to be in, brother. He's also got this other problem: he has to survive, even if by vending his memories."

St Notorious and his group also made use of Bantu in their own way. Sometimes, one of them would throw a question at him that took him away from his narration.

"Have you been to Memphis?"

"Are you kidding me?"

"Do you know The Memphis Pyramid?"

"Come on, man, you're talking to Captain Black here."

"Do you know those behind it?"

Bantu would launch into a long narrative.

On some nights, he would appear to fall into a short trance in which his every gesture was a language – after naming the city on his mind. Sometimes, he would tell his story by simply referring to one arrested moment.

"Rome. Man, it touched me when I saw them people crowding to St Peter's Basilica waiting for a sign from the pope."

"But St Peter's Basilica is in Vatican City," someone observed.

"Sure, man. Vatican City is Rome reborn."

Everyone laughed.

Whenever New York was on Bantu's mind, he never

named it once. It was always "New York, New York" around that table.

With me, however, Bantu was Bantu. We had been on "hello" terms until he stopped me one night.

"I've been wondering about you, man. Whatever did you do for Don to be getting this royal treatment from him?"

"What do you mean?"

"I know you were in the same class with him, but he must have been in the same class with about hundreds of other fellas. You ever seen any of them here?"

"Yes, a couple of times."

"You see what I mean? The Don I know is a hard businessman, but here you are all the time like some kind of mascot. Don't get me wrong, man. I'm only saying you're someone kind of special. What did you ever do for Don?"

I laughed the question away, and he did not press it. From then, we started talking a little bit more – and more. He told me Bantu was his final corruption of his much-corrupted given name, Obu iba na etulum: Is it fever that is boastful toward me? His mother had been down with a debilitating fever at the time she gave birth to him, and that had been her way of thumbing her nose at the fever. But she did not live long to do much else. Fortunately for him, he had a father who cared for him and sent him abroad to study for a degree in linguistics.

"That was the last time I saw him alive. The next thing you know, I had a letter telling me he was gone too. And there I was in the capital of desperation wondering if I was breathing or sneezing. Man, it was crazy. It was weird. I realized soon enough that life is a sea of sharks, but thank God I knew how to swim. It was Bantu for himself. I threw myself into the school of pains called the job market. My life depended on it. Don't ever let anybody kid you, man. Working your way through school is a painful road to travel. The best job I ever had in them days was in the campus library. It was there I read this great fella called Shakespeare. There was a shelf of his books, and then rows and rows of books on his books.

What more is greatness? And he had these lines that sent me into crazy spins. I think he must have been some smart fella who went to the factory for metaphors and staged a buyout. If literature had stopped with him, I don't think it would have lost much."

My mind raced immediately to the disputation that had preceded a change in Tamuno's original thesis proposal from "The *End* of Popular Culture" to "The *Ends* of Popular Culture."

"That's not the sort of thing I expect to hear from you, Bantu. If the world, or any aspect of it, stops at any point, it loses something vital – its future."

"If there is one, man. After Shakespeare, then maybe you have a couple of fellas trying..."

"What are you even trying to tell me – that the whole of modern literature amounts to nothing?"

"I don't want to get into them academic fogs, man. What I'm trying to tell you is that after I read Shakespeare, I never read another fella who sent me into crazy spins – well, until this character came along from somewhere in Latin America. He calls himself La Luna: the moon. I call him El Diablito: the little devil. He took my wife away."

I sensed a story, so I managed not to say anything.

"Look, I'll show you, man. I'll show you. I've never shown this around before, but I'll show it to you."

He dug his hand deep into the pocket of his faded jeans, brought out a wallet, extracted a neatly folded paper from it and gave it to me without another word. On the paper was a poem, written in a stylish handwriting, entitled "Naomi":

> Tonight
> When the air smells of rose banquets
> And the moon is as supple as a bulbous breast
> In the shade of ancient poplars
> Where wizened matrons
> Speak of bygone boyfriends
> With girlish giggles
> You are the song of the wind

That I must sing, Naomi

Tonight
When hallelujah messiahs float on Easter wings
And heedless songs of salvation
Tinkle the whoosh of snuffing breezes
I finally understand the anonymity of Golgotha
And the nails bleed my heart
You are the crucifix of blinding jeremiads, Naomi
A conquest of deaths
And life begins anew in twilight surges of faith

I read it all over again, which was not exactly an easy thing to do at The Owl.

"This fellow sounds confused to me, confused even as a poet," I said to Bantu. "This poem took your wife away?"

"It gave her the crazy spins, man. I'll tell you the story. She had been my classmate. In that class, I think I was ahead of a lot of them fellas, so I helped some out with their schoolwork. I helped her out a couple of times. She seemed clearheaded. In my situation, I was desperately looking for someone to share my apartment with – with both of us splitting them rent and bills down the middle. I told this to anyone who cared to listen. She had her own problems from home, so she took up the offer. There was nothing between us then. It was convenience, that damned word! In any case, I was hardly ever there.

"For two years, we were plain roommates. She never brought anyone into that room. I never did. I was never there really. But then one night a colleague in the library made what I considered an overtly racist remark. I could deal with the pretense but not that sort of stuff. I gave it to him, man, and I left there in a huff. Obviously, she was not expecting me back that night. There she was puttering about the room, without the door locked and without a stitch on. You would have thought she would scurry for cover on my walking in, but apparently there had been the same hunger eating both of us up. It's easier to deal with when you love someone and you know it. When you love someone and you don't really know it, man, everything happens like in a spacey movie. We were married that same semester.

"We had two beautiful kids, a son and a daughter. But then I began to sense that everything was not what it should be. Suddenly, she had a way of not being there when she should. One night, I searched her handbag out of frustration, and I discovered this poem. It surely sent me into a crazy spin.

"'What's this?' I demanded.

"'What's what? I won't have you searching my bag. I'm not going to stand for it. Give it back.'

"'That I will not do, but that's not the issue here. Who's this fella writing you love poems filled with death?'

"'Okay, so now you know. I'm in love.'

"Can you imagine your wife telling you that, your clearheaded wife and mother of your two beautiful kids?

"'You are in love *now*? What has our marriage been all about since?'

"'Our relationship was convenience. I realize that now. I thought I was in love with you, but now I'm truly in love – with someone else.'

"Life is a sea of sharks, but thank God I know how to swim. We had a divorce, and a big custody battle. She won, of course. I turned my back on New York, New York and I went to sea. New York, New York! Goodbye, dear heart. I was really in love with her. I really loved her, man. But one of the greatest lessons we all have to learn is not to be too hard on ourselves."

I became close to Bantu. After entertaining St Notorious, who favored him with cash handouts, he would retire with me to the bar or to another table. Sometimes, he would offer to buy me a drink. I never accepted, not that that stopped him. On my part, I rarely ever made any such offer, and when I did I insisted on paying for the drink. I did not want to experiment with Tamuno's generosity.

But it appeared I was abusing my maternal uncle's. I had

supposed that since I had previously been coming home late that no one had noticed that I had recently been returning even later. Sometimes, I took the precaution of going home straight from the office, parading myself about and then disappearing to The Owl after everyone else had gone to bed. I had a paying departure and arrival protocol with the senior housemaid, Josephine. She normally let me out, and she usually let me in – upon my knocking in an agreed manner.

On this night, however, when I returned home reeking of alcohol and cigarette smoke, and smartly executed my Josephine code, my maternal uncle unlocked the door. He filled the doorway in his pajamas. Behind him stood his equally burly wife, similarly attired. Without a word, they made way for me to enter. My maternal uncle bolted the door again, then he summoned me to the living room. Before he said anything, he first shone his torchlight on the wall clock as if to reconfirm the time. It was half past three.

"Sit down."

We all did.

"Where are you coming from? Anyway, it's either you're coming from a den of thieves or from a brothel. No decent person stays out until this time."

"Now, I'm disappointed in you, Taneba," his wife said. "Your father's second wife, *second* wife, and her children have taken over whatever your father had, and here you are living a useless life!"

"You will still go to work this morning in this state?" my maternal uncle wondered.

I misunderstood the question or comment. "My office record is beyond reproach," I said.

"Why would it not be when ..." my uncle's wife began.

"Easy, my dear," cautioned the husband. "Don't let this boy give you a heart attack." Then he turned to me: "You must be out of your senses as well as suicidal. What man will come back in this state and go to work after three hours of sleep, work through the day and not be breaking down his body? Everything I do for you,

I do for your mother – my only sister – but this is too much. I told you right from the beginning, and I'm telling you for the last time: you are to come back to this house no later than ten p.m. Ten p.m. Not a second more. I have warned Josephine: the next time she opens the door for you later than ten p.m., I will send her back to her village. Do you completely understand me?"

My maternal uncle and the completeness of things!

Something stirred in my brain. "There's something I've been meaning to tell you, uncle. I'm going to Liberia."

Was it the drink, or my anger at being caught, or the continual reference to my father? I had not been meaning to tell him any such thing. In fact, I had dismissed the idea when Bantu had invited me to sail with him – to Liberia.

"And leave my job?" I had asked him scornfully.

"What job – licking postage stamps?"

"At least, it's better, far better, than living your own sort of life on the streets."

He gave me a royal smile when I thought he would be offended. "Sure, man, I'm a street element. But smell me. I smell of freedom, of the open sea."

"You can smell of fuel for all I care. Or even of Liberia. I'm doing well in my office. In another year or two, I could become a section head. I've got a great record."

"You're jumping to conclusion, man, without even hearing me out. There's this ship that makes a routine trip to Liberia. Unfortunately, we won't be going as sailors, but then you can't always win them all. I know the woman who's got the catering contract, so we'll be sailing as stewards..."

"Me?"

"Hear me out, man. The pay is twenty-two American dollars a day, on top of the free food and lodging. How about that? In a week, you'll make more than you earn in a month."

I began to listen to Bantu with a bit more attention.

"Probably good for you, Bantu, but I've got a job and a pension plan to look forward to."

"I'm only telling you this because I like you, man, but I don't think you're listening to me very well. We sail with this ship to and fro, we rest awhile and then we make the trip again. I know this woman, so I know what I'm talking about. If you want, you can come along with me to see her, then we straighten everything out. How about that, man?"

"I'll think about it." At least, that would keep him off my back for some time.

But there I was telling my maternal uncle and his wife that I would be sailing to Liberia – without having even secured the job, if at all it existed.

"You're going to where?" asked my uncle.

His wife had been struck speechless. She could only clap her hands together, raising them upwards as if in silent supplication to the heavens. I believe that I even enjoyed the consternation I had caused. But I was also touched by their concern.

"I'm sailing to Liberia, uncle."

"To do what? What about your job? Even if you've gone out of your mind, is there no method to your own madness?"

"I'm sailing to Liberia, working on a ship. I'll resign from the post office. God will bless you for everything you've done for me."

A deep stillness descended on that room. It was the first conflict the night had imposed on me, and I had blundered to a decision without serious thought.

"Everything I do for you I do for my sister," my maternal uncle said, slowly, when he regained his speech. "But God will not allow you to kill me, Taneba. God will not allow you to give me high blood pressure. The only thing I will tell you is that the day you leave the post office to go working on a ship that is the day you will leave my house. Do you completely understand me?"

There was no completeness about my understanding, but I think the decision was not so much between the post office and the ship. It was more between my maternal uncle's house and The Owl, between the 'vaganza of Tamuno's world and the tame nights of my neighborhood.

The neighborhood itself was throbbing with questions over my absence from my regular haunts once upon a time. The day I stopped by Isa's "suya spot," he stiffened in mid-motion as if he had seen an apparition.

"Taneba! Where I go?" he queried me in his peculiar English. "*Abi* I dey vex for Isa?"

I assured him that that was not the case.

"Isa I no dey see you again. I travel?"

"Yes, I went to Liberia," I said, transporting the future into the past.

"Liberia? Wetin e happen?"

"I went to work." There was nothing else than to elaborate on the fiction.

"I no dey work for post office again?"

I nodded a confirmation.

"I no dey live with postmaster again? Ah, postmaster na better man, *wallahi!* Wetin I dey do now?"

Telling him I was going to be a steward on a ship would be belittling myself, my maternal uncle, and the idea of traveling to Liberia. So, I told him I was buying and selling ships in Liberia. He pondered the idea for some time, then he invited me to sit down and eat some grilled meat. As he tended the charcoal grill, he launched into an account of how his side and the other had fought the civil war even after it had ended. Both had been ignorant of that fact and had consequently terminated a few lives in the shelling and raiding that continued after the surrender.

Why Isa went on and on about the war, I really could not fathom. Perhaps the war had been the peak experience of his life, after which Isa the *mai suya* amounted to no more than a charcoal grill at night. Perhaps to him the war had ended without peace. Maybe that was also why some people in the neighborhood had insisted on associations between the war and January 15. Whichever, Isa was the one who gave me the warmest welcome. Mama Senegal was cold, initially. I had expected to be welcomed like a prodigal son. I was accosted like the debtor I was.

"Taneba, you don run finish?"

It occurred to me powerfully that a debtor who had vanished for months should not expect any other kind of welcome.

"Ah, Mama, why would you think such a thing?"

"You wey dey come here every day before, you just vanish like that. Why I no go think so? The thing wey you do e good?"

"Everything happened very fast. I'm sorry. I traveled – to Liberia."

"No, you go Japan. You wey Mabel my daughter see near your uncle house. Na your uncle I respect wey I no come drag you for house."

"True, I went to Liberia. How can I lie to you? Maybe she saw me when I dashed into Lagos. But it's your fault, Mama. You refused to let me marry any of your daughters."

The magic in those words is still beyond my comprehension, but it always worked.

"Person wey see you go think say you no dey talk, but na so your eyes sharp like headlamp. My daughters na special reserve. No worry, you hear, when you settle we fit talk reach that side. Person wey go school like you, come still cool for head, one day e go surely make am. That's why I trust you. So, wetin you go do for Liberia?"

I could not tell her I was buying and selling ships. That would unmask my entire posturing. I had gone, I told her, on an exchange program between my office and...yes, the Liberia Board of Letters.

She was suitably impressed. "You don dey climb be that. I talk am! Mabel, you no go bring drink for your husband? Na because I dey here, *abi*?"

I downed my drink quickly, glanced at my wristwatch and excused myself because, knowing her, the next stage of the conversation might lead to her figuring out the truth. I fled to Silas Peter's pepper soup joint instead, where the highlife music was so loud that conversation was mostly conducted with gestures. But the area was uncannily silent. In the months of my absence, the "feel good" Silas Peter and his wife had finally run themselves out of business. I had often wondered how such a place could survive with husband and wife seemingly locked in competition over who would out-eat and out-drink the other.

I then wandered toward the region of the telephone booths where one could be entertained by listening to young girls, just barely beyond puberty but confident in their assumed knowledge of everything, calling their old and new boyfriends.

Yellow was there, vending dubiously acquired telephone cards as if he was the telephone company. He was an albino, hence the name. But the mystery around him was beyond his skin pigmentation. Yellow was always up and about at all times of the day and the night, waving his stark walking stick like a wand.

"In the night, you are here. And in the day too. When do you sleep?" I had asked him one day.

"I no dey fit sleep. Na the problem wey I get be that."

"What do you mean you don't sleep? Everybody sleeps."

"I no dey fit sleep, true. Even, the time when I dey Aro, na the thing wey dey write for my file: 'Sleepless.'"

So, he had been in a mental hospital?

"You slept yesterday, didn't you?"

"No, I no fit sleep."

"You slept the day before yesterday then?"

"No, I no fit."

"When was the last time you slept?"

He actually paused to consider. "Maybe like four months now. That time, I drink plenty assorted sleeping tablets."

I was sure I had nailed him. "Whom do you think you're talking to – some kind of mushroom? You drank 'plenty assorted sleeping tablets' and you're still alive? And whoever heard of anyone sleeping three times a year?"

"Na true I dey tell you. If I lie, make trailer crush me." He bit his walking stick with his tobacco-stained teeth as the sign of his oath.

I decided there was no point stretching the matter further. I would monitor him, and the day I would knock him up from sleep I would take his walking stick away as an irrevocable testimony. I even conscripted the vigilant Isa, who lived in his kiosk, into the Yellow watch. But neither of us ever caught him asleep or away from the streets. That was not how it should be. Short of asking him to swallow assorted sleeping tablets in my presence, I confronted him again.

"How is it that you don't sleep?"

"I been go steal dream. Na inside am they tell me say I don break one heavy rule, say I no go dey sleep again."

I did not want him to draw me back into the world of my misadventure with Mama Rekia, so I left him well alone. But I often pondered: if indeed he was not sneaking naps in-between his eternal presence on the streets, then he must be one of the living wonders on earth. And if indeed he slept sometimes, why would he lie about it? But then several things on the streets are not what they seem, I had learned. I chose, therefore, not to dwell on Yellow and his habit – or curse – of sleeplessness.

That night, he was very surprised to see me.

"Oga Taneba! I been hear say you don go Liberia. Which time you come back?"

"Where did you hear that?"

"You no know say talk dey waka for street?"

"I don't doubt that, but whoever told you that is spreading a rumor. I'm yet to leave for Liberia."

"Small matter. Something wey remain small don finish be that. When you get to Liberia, make you sharp, dey very sharp. You go just sharp make your money, then you go sharp duck out. As e be say na dollar them dey use there, when you come back change the money na you get Lagos be that. But make you no forget Yellow-o!"

His optimism aided nothing. The trip to Liberia was a disaster. There was indeed a caterer with a contract on a ship that sailed and docked safely in Monrovia. And we were indeed engaged in the vexatious occupation of toiling as ship stewards. I did not see what the hoopla about sailing was all about. For all I cared, we could as well have been sailing on stones. I needed the twenty-two dollars a day like the ship needed its compass.

We were told, however, that the money would be paid in bulk upon docking. That was the first and minor disappointment. Upon docking safely, however, the story took an ominous turn. The sight of the caterer and the captain shouting at each other furiously was like a suspended disappointment. The ship, we were told, was not making the expected return journey to Lagos immediately. It had been ordered to sail to Casablanca or someplace that sounded like that. The caterer insisted she was sailing no farther because she had pressing engagements back home. Before we even properly understood that she had terminated her contract herself, she had become a harrowing absence. A new caterer was contracted, and she arrived with her own cooks and stewards. The short of it was that we were marooned.

I was shattered. To make that trip, I had resigned from the post office, paid off my debts, and moved out of my maternal uncle's house. My entire belongings were contained in the bag I toted along – an assortment of clothes and other such. Bantu did not have half as much, but he had something more valuable then – his familiarity with the rough sea of life. I was almost twenty-six years old, and the trip had seemed like both an adventure and a fail-safe lottery. I had missed both.

Youth is madness, but then I would rather be young again because youth is also freedom. Age is wisdom – and decline.

"Life, always a sea of sharks!" Bantu kept muttering. "But I know how to swim. Once more, it's Bantu for himself."

I did not like the sound of that. "You better be careful what you're saying. You were the one that got me into this in the first place."

"Don't worry, man. You just stay close to Bantu, and we'll make it back to Lagos before that ship gets to Casablanca – if it does."

The caterer had invoked high tides on the ship. But how would that help us?

"There's only one thing to it, man. We have to make it to the Nigerian embassy, but we can't go looking like beggars."

So, we dressed ourselves in my best clothes. But the embassy guards were not impressed. We had sailed on that ship without a passport, and as far as they were concerned we were shipwrecks of no nation. We must have made quite a spectacle of ourselves outside that embassy singing the national anthem, reciting the national pledge, calling out in several Nigerian languages – all in a bid to prove our nationality. It was free theater, but we were no less marooned.

"There's only one thing to it, man. We go back the same way we came – this time in the fourth-class compartment."

"Where's that?"

"In the cargo section."

"Not me, Bantu. Do you want to commit suicide or what?"

"Well then, man, so long. I'll tell them in Lagos that Monrovia has you now."

What was there then to decide? We made the journey back as fake cargoes. Our success was entirely due to Bantu's savvy as a sailor over many years and across many seas. But by the time we arrived, we could as well truly have been cargoes – damaged cargoes. In my own case, I was also bleeding – inside. Bantu gave me a five-finger salute and vanished. He was going in search of the caterer, he told me in a barely audible voice.

When I presented myself at Tamuno's hotel suite, he laughed himself into a serial cough. After he had heard my story, he gave me a set answer: "Tomorrow, robins will sing, brother. It really is no big deal."

It was, for me. I needed accommodation, and I needed an income. So, I asked him for a temporary job of sorts – a request prefaced by a long speech about my gratitude to him and how I hoped that one day I would be able to pay him back.

"Don't do it, brother. Some things are beyond money. I

told you you'll make it. I see myself in your eyes, Taneba, and it's a better picture."

It was the only time he ever gave me money – enough to get a small room in a truly overpopulated house, where the decrepit toilet facility was often a battlefront. But I had also learned something from Tamuno. Sometimes, you are as good as your presentation of yourself. So, I named my residence House Number 25, and I made it seem as if it had twenty-five staircases.

Our search for the caterer was not a long one, but she insisted she would not pay us until she received her own payment.

"How are we supposed to know about that?" queried Bantu. "In any case, you employed us, not the shipping company."

She was unmoved.

"What do you think, man?" Bantu asked me. "The only thing to it is some hard tackle. I know a couple of fellas who can cut up them pretty fingers of hers, and then she'll be in a crazy hurry to pay that money."

I had never associated him with violence, but then on the streets several things are not at all what they seem. The hard life out there sometimes makes people what they are really not or would rather not be.

"Let it go, Bantu. I probably need that money more than you do, but I tell you: we've just benefited so much from the mercy of God that to do what you're suggesting would be to fly in the face of providence."

"Hey man, I'm not getting into them religious fogs with you."

"Bantu, blood has a way of coming back at you."

That touched him, so I drove on: "The time you said your captain was quoting to the sea: 'I would rather be ash than dust.' You know what that means?"

It pained him very much to let go of that money. We were now closer than ever before, and he soon moved in with me. He was tired of being a "performing monkey," he told me – obviously referring to his tales for St Notorious and his group.

"I'm tired of knowing about the sea of sharks, man. Why not the sea of seas? I've got about twenty-eight gray hairs on my head, man. It's about time I made some money to feed them. They're crying in my sleep."

Even in my poverty, I began to pray fervently to God to cast a treasure chest in Bantu's direction before he went berserk in my small room – with me in it. So, when he woke up one morning in a state of excitement, I felt relieved.

"You know what's going on all over the world, man? Governments are getting smaller. That's the new craze – divestment, deregulation, privatization, and all them jargon. What do you expect? As governments are getting smaller, non-governmental organizations are getting bigger. There must be thousands of them in Lagos alone, drawing from a sea of funds."

Once he was set on that course, there was no stopping him. He investigated the possibilities of several NGOs – for domestic pets, for intestinal disorders, for seasickness, for mortuary workers, for traffic regulations, perhaps even for masquerades and night markets.

"I think the problem is that we've stayed in this town too long, man. There's a way a town begins to close in on you after a while. The first thing people ask me before they even listen to me is 'How is Monaco?' or 'How's San Cristóbal?' – as if I'm a mobile travel agency. I've got to get out of this town, man, before my gray hairs begin to mutiny in my sleep."

Again?

"We've got to take a lesson from the queens of the night, man. These girls understand the value of mobility. The moment they hang around one place for some time, they graduate from there and move on – arriving at their next destination as freshers. We have to move, man. Lagos is overpopulated with everything imaginable, even everything unimaginable for that matter."

With his power of persuasion and because my job search had yielded nothing, Bantu soon convinced me to set out with him again. At the least, I thought, I would get to see more of the country.

And I was still young anyway. While I made ready once more to set off with everything I had, which was still not more than my bag could carry, Bantu as usual did not travel with much besides the numerous proposals and surveys he had spent some time preparing. When he wanted, he could really get down to the arithmetic of things.

We toured the country extensively, as if we were searching for hollow worlds. We were the unanointed high priests of non-governmental organizations – preaching, in a rapid relay, an agency for the enlightenment of kola nut consumers, for the advancement of lorry drivers, the legalization of prostitution and gambling, the beautification of graveyards, the protection of the desert. Bantu's idea was that if everyone was going in a particular direction, the right thing for us to do was to proceed noisily in the opposite fashion.

"It's the history of the world, man. Everything that is a fad today will die out, and whatever is not now will eventually become fashionable."

"Why don't we simply follow the fashion of the day?"

"The beauty of this whole NGO riot is that there's a reason for everything. Even if you start an NGO for the encouragement of suicide or the immediate destruction of the world, and you're ready with your arguments, you'll find some supporters, man."

And he was not very wrong. In between the horror of starvation and exhaustion that was the sum of our life in that period, we did have minor successes – up until the time we settled down somewhat to run a poor nightclub. Bantu could think of only one name: Naomi's. All I cared about was that the place should elevate us above our existence as low beggars with high dignity. But how do you nourish flowers on desert sand?

One afternoon – about the time we normally woke up from sleep after the exertions of the night – I discovered a gray hair on my head. I must have been paralyzed for the first five minutes, then I spent another five studying it and verifying its existence.

"I'm leaving, Bantu," I announced slowly. "I'm going back

to Lagos."

"To do what, man? This is our thing. I tell you: it's going to work out in the long run."

The thought fleeted through my mind that Bantu might have made all those trips of his in a ship sanatorium.

"I've just noticed a gray hair on my head – at twenty-seven. I don't think that's the natural order of things."

"We live in the sun, man. That's why we gray early."

"So, how come our brothers in the colder regions haven't frozen out their dark skin?"

"You're a great one for them academic fogs, man. But I'll tell you something. We're all God's children, right? All this color stuff is because some people stayed in the cold while others went into the sun, or in whichever direction the movement was. It's not something that happens in a century or two. We're talking centuries or even millenniums, man. Give them brothers and sisters over there some more time. They've already made a lot of progress."

"My mind is made up, Bantu. I'm leaving before my gray hair starts whining in my sleep."

"Well, so long, man. Once more, it's Bantu for himself."

I returned to Lagos in the third-class compartment of a train right out of antiquity. And I discovered that the world as I knew it had changed.

Listen to me, Mojida. My dreams pursued me, again. I took the camel route, and I crossed the desert. I dared everything. In the oasis where I stopped to drink, there was a dead camel. You know what that means – a dead camel in the only watering hole for miles around? But I crossed that desert, powered by thoughts of you. When I arrived, however, you were gone. I will not give up on simple dreams because I know the camel route is not the only way across the desert. Am I to believe that all those lavender afternoons were dream hazes in which I was only a sole traveler multiplying himself? I dreamed you once ago. I will dream you again – into being.

Mairo

We all live in moments in history that are unrepeatable. The Owl of Tamuno was gone. The story on the streets was that things had fallen apart between him and St Notorious. Consequently, he had moved out of the hotel suite and away from the nightclub he had loved with a passion. It was a situation I had not imagined. But when I was refused entrance by the very same Iron who would usually open the gate for me without hesitation, I did not require any leap of the imagination to tell me that the world of the night as I knew it had changed.

I had arrived Lagos that night, dumped my bag at Isa's kiosk, freshened up in the toilet of a roadside hotel, and hastened to The Owl. I was deflated by my encounter with Iron. I walked away from the gate and its steely attendant and began to negotiate my own corner of the night – away from the street army that normally hung around outside the club either as unofficial car attendants or as beggars. It was then that I saw André. He also noticed me and came toward me.

Among Tamuno's three assistants, the ebullient Alonzo had perhaps been the one closest to me. The wiry Lucas was so wrapped up in the labyrinth of figures that he had an accountant's suspicion of everything. Between the shadowy André and me, there had always been a cautious distance. That night, however, there was no hesitation either on his part or mine.

"Oga Taneba, which time you come?"

"Forget about that. What's going on here?"

"Don and Saint get palaver, so we no dey here again."

"But Iron is still here."

"Iron no dey work for Don. Na Alonzo, Lucas, and me."

"What happened?"

"That na long story. Na between Don and Saint."

I knew better than to press him. "Where's Tamuno now?" I asked instead.

"I no know."

"Where's Alonzo or Lucas?"

"They dey with Don."

Interviewing André was of no further use, so I dismissed him and found a corner from where I could observe and ponder. I did not need an oracle to tell me I would spend that night on the streets the hard way. Should I return to Isa's place and spend the night there? I perished the thought. He had such a high view of me that it would pain even me to betray his illusions. Besides, if he began to see me as a tramp, I might not be so welcome in his place anymore. To even keep my bag there, I had told him a tall tale about ship markets and midnight prospects.

In my sad corner, with everyone else bustling after one peak experience or grand illusion, I contemplated the great times I had had at The Owl – especially at month-ends. Love had ironically turned out to be one of the revelations I had experienced there. From deciding I would never speak to her again, after her tonal "Excuse me," I had actually started taking a fancy to her. It was a wonder how she could coordinate her different bulging aspects on the dance floor. And she was like a gift that had defeated me.

I knew she would give me another tonal "Excuse me" if I approached her directly again. So, I made an arrangement with Esther to give her a drink on my account whenever she entered the club. Initially, she took my drinks, then looked through me as if focusing on someone behind me. I let her be, until one night when she was in that mood in which you feel an overwhelming kindness to the entire world, especially those you had previously neglected unfairly. She came to where I was then and gave me a warm expression of gratitude: "Thanks."

It was a moment to seize and nourish. That night, we talked about dress-sense, moot trials, campus gangs, hair colors, body piercing, and all sorts of things that I knew little about. I guess it is easy to talk about everything with a fair measure of alcohol in your system, a little knowledge of things, and a rich language. I could not ask her out because it was not the end of the month yet. But at least we were talking, and that night led to other such nights.

One night, I asked her the question I had been carefully avoiding.

"You're a law student, right?"

"You know that already, don't you? I have one more year to go. I can hardly wait."

"Then what are you doing here?"

She regarded me for some time, then she retorted: "You *nko*, what are you doing here? In short, ask my back."

She walked away, wriggling her waist. The next night, she tried to avoid me. I wondered then: what was it about this girl anyway that our relationship kept moving from brink to brink?

"I'm sorry, Love," I said to her. "Asking you that what you're doing here only shows that I care about you. But I guess salvation is personal, and what we do with ourselves is our business."

She smiled at me as if I had achieved unexpected brilliance. "It's my life, and I will live it the way I can, okay? How else do you want me to survive when all these government-miss-road people are making life hellish for everyone? How do you want me to train myself in school?"

She told me a hard-luck story about why she had taken to the streets. Her real name was Elizabeth. Love was only a trade name. She had a complex marriage between her parents behind her, and only herself and her younger siblings before her. And it was either she took care of them or no one else would. I knew she had no patience for my answers, only my acknowledgement. So, I calmed her down with a short monologue on how the school of suffering produces desperate graduates. I then invited her out.

"Ah-ah, Taneba, you're my brother now. Look, any girl you want here, just show her to me and I'll get her for you."

Was this girl a candidate for a mental hospital, or was she trying to up her price?

"I don't want anyone else, Love."

"I think I would have preferred it the way it was, but your

wish is my command."

That cliché should have forewarned me it would be an ordinary sort of experience. But sexual passion is a poor philosopher of language. After that night, our relationship cooled off. I still bought her an occasional drink, and we still had an occasional conversation – until Bianca drifted in.

She was obviously a newcomer, with all the glamour of newness in a place where many of the men were hunting for new conquests and the familiar girls were striving breathlessly to reinvent themselves. She had tall, elegant legs that someone joked could stop even a speed train, the well-chiseled shape of a mannequin, and a fondness for long hair and big earrings. Her face was not correspondingly beautiful – the cheekbones were rather too high – but there was so much to admire in her that it was easy to discount that detail. She was not a great one for dancing, perhaps because she had so much attention to contend with.

My attempts to get her interested in me received only half-hearted responses because there were other men in that nightclub amply equipped with the new tools of pacification – gold and atmosphere. I let them seize their day. At month-end, I sought Esther's assistance. I was glad then that I had not gone ahead with my previous intention to ask Esther out.

"Bianca? No worry, I'll get her for you. But you go settle me-o."

"Why are you talking like that? You know me, don't you?"

"I just dey talk. I trust you."

I really wondered how she would accomplish her mission that night, considering all the attention Bianca was receiving.

"I say make you no worry. She will go with you."

"With this whole market around her?"

"I say: no worry. Only you go take care of her well-o."

I knew Esther had her ways with the girls, but I was doubtful about this particular plot. Bianca hardly ever looked my way, and when she did it was in a general fashion. I was contemplating an honorable exit when the dutiful Esther came and whispered to me that they had agreed on the mode of departure. Bianca would meet me outside the gate. It was a curious procedure to me. But Bianca soon joined me outside, having stolen away from the market closing in on her. I did not have a car, but there were taxi drivers holding the doors of their cars open like certified doormen.

"No mind all those people. They no want let me go, like say na by force."

"Why didn't you just tell them off, or even go with one of them?" I inquired, secure in the knowledge that I had her beside me in a taxi already speeding to my chosen destination.

"No be like that. At first, na only one of them I been dey talk to, before im friends come join us. And e say all of them dey live together. I no want make anybody cut off my head because I dey do *ashawo*."

She was just a prettified temptress right out of the gutter, I surmised.

She told me a story about how her friend had gone with a group of friends like that – with the principal actor telling her not to worry, that his friends were not part of the arrangement. Her friend, she said, only managed to escape with her head intact because the old man who was invited to inspect her announced that her head was "too strong" for their purpose.

"Na so they just push her out. And na for inside inside Victoria Island. She waka tire before she fit even see motor."

"So, why are you going with me?"

"At least, Esther know you well – as Don friend. And na only me and you."

Bianca was a nymphomaniac – and a masochist. The first time, she wanted me to tie her, spread-eagled, to the bedpost. In the state I was in then, I would have tied her to the roof beam if that had been required of me. But the thought also struck me that it was like making love to a female Jesus on the cross. And if she was so enamored of the dramatics of pain, why was she wary of possible headhunters?

The second time, she wanted me to "handcuff" her, then flog her and yell at her. With each occasion of pain, she would fall into a delirium in which she moaned with blissful abandonment.

I fled from her, the same way she had fled to me. During the incredible naps she fell into in-between, I stealthily put on my clothes, left what I considered enough money for her on the bed and sneaked out of the room. I needed the fresh air more than anything else in the world. How could I even have trussed her up and all that? In the name of pleasure, this girl who summed herself up very starkly had turned me into an animal – very easily. Who was I then to judge her?

After that night, we never spoke to each other again. The way she carried on, it was as if I did not exist any longer.

After Bianca, I tended to look at every girl there with great suspicion – wondering what devilry each was capable of, despite the prettified exterior. My experience with Bianca, which had started off as a great erotic adventure, had erected walls of celibacy around me. Her Majesty broke down those walls without even trying.

Once in a while, I suppose, there appears a girl on such a scene who so captures the verve of its hours and the radiance of its spirit that she becomes the scene itself. For those who witness this appearance, everything before her becomes like a questing prologue, everything afterwards a perspiring epilogue. That girl was Aisha, whom everyone called Her Majesty. She deserved the name. She had Bianca's beauty, made even more so by the exacting proportionality of her construction – right up to the face. Her face shone – every aspect of its careful, oval features – with the polish of unblemished youth, tanned by the sheen of well-being.

She was such a great dancer that she even had a special way of welcoming any man she danced with – a floorward sass followed by a graduated ascension in which her body became a delicate, spasmodic salute. With her fondness for the shortest miniskirts I ever saw, barely covering her lower region only in order to praise it, I wondered why I never saw more than I did.

There were all sorts of stories about her. In one, she was the daughter of a famous medical doctor who had run wild. In another, she was a medical student moonlighting at The Owl and other such places. Yet in another she was a model who was vacationing before taking up a major international assignment. I chose to believe all the stories. She had both a model's comeliness and a student's coquetry.

Usually, she never waited for anyone to ask her to dance. She prompted herself. I gravitated toward her on one such occasion, and she gave me the pleasure of dancing with her.

"I guess you must have heard this over and over," I told her afterward, "but then the truth can bear repeating. You must be one of the most beautiful girls anywhere, certainly the most beautiful I've ever seen. And you dance as if each song was made especially for you. When you leave the dance floor, it's as if the music loses its rhythm."

She fluttered a "thank you" in my direction as if she had a band that sung that anthem to her every morning.

"Can I buy you a drink? Please."

"Thank you, but I already have too many drinks on the way. So, who are you?"

"Taneba. I don't have to ask you who you are, Her Majesty."

"Oh, thanks. What does Taneba do?"

An alarm went off in my head, but I have never learned to pass myself off as what I am not. "Come on, you're almost sounding like a detective," I parried the question with a weak attempt at humor that did not succeed.

"Well, I'll see you around."

It was the only chance I ever had. After that, she never gave me the opportunity of getting close to her, much less of a conversation or a dance. Once more, I sought Esther's assistance.

"That girl?" she said, as if she was referring to a spirit. "I go try."

That was what I wanted to hear, but she only came back to

report that Her Majesty had told her bluntly that she had no business at the post office. She must have found out my occupation, which was an easy thing to do with everyone whispering about everyone else.

"I don't think you understood me well, Esther. Tell her to forget where I work. I'll give her anything at all she wants."

"Ah-ah. Na that kin' thing you want promise girl? She go kill you-o."

If Esther was moved, Her Majesty was not. "I no know as that girl dey do," Esther reported back to me. "She don tell me say she dey come meet you reach three times. *Abi* she come here?"

I decided this was beyond Esther, and I soon found myself swept into a racket I did not know existed. I implored one of the female hangers-on around Her Majesty to speak with her on my behalf and to explain my offer. I had to part with some money to get her to agree to be my messenger. I doubt she even remembered half a word once she tucked my money away into a deep pocket. All I got afterward was suspense unto suspense: "She go soon come," "No worry, she dey come," "She never come?" I was duped in that manner twice. I then broke my own rule and engaged Alonzo to help me win Her Majesty over.

"Oga Taneba, e get as e be," he reported back to me.

"What do you mean?"

"She say she no want another wardrobe case."

She had once gone out with a fellow who worked in a garment industry, and he had thrown open his wardrobe to her the next morning and asked her to take her choice of his clothes in lieu of cash.

"What did she do?" I asked, interested.

"E be like say she pack plenty of im clothes. But she say she no ready for that kin' thing again."

I tried to rally myself to anger. It was no use: I still wanted her. With every indication that I could not have her, I wanted her all the more. I surprised myself: I approached Tamuno. It was the only time I ever did.

"She's a cute girl any day, sure. You've got great eyes, brother."

"Just help me win her over. I'll always be in your debt."

"Don't do it, brother. Don't be so easy with your pledges. She's a great girl, sure, but then she's just a girl like many others. And maybe she's not for you, brother."

"How's that? I believe I was making progress before I blew my chance."

"Maybe you were, maybe you weren't. Maybe a lot of things, brother."

It was not Tamuno's normal manner of speech. And I had learned that whenever he started speaking like an oracle, it meant the matter was deeper than it seemed. It was best at such times to let him be. But how was I ever going to forget Her Majesty? She had gone to my head like a century-old wine. I could have lived without her if I had never seen her.

My obsession ended in an unexpected manner. Since cigarettes were not on sale inside The Owl, I usually replenished my supply from the vendor down the road. I was on that mission when I saw Her Majesty almost run out of the club toward a waiting sports car on the other side of the road. In the driver's seat sat a notorious character called Zanda who sometimes hung around with St Notorious. His friends called him Above the Law.

When she got to the waiting car, she reached across to hug or kiss the character inside. He put a hand around her waist. Her micro skirt was further drawn up. She must have been wearing a G-string or something like that because what I saw that night was proud flesh with only a hint of white in-between. I stood rooted where I was even after the car had driven away – with Her Majesty in it. The reality had struck me where even my ravenous hunger could not dialogue with it any longer. Her Majesty was only a majestic deception – no better, in essence, than the girls who wore their trade like flags. And because I had placed her on a pedestal stretching up to the heavens, she was only rubble when she came crashing down.

I still admired her, but I was no longer as hungry as the sea.

Better to forget and smile than to remember and be sad.

Love. Bianca. Her Majesty. And some others. Each had in her own way highlighted the 'vaganza of the night for me, in a way that nothing else but actual experience could have done. Those days were suddenly far away, deep in the past. What was ahead of me? I had no answer, even a simple one. As the night wore out and daylight began to impose its sort of sanity, or insanity, around The Owl, I came to the decision I had been postponing. Once more, I stole into the toilet of a roadside hotel and freshened up, then I headed to the general post office for what I expected would be a bitter encounter.

On the contrary, my maternal uncle welcomed me into his office calmly and asked me to sit down as if he had been expecting me.

"I knew you would come back," he said. "I regard you as my blood, Taneba. Everything I do for you I do for my sister."

I could not have cared less if he was doing it for the devil, as long as he took me back.

"You thoroughly disappointed me, but then you think you're still too young to be responsible. You think you know all the answers, when you don't even understand the questions. It's the affliction of youth. Anyway, where have you been all this while – in prison?"

I told him my story as best as I could without making my nights sound like his daylight.

"So, have you completely learned your lesson now? There's an old saying you'll do well to remember: when you lose, don't lose the lesson."

"I'm sorry, uncle. I'm very sorry. I want you to take me back."

He appeared to consider that for a while, during which time my heart raced in all directions.

"Take you back as what? As Taneba who lived in my house or as Taneba who worked in the post office?"

"I want to come back to the post office."

"Listen: I have nothing, completely nothing, against your getting a place of your own. You're old enough to do so. You're even old enough to be thinking of getting married and settling down. What I'm against is your getting mixed up with low characters all over the place who think there's a pot of gold around the corner and the only way to get to it is to mow down everyone in sight."

"I appreciate your concern and kindness, uncle."

"As for the post office, I think I can get you in again, but as what? Some of your mates have since moved up, and you were ahead of most of them. The only way I can see is for you to go for management training. It won't be easy, but it can be done. Are you prepared to take that route?"

I had expected much worse, so it was not difficult at all to assent vigorously.

"One last thing. We all make mistakes. I even believe that every person is entitled to one honest mistake. I will never do this again. The next time you abandon your job and go to farm gold on the moon, don't bother to come back to earth. But if you do, don't ever come back to ask for my help again. I will not do it even for the sake of my mother. Do you completely understand me?"

Once more, I was a citizen of daylight. I spent four months at a center for management training in the middle of nowhere. Four months in which all I had, mostly, was silence. Four months in which I constantly prayed that the pitch of that silence would not strike me deaf. Four months in which I was once more wailing, unheard, in the desert of chastity.

I returned to Lagos a few months to my twenty-eighth birthday. My first gray hair had since advanced inward on an evangelizing mission. I chose to ignore this invasion, especially as I was posted to the express mail section as an assistant manager. The good thing about the job was that, with all the allowances I was entitled to, my take-home pay was almost three times what I had earned in my days in the sorting department. The great thing about it was that I had an official car to myself for all the running around that I now had to do. I soon converted that car into a personal utility vehicle. And it was with it that I once more reentered the world of the night, which I had missed very much.

Suddenly, women who had never taken a second look at me previously began to invite my attention. Driving to work, I could see well-dressed women, wearing the tight-lipped expression of workers stranded at the bus stop, shooting four-letter telegraphs at me: Stop! Sometimes, even ten letters: Stop, please! The bolder or more desperate ones sometimes actually made signals ranging from a raised finger to lewd winks. But the promising service to humanity that I embarked on was benefiting everyone else except me. All I got were addresses, some of which turned out to be fake.

Going back at night or just driving around, it was a wonder to see streetwalkers, who had previously contemplated me with know-all scorn, trying to flag me down. It was on one such drive, down the famous Allen Avenue, that I saw this innocent-looking girl standing by the side of the road. She was slender and carried her strap-on bag like a school kit. With her sleeveless black shirt, bright blue jeans and white sneakers, she could have been a student on a holiday tour. She could have been, but then it was almost eleven o'clock at night. What was this girl, who should be asleep in the room next to her mother's by that time, doing on Allen Avenue?

I screeched to a stop beside her before I had thought the matter through. I had never had anything to do with this roadside universe before. In my estimation, there were three classes of women in the flesh market: those in brothels, those by the roadsides, and those in the clubs. In some cases, these distinctions were not exact because of flux, but I believed they were mostly so. I had always aimed at scooping the cream, nothing less. One night with Bantu, we had even reckoned that if those in the clubs could manage a lifespan of perhaps a decade before the marks of usage transformed them into living artifacts in the museum of time, those in rooming houses could only manage much less.

As soon as I stopped, she came toward me.

"What are you doing here?" I asked, almost as if I were her father.

The question briefly left her speechless.

"Na question you want ask? You miss road?" she queried back.

"Sorry, get in."

"To where?" she asked me when she was seated beside me.

I had rented a small apartment in a more decent and less populated house than House 25. This time, it was House 18. I told her that I would take her there.

"How much you go give me?"

It was the thing that I truly disliked – that sort of haggling.

"Don't worry. Whatever you want."

"No, make we talk am well here."

Was it desperation or bitter experience or even craft that was driving this girl so? Could she be that innocent if she was so schooled?

"I said: whatever you want. Do you want the money here?"

She came with me then without further argument. In my mind, I really had only one thing to say to her: "Whatever your problems are, I'm going to take you off the streets before you age into nothingness." In the same way that I had been adopted – by my maternal uncle, by Mama Senegal, by Tamuno – I had adopted her in my heart, perhaps as the sister that I never had. Sometimes, we surprise ourselves. In my mind, I could already see this girl stepping out in the future as a stable success – with me having engineered the momentum. In as much as I loved the night, I also knew it doled out glories and scars in almost equal measure. If ever I did nothing else, this was one girl I would save from those indelible scars.

The love we give away is the only one we keep.

I failed myself, however, because I could not resist her when we got to my apartment and she herself seized the initiative. She had obviously been schooled. I pampered myself with the thought that that was about the only way to get her to relax and stop being suspicious of me. Perhaps it was, because it was only afterward that we could talk – with her paying any attention other than worrying about her pay.

Her name was Mairo, so chosen by her father because she had been born in the North. She was eighteen and had been on the streets – on and off – for almost two years. To her, her story was enough justification for anything.

Her father had been a factory worker, and he had had two wives. His death, more than two years ago, had interrupted her almost completed high school education. Her mother had been accused of causing his death, and she had fled with her children to her maternal home. There was only her aged mother to receive her, so she took up the unrewarding business of hawking fish and pepper. For Mairo and her younger siblings, it was a difficult existence. Her elder brother was a bus conductor somewhere in the North and was having such a hard time taking care of himself that he never bothered to maintain contact with home.

Her own problem started when, two years ago, her mother started goading her toward joining the ring of Nigerian girls who went abroad, to Europe in particular, to earn money in the flesh market. She even made the necessary contacts because she reckoned that the money her daughter would send home would save the family from destitution. Mairo would have none of that because she had heard stories that those girls were sometimes forced into liaisons with animals. Her decision created disaffection between her and her mother.

"Na so I kneel down dey beg am, say: mama, a-beg, no send me away; please let me be your little girl again."

As far as her mother was concerned, she was ungrateful and stupid. When she could no longer bear the coldness, she ran away to the Mecca of opportunity prospectors: Lagos. She had the address of an old school friend from her village. Her friend took her in and introduced her to the streets at night. Running from going abroad to trade herself, she ended up doing that in Lagos.

"You mean you were on the streets at sixteen and men were going out with you?"

"Them dey rush me sef. Na so I begin see the kin' money wey I never see before. Na the thing wey spoil me be that."

The tide ebbed one day when she woke up with a corpse.

"What do you mean? You went home with a man and he died? What killed him?"

"I no know. When I woke up, come dey try to wake am make e pay me, na so im body just cold. I ran. I tear race from there, straight to the motor park."

Her mother was happy to see her, especially as she came back with some money. It was not much, so it soon ran out. The talk about going abroad came up again. Then her grandmother died. It was up to her mother to see to the burial, but she was too poor. So, she turned to her daughter.

"Na so my mother kneel down dey beg me, say: please, my daughter, if you fit even raise the money for the coffin for me, that go save me from total disgrace."

So, she had returned to Lagos on that mission – about a year after her flight. And I had met her.

"This is a little more complicated than I had expected, but the solution is entirely up to you," I told her. "Now, tell me the truth: do you think you can leave the streets, finish your education and try and make a success of your life?"

"Is that a question? You think say I like as I be? Na condition na im cause am."

"Let the past bury the past. I want to help you."

"Why?"

"I don't even know, but I think I want to save you from the streets. You don't belong there. Whatever. That's not really important now. First, you have to leave the guesthouse where you stay with your friend. Unless you break that link, you'll always be drawn back."

"Where you want make I dey stay? Make I come live with you, na your plan be that?"

"No, I don't want a repeat of this night. Look, I don't want to make you my sex slave, okay? I'll do everything I can for you, on one condition: you're never to return to the streets."

I gave her as much as I could under the circumstances to see to her mother, and we agreed she would return within two weeks. I would then give her a weekly stipend.

"I can only try my best. I'm not rich. So, don't start comparing what I give you to what you sometimes get in a week. You must help yourself too."

The more we straightened out the details, the more I felt like a royal fool. What was I getting myself into – a paternity arrangement? Why? I actually began to wish that Mairo would not return from the village or that she would return after two weeks, which would give me a reason to cancel the arrangement. What if she even returned on time? I could give her some money, an overdose of advice, and bid her farewell. Why should anyone who cannot save herself be saved by anyone else?

She was back within two weeks – with a basket of dry fish and a plenitude of good wishes from her mother, and a large "thank you" card from herself. I accepted the situation as my self-attracted fate. However, getting an accommodation for her proved to be more difficult than I had imagined. Many of the landlords we approached did not want a single girl her age. And if she was my sister, which was the story I told, why could she not stay with me? But we eventually found a landlord who believed or did not care about my story concerning the uneasy relationship between my younger sister and my wife. After that, there was the matter of the basic furniture to attend to.

Getting her into school was harder. She was admitted as a second-year senior high school student. The first day she went to school, looking every bit a student, I experienced a feeling of pride that God must have felt on creation day. My finances and morality were nothing to sing about, however. To get her that far, I had had to use my position in the office to commit fraud – something I had never ever done before.

You must be surprised to receive this postcard from me, after I had sent you my 'suicide note.' I changed my mind. I had already closed the chapter on my life, and I was taking what would have been my last walk on earth – after dispatching that note to you. At the bus stop, I ran into an old woman shivering in the cold. Of course, she was wearing gloves and a long winter jacket, but then it was snowing enough to frighten even the devil. As I passed by her, she grabbed my hand with unexpected energy. 'Thank God you have come back to me, my son,' she cried. 'Where have you been all these years, Alexander? And you left your poor mother forsaken!' She was not blind, so she could see that I was not white. What sort of loneliness or desperation then would make a white woman hold on to a black man, pleading kinship? I was touched. I gave her my own jacket, comforted her and put her on the bus. As I went on, the fog of racism that had almost driven me to suicide dissipated enough for me to regain clarity. If that old woman – frail in age and destitute at heart – could still face this life, then why not me? Of course, my situation is probably worse. Beyond color, I have already given everything I ever had away, so it is like starting from scratch all over again. But now my spirit is strong. And my spirit will lead me on.

Renting a room for Mairo and putting her in school soon turned out to be easier than the other challenges. She complained of boredom and told me she had had to restrain herself several times from visiting her former associates because I had insisted she should not. She could not sleep until very late at night, she said, and this meant her concentration at school in the early hours was very poor. I counseled her once more about the virtue of making new friends and facing the process of adjustment as a battle for her life.

I soon found myself turned into a night nurse. I consented to take her out in the evenings or early hours of the night – not to the clubs, but mostly to roadside eateries and bars. She neither smoked nor drank, so I did not have to legislate against those. But mostly she favored the open-air bars where local bands or traveling minstrels performed. She particularly liked the refrain of a popular drinking song:

Silo silo silo-o
Silololo-o

Whenever she heard the song, she would echo the refrain with such zest and drum on the table with such vigor that I wondered if I was not trying to wrench her away from where her heart truly was.

I inspected her schoolwork regularly. As far as I could tell, she was not missing classes and generally appeared to be taking her studies seriously. It was from this routine inspection that I noticed she had stopped attending her Geography class altogether.

"Have they struck Geography off the curriculum in your school?" I asked her.

"No, but na every time na im that teacher dey flog me."

"Why?"

"Na since na im the man dey chase me, since I enter that school."

"And you never told me?"

"I dey think say I go fit handle am. I no want to dey worry you all the time. I'm not a baby. I can take care of myself."

"When you're no longer a baby, you won't need to announce it."

So it was that I forgot about my punctuality record in my office and marched to the school the next morning to demand an explanation from the principal. When the old scarecrow that was the Geography teacher was summoned, he denied ever making any "overtures of friendship" to Mairo. He had flogged her, he said, because he had caught her and a classmate of hers, Daniel, necking behind the school toilet. Why had he not reported the matter to the principal? Because having disciplined them, he said, he wanted to give them a chance instead of having them suspended from the school.

Both Mairo and Daniel swore that the teacher was lying and was only mentioning their names together because Daniel had caught him struggling to kiss Mairo. Even the principal did not know what to do, whom to believe, much less my confounded self.

"Tell me the truth: were you ever caught, or were you even with Daniel behind the toilet?" I asked Mairo later.

"What for? He's too small for me. I no fit friend anybody for that school."

I once more began my sermon on the need for her to make new friends her age.

The next thing that happened was that on visiting her one evening, she solemnly told me she had something to discuss with me, something that had been worrying her.

"Go ahead," I said. "You don't need any prologue to talk with me."

"Why you no dey make love to me? I too small for you?"

"The question I should ask you is: do you feel you have to pay me back by offering yourself to me?"

"No be like that. I love you. I don give my heart to you, that's why I no fit get another boyfriend."

She got up and began to undress. I believe I wished I could love her. That might have made things easier. But I was in that stage of my life when I was guarding my freedom, guarding myself against love. We were back to that first night, with her now spending more time in my apartment.

"Doesn't your landlord wonder where you go?" I asked her.

"I tell am say your wife don travel. I'm not a baby."

"Listen to me, Mairo. The problem with this is that you'll never start a new life. You're building your life around me. I think the best thing will be for you to go to a boarding school outside Lagos."

"How I go dey see you?"

"You'll see me once in a while, but not in this manner."

"You want to send me away." It was an accusation. "Why you no fit marry me? Na only you be the better man wey I don meet for this Lagos, and I'll take good care of you. I swear."

"The important thing now is for you to get a proper

education."

"As long as you no go leave me."

"I'm not leaving you. I'm only telling you to expand your life."

She appeared to accept that, and I began to feel better. But when I returned to my apartment the next day, her landlord was waiting impatiently outside my door.

"Something is wrong with your sister," he told me animatedly. "We heard her in her room shouting, something like 'Leave me alone,' 'I no want.' Knowing she was alone in that room, we were alarmed. Then we heard a loud crash, like something falling. By the time we broke down the door, she was sprawled on the floor like a corpse. We rushed her to a hospital. They say she's still alive."

We drove to the hospital. Mairo was in a coma. She remained in that state for four days, with me spending a great deal of time beside her. When she regained consciousness, she gave me a coy smile that could only have meant "Thank you, Taneba" and "I love you, Taneba" – together.

"I'm sorry," she told me. "Na my husband cause am. Na so e dey do when e dey vex for me."

I put my head in my hands, wondering where my next station would be – on a bedside chair in a mental hospital?

"What are you talking about? You never told me you have a husband."

"I'm sorry. I no want worry you too much."

"I asked you, several times, to tell me everything about you, everything I need to know."

"I dey sorry. But all the time when I dey for street, e no dey worry me. I think say that one don pass, because im get other wives. But e say e no like the thing wey we dey do; e no want make I marry you."

"What, in God's name, are you talking about?"

According to her, her paternal grandmother had been the priestess of a river deity, and she had given her out in marriage to her deity. She had been so related to the water that when it was time for her to die, she had simply waded far into the water and no one ever saw her again. After her departure, it had rained without ceasing for four market days. Ever since then, her river husband – Mairo's – would come and carry her off for four days any time he needed her.

I was greatly comforted by the doctor, who told me that Mairo was only showing symptoms of post-coma hallucination or something like that. In his own explanation, she was suffering from a rare blood disease, and he strongly recommended that she should remain under observation for some time. The problem was that his estimation of the bill was a question that would require my salary for several months to answer. Fortunately, he was agreeable to my payment plan.

With Mairo in hospital, I deliriously returned to the night. I would visit her for a few hours after work, then I would become one with the night. It was then I finally revisited Sundown! It was not such a great experience. Apart from the fact that everything there was scandalously expensive, it lacked the verve of The Owl. Everything was so formal and mannered that it would not have been out of place for a bell to sound and all the guests there invited to the dinner table.

So, I settled for 24. It was located in a part of Lagos, near the seaport, that I had hardly ever visited previously. The allure of 24 was that, with its shift system, it never closed.

It was there that I finally saw Tamuno again, the shadow of Tamuno. Both his pendant and all the gold rings were gone. He had lost weight and his fancy haircut looked forsaken. Perhaps as a mockery of his fate or in an attempt at self-assertion, he now sported a large earring, copper-plated.

"My brother, Taneba! Where have you been?" he exclaimed when he saw me, overwhelming me with an embrace. There was no fear this time of my being swept off my feet.

Even his language had undergone a change. Ever since we left school, I had never heard Tamuno's "brother" preceded by any possessive pronoun. But the gleam of his smile was still there. Nothing could take that away.

"I've been looking all over for you," I told him.

"André told me he saw you outside The Owl."

"He did? But he said he didn't know where you were."

"There are some things he doesn't understand."

"What happened?"

"Tomorrow, robins will sing, my brother. It really is no big deal."

It occurred to me then that he had chosen the song as much as it had chosen him. He was living his life as a song, according to a song. He was no longer in show business; he had become a show – with or without a business.

"I had a run-in with Saint. You don't want to know the details. We didn't rhyme anymore, so I moved on. But you know what pains me, my brother? They've killed The Owl. It's free-for-all there these days; they even fight with bottles. That could never have happened in my time."

He had tried to run two other nightclubs after that. Both had started with flourish but had closed without fanfare. The first had been in a restaurant; it opened when the restaurant closed. According to Tamuno, the smell of food had been too thick for the patrons, despite his air-freshening measures. Besides, it was on a street where there were already two established dancing restaurants – the preference of most residents in the area. The second, by the waterfront, had been closed down because he had tried to turn it into a striptease club.

"But the robins will still sing, my brother. I'm coming back with a bang."

I had no doubt that he would. If anyone was indeed born for that life, it was Tamuno. Before I left, he took my address.

"I'm going to invite you to the opening, as soon as everything is set. This time, my brother, I'm going to stay on top until I die. You'll see."

On my way out, I saw Alonzo beside a taxi.

"I dey wait for Don," he told me.

"Beside a taxi? What happened to the cars?"

"Life na gamble."

It was meeting Tamuno that led Bantu to me. Two nights afterward, he knocked on my door at almost four o'clock in the morning – banged on it as if he was the tenant and I was a squatter. I was exceedingly happy to see him. I was also mystified about how he had managed to make it to my door at that hour since our neighborhood guards did not know him and he had a thick nightclub smell about him.

"How did you get here, Bantu? How did you manage to pass the street gate?" I asked him, after I made him welcome.

"A sea of sharks, and it's Bantu for himself."

"I just hope there's no search party on its way to my apartment right now."

"It's the low tide, man, but let's still make up for the time we'll lose in the day. A very cold beer would be an inspired thought."

He was referring to his theory that, for nightclub patrons, the high tide of the night began at midnight. It was within the next three hours that they experienced that nirvana of the night that made it all worthwhile. As from three o'clock, when the low tide commenced, it was time to go home, time to begin to reconcile the night with the day.

"So, how did you locate my place?" I asked, after I had fulfilled his request.

"I met Don at 24, only now it looks as if it's Don as in d-o-n-e. He's taken a mighty fall, man."

"He'll come up again."

"Sure, he will. He's a hard businessman, only he's also hard in the gaming division. But I like his spirit, man. He's not giving up on himself at all."

"Now, the main question: what are you doing in Lagos? I didn't hear the noise of your jet landing on my roof."

"It's coming after me," he said with a boisterous laugh. "I'm in what they call the advance party, man. Well, I had to leave that place for them rioters. I don't know what the attraction is, but they moved in there like it's paradise."

"What would they be looking for in a place called Naomi's?"

"You're asking the wrong person, man. They've got their life. I've got mine."

"You left the place just like that? What sort of management practice is that?"

"It's the Bantu Practice, I guess," he said. "The Bantu Practice, man. I'm right in them fogs these days."

"I can see you're in very good cheer. What happened – your gray hairs stopped marching in your sleep?"

"They had to, man, after the revelation. I court-martialed all of them. A very strange thing happened to me. This figure without a face rode up to the club..."

"What are you talking about?"

"Well, maybe it had a face, but it was invisible. And it came on top of this camel that looked older than time itself."

"How could this figure see if..."

"If you've got the revelation, you can see very well without them tired eyes of ours. But why don't you hear me out first before you start wandering in them academic laboratories? This figure rode up to the club and gave me the sign. I got on the camel and it took us inside the desert, deep inside. We stopped by a valley, and we rode right down. Then it happened to me – like being struck by a thunderbolt. I must have gone back to the origin of the world. I was in this vast palace in the kingdom of a people who were neither white nor black – the Ams. And this king in a truly splendid throne beckoned to me: 'Come, my son, in whom I am well pleased.' By the way, I'm *Am* Bantu now because I'm the son of a king. But you can rest easy. I don't insist on the title. I know what I know.

"In that valley, I went past that little garden called Eden, no bigger than the nursery where my kids learned the alphabets..."

"That garden, Bantu, was the first garden. You went past it

– to where?"

"Is that what your history tells you, man? The problem with history is that it's been so torn apart – indigenized, colonized, gassed up, whatever – that it hardly knows what it is anymore. It's all messed up and abridged. I'm telling you, man: I saw Adam's grandfather being readied for the initiation rite. I saw Christ chewing his nails at Golgotha. I saw Noah complaining about the size of his ark. I came across a pharaoh rising from the dead. I saw the Igbo captives who would rather die than be slaves merge with the water at Igbo Landing, singing 'Orimiri Omambala bu anyi bia. Orimiri Omambala ka anyi ga ejina.'"

"You saw all these in that little valley?" In my estimation, the situation was way beyond asking God to cast a treasure chest in Bantu's direction. I had to reason with him.

"It's a relay vision, man, deep into history, beyond history even. Then I heard the song:

> By the rivers of Babylon
> There we sat down
> And there we wept
> When we remembered Zion
>
> But the wicked carried us away
> Captivity required from us a song
> But how can we sing the alpha song
> In a strange land?

"That's the song I heard from the water at Igbo Landing, the alpha song. It's the first stage: self-awareness, self-reclamation. After that, there is the meridian song: the conquest of the spheres, the power of miracles. And then the omega song: the immortality of the self. My people perish for lack of knowledge, don't you understand? But I'm jumping ahead. After Igbo Landing..."

"I get your drift. You saw everything in this relay vision, right?"

"Everything, man. And don't be talking about 'vision' as if I'm on the borderline. I only used that to comfort you. It was an experience, with the figure without a face leading me to it."

"I don't know what happened to you up there, Bantu, but I think you probably took a mightier fall than Tamuno and you've gone way beyond storytelling now. You're into mythmaking."

"There you go. Mythmaking. You almost make it sound like madness or muddling up everything. But we're all in it. It's your myth against mine. You're a myth, man, you know that? Life itself is a myth. We don't live, man. We only go through the motions. Every man's life is a myth he tries to personalize. He doesn't own it, he doesn't even understand it. Our lives could as well be fables or nightdreams to us. We're all mythmakers, so I'd rather be bold about it."

"So, you agree you're into mythmaking now?"

"No, not with my story. I'm just helping you out with throwing names around. Here I come telling you about the truest peak experience and the first thing you do is to scurry behind them textbook fogs where name-calling jargons make you a professor faster than anything else. Better for you, you think, because you don't want your universe disturbed. You've been tidied in, tucked in with a lot of airbrushed myths you're just like all them sell-outs in Babylon who mistook them whips for soup ladles."

"Hey, Bantu, what's this? Did you come here to attack me?"

He laughed then. "You know me, man. I've never attacked anybody in my life, not even El Diablito, not even them pretty fingers that left us stranded in Monrovia. You're my partner, always. But I'm telling you: I'm going to disturb your tidy universe. I'm going to wait for the meridian hour singing the alpha song."

What he was up to I did not know. But he stayed in my apartment for two days, and then he vanished – without any notice or departure note. He left without his bag of clothes and other personal items. In those two days, he came across a letter from Mairo that I suspect she must have copied from somewhere.

"I promise. I promise you things any time I'm with you and I wish I could promise you everything this world can hold. I promise I'll always love you even if you break up with me. I

promise I'll always share everything I have with you. I promise any time you need me I'll always be there. I promise kisses any time your lips are dry. I promise I'll always say the truth any time you need it. I promise I'll always satisfy you any time we're on. I promise I'll always spend time with you, no one else. I promise I'll never make you regret anything. Can you promise me these things too? Love, Mairo."

"Hey, man. What's this? How old is she?"

I told him.

"Are you snatching babies from them mothers these days?"

"She's not a baby, and I'm only trying to help her." I felt that Bantu, in his new state, would understand, so I told him the story.

"You've got a great soul, man, but how are you going to help this kid with all them kisses and monkeying in bed?"

"Maybe I'm waiting for my own alpha song," I said teasingly.

"It's not about you no longer being you. It's about you being you. The turning of water into wine was not religion, man. It was chemistry. The walking on the water was not about commandments. It was physics."

"Going against the law of gravity is physics?"

"Physics ahead of its time, chemistry ahead of its time. That's what happens when you conquer the spheres: you're ahead of time. Well, you take care of that kid as best as you can. She may indeed lead you to your alpha song."

If there was a song about Mairo, it turned out to be of a different sort. When she came out of hospital, she was more restless than ever. I told her to be thankful rather than go on moaning about her hospital experience and to concentrate on finishing the remaining weeks of the academic year with a good result that would enable her to transfer to a reputable boarding school. I had already made the financial provision.

"You promise say you no go leave me?"

"How you go on about this matter! I'm not leaving you, as

long as you follow the path we've discussed."

"I promise."

Shortly afterward, I had to travel for a two-week refresher course outside Lagos. Mairo was very sad. So, I promised her that on the very night of my return I would take her dancing – in a nightclub.

The information I had been given about the course turned out to be incorrect. It was only for ten days. I returned to Lagos four days earlier than I had expected. I considered going to see Mairo, but I had not come up with a winning idea on how to mollify her since I had no intention of keeping the promise I had made to her. I took to the night instead.

I did not really want to go to 24 for fear of running into Tamuno there. Seeing him in the state he was in was a painful experience. But my thoughts kept traveling in the direction of 24. Although it had no admission code, it best suited my mood.

It was there that I saw Mairo – wearing a spaghetti top, bell-bottoms, and snub-nosed platform shoes that made her look like a renegade princess – dancing away with her soul on her hips as if there was no tomorrow. When she saw me, she screamed and took to her heels, leaving her friend, Jovita, studying me coldly.

The night was ruined for me. I had a beer, nonetheless, before I left for home. She was waiting for me outside my door, spouting apologies like a fountain. I unlocked the door, and she followed me inside. She threw herself at my feet and held on to my trouser as if her life depended on it. I invited her to sit down instead, but that only provoked a fresh outburst of tears. I did manage to free myself enough to sit down.

"I'm sorry, Taneba. I take God beg you. Na as you no dey na im my friend say make I follow am out. I just go there to dance, not to look for man."

"What am I to say to you, Mairo: get angry with you or get angry with myself? Take a look at yourself. The top you're wearing barely manages to cover your breasts. I thought you said you had thrown all these things away? And your friend, Jovita, when did you start going out with her again?”

"Na as you no dey. I come dey lonely. No one to talk to..."

“How many times did I counsel you to become a student both in motion and in notion? Those girls in your class are not non-living things. Why can’t you find a friend among them? What is the great thing you’re looking for on the streets?”

“I take God beg you. It will never happen again. I am sorry. You no say even God in heaven dey still forgive us our sins...”

“Your addiction to the streets has entered your spirit, Mairo, and you’re not ready yet to fight for your life. How can you win a battle that you’re not even fighting? But who am I to judge you? To do that is to judge myself. It’s your life to live, but I’ll take no further responsibility for you. The only thing I can do now is to advise you to at least finish high school – no matter what else you do.”

The tears and pleas went on and on, for the next hour or two, and I did not have the heart to turn her out. Over the months I had known her, I had become very fond of Mairo. However, that night had illuminated for me the fact that we were embarked on an impossible venture because she did not have the drive and the vision to make a clean break with the life of the streets at night.

When she finally wore herself out, I insisted on taking her home. I took the money I had saved for her boarding school fees, stuffed it into her bag, then I drove her home – with her writhing and muttering something like “I don kill myself be that” over the quarter-mile or so of that terribly sad journey.

Toshiba

After the incident with Mairo, I was like a valley of pain hemmed in by regrets. I blamed the stunting politics of the day that had steered her into the refuge of the night. I blamed the dazzle of the night that had blinded her to other possibilities. And I blamed her for forsaking in the bald land of self-pity my oft-repeated lesson that the greatest power for our own salvation must come from within us. Did she suppose that running with the night would take her farther than the Epicurean signposts of male patrons, like me, who only wanted her for a time out of mostly exaggerated necessity? Was it that difficult for her to rise above her circumstances or was it easy for her to discount my sermons because she could not reconcile my sermons with my own lifestyle?

I blamed myself even more. Really, I should have figured out early enough that it would end the way it did. The spirit of the night can be a terrible demon to exorcise – terrible because, to the possessed, it is a pleasurable addiction. And I had merely given her a stone tablet of commandments and expected everything else to fall into place. Had I altogether been fair to Mairo, especially in abandoning her upon her missing her first step in the journey we had set out on? If I really wanted her to turn out well, why had I not taken the confidence-boosting step of keeping her as my girlfriend? Had I restrained myself because I had met her as a prostitute?

I found myself rereading some of her letters to me. She had certainly loved expressing her emotions in writing, often sending me cards and letters that she probably copied from somewhere.

Reliving those moments saddened me. It was not difficult to see that, whatever else had happened between us, Mairo had gravitated to me powerfully. Had we been on the road to something greater than both of us had imagined, and could I not forgive and forget the incident at 24? But was there any insurance against any such future weakness? Although I felt the weight of approximate paternity lifted off my shoulders, I was also burdened by a sense of loss.

For Mairo, the matter was not that complicated. Many were the days she sought me out after the incident, tearfully soliciting my forgiveness and swearing great oaths that she would never err in such a fashion again.

"I take God beg you, Taneba, that na devil work. E no go ever happen again, otherwise make Satan eat me. You know say I love you, no be just say you dey help me. I love you with all my heart. God na im be my witness: I just go there that day because I dey feel lonely, no be any other thing."

My resolve was shaken, especially as she had evidently lost weight in so short a time. But there was something in me that was resolute that both of us would fare better in our different spheres without each other. Without her, I would return to my life. Without me, she would have to deal with the starkness of a decision that she must confront, especially now that I had validated an option for her.

The next thing that happened was that she turned up with her landlord. He came with a bottle of wine to oil his intercession. Right away, he told me he had suspected from the beginning that we were not related but that he had been impressed by my mission. "Will you abandon her now, now that she's acquired that determination to be true to everything that you've taught her? Apart from the fact that I fear for her health and even her life, remember: to profess love without showing mercy is meaningless."

He was one of the few people who could go on and on without losing their clarity of focus. He delved into all sorts of private and public histories, even religious prophecies, to make the most sustained appeal that has ever been directed to me. I promised to reconsider the matter.

"Remember: although we all live by God's grace, we all are children of our own grace."

There was only one thing to do. As soon as they left, I threw my things into a bag and fled my apartment. I knew there was no way I would face Mairo again – especially Mairo and Mr Samuel, her landlord – and not take her back.

On the third day of my flight, a card arrived for me in my office. It was from Mairo. On the cover was the picture of a heart splitting into two; inside was the message 'I love you' – in small letters. In all, I received thirty cards, one every day. As the heart on the cover split up all the more, the message of love within grew bigger. In the final card, the heart had become entirely shattered whereas the plaintive cry of love had filled up every available space inside.

The shattering was prophetic in another sense. The day that last card arrived was the day I lost my job in the express mail section of the postal service. My fraud had been discovered. Of course, I had a well-rehearsed explanation and my unblemished record to cite as further proof of my honesty. I might have triumphed, had things gone according to my disaster scenarios.

But they did not. In that service, there were eyes and ears that were not happy with the way I had arrived at my position. So, there were brains doubly verifying my figures. The purpose was to amass enough evidence for the in-house "tribunal" ever ready to levy justice on frauds like me.

I did not immediately make this connection, but when my maternal uncle walked into my office that afternoon, I sensed that something was out of order. Usually, he invited me to his office. Ignoring my greeting, he surveyed my flustered presence calmly, then he sat down.

"I will get to the point immediately. It has been brought to my notice – and the evidence is strong – that you have been gambling with your figures and stealing money from the postal service. Is this a correct summation of the situation?"

"There must be a mistake, uncle. No one has even queried me, instead they're going behind my back..."

"If the matter weren't so serious, I believe I might have found your low comedy funny. Have you forgotten that I was the one who brought you into the postal service? Before you started work here, I had already spent fourteen years in the service.

Fourteen years. I know postal fraud when I see one. That's why I am a respected postal fraud examiner. And now you have gone from stealing to lying, or is it from lying to stealing?"

I said nothing.

"You require a query, do you? That's in order then. I really do not have to deal with this. There's an internal disciplinary mechanism that will take care of you. Do you understand me completely?"

"Uncle, please, it's not like that," I heard myself say as he made to get up.

"It's like how? Did you or did you not steal all that money?"

"I did."

"And what did you do with the money? Where is the house that you are building, where is the land that you bought, where is the wife you married, where is the car you bought?"

What was there to say? My maternal uncle would not have had a royal laugh if I had told him my story. He would have had a fit.

"And even if you did all or any of these things, what still would be the justification to steal like a common criminal? I regard you as my blood, Taneba. I will not deny it even now, but I think yours is corrupted blood, especially with the low life that you live and the low lives you prefer to associate with. When was the last time you came to my house? The moment I suggested you should think of getting married, you chose to stay away because – even as old as you are – you still think you are too young to be responsible. Not anymore. Right now, you are looking at a long prison term because the postal service wants to set an example with you."

I knew my uncle did not play around with the truth. I began to perspire seriously – cold sweat, although it was a blistering afternoon.

"Uncle, please, I'm sorry."

"What did you do with the money?"

He actually paused for an answer. I licked my lips over and over again, moistening them helplessly.

"How would you know or tell me? I only hope you do not end up before a firing squad one day, convicted of a capital crime. Right now, to say I'm ashamed of you is an understatement. You have brought disgrace to yourself, and to me. If it were not for the sake of my sister, who made me swear to take care of you, I would leave you to your fate. Anyway, you can remain at your post and wait for a query. It will come soon enough, and you will be fully prosecuted thereafter. The alternative is for you to put in your resignation immediately. Either way, you'll still be required to pay back the money you stole. One road leads you to prison certainly. The other leads you to yourself, doubtfully. Do you completely understand me?"

I began a jerky expression of gratitude.

"God damn you, Taneba!"

It was the strongest language I had ever heard him use.

"You are forcing me to stick out my neck for you again and almost turning me into an accomplice! Right here and now, I tell you: I will have nothing to do with you henceforth, except as my sister's son – when you decide to become one. Nothing more in the public service. If you require any further telling, then let me spell it out for you, you are a complete f-o-o-l and you are traveling on the thoroughfare to ruin and agony. May God have mercy on you!"

It sounded like a prayer for the condemned. I put in my letter that same afternoon – just a sentence that read "I hereby beg to resign" – and left the postal service forever.

Once more, I was jobless. It was harder this time because I was no longer twenty-five. I was past twenty-eight, and I had been out of school for seven years. There was really no point trying to take stock because I knew there was nothing much to reckon.

I sorely missed Bantu. He would have had something uplifting to say, even if only to pat me on the back and speak of seas and sharks and about knowing how to swim. I found myself pondering once more where he could have disappeared to. Although I had asked around, I had found no one who was any wiser. In fact, my asking about him only earned me suspicious looks because everyone believed I was the one who should be doing the answering – perhaps at the police station. It was an uneasy state to be in, and this time around I did not have my maternal uncle as my guardian angel.

Mercifully, the situation did not persist. It lasted three unnerving months. Then I received an ornate invitation to the "grand opening" of Tamuno's new nightclub, Seventh Heaven. It was the song of the season everywhere, especially in the media. On one television program, the presenter spoke glowingly of Tamuno's thesis. According to her, he had subsequently received a deserved invitation to give a lecture on subcultures at a university in Ghana.

Tamuno himself later appeared on the program, looking like a beefy resurrection and glittering more than ever before. He must have decided to keep the earring motif, this time with a gold-plated earring that could have passed for a stopwatch.

"Owl was like Third Heaven, sister. The idea was to lift people up above the drudgery of their everyday lives. But we didn't go high enough. Now, we're going all the way. Some people think a nightclub is all about dancing and people connecting. It's a language too, and that's important. It should give you a feeling of flotation that says to you: what's this grand act telling me about my life, about the largesse of life? It's a great way of life, and it's the only one I know."

The effect of the buildup was that on the opening night all the arteries of Lagos led to Seventh Heaven, which was located deep in the Government Reserved Area. Tamuno gave me a heart-warming embrace when he saw me and asked Alonzo to introduce me to the key workers.

The place must have been designed as an ode to magnificence. Not only was it the biggest club in Lagos, it made Sundown! seem frugal and The Owl tame. There was a "maximum" revolving dance floor that was quite a spectacle. Apart from the male bouncers at the gate, all the workers within – disc jockeys, waitresses, barkeepers, game-table attendants – were female. And their dress mode was fascinating – an attempt to dress everything that should be undressed and undress everything that should be dressed. Although the girls wore high sombreros and almost knee-length boots, their blouse and skirt consisted of only a leather bra and pant, with a money-belt. After more than a year of being in the doldrums, Tamuno had returned to reckoning with an instant sensation.

My supposition was that he would be too busy that night for us to talk. But it was not too long before I saw him escorting a well-dressed man that looked like a boxer and his train of male and female companions. Another St Notorious? They passed by my table, and Tamuno caused the train to stop.

"What's the problem, brother, sitting all alone and looking as bland as ice?" he asked me.

"This is not the time..."

"Come on, we're brothers, right?"

"Well, I lost my job about three months ago."

"We'll sort that out. Here, meet my partner, Chief Stephens. Taneba."

"Oh, you're the genius Taneba?" Chief Stephens said familiarly, extending a hand that could have been a paw.

I smiled then and felt better.

"Tamuno thinks you're a genius, and I know him enough to believe him. Why don't you come and see me in my office and we'll do something about a job for you?" He spoke in measured tones, as if reciting by rote.

One of his companions slipped a business card into my hand, and the train moved on. Tamuno returned much later with a tall, pretty girl in a very revealing dress. In this case, the naked flesh appeared to clothe the dress. I had never seen her before, and I told myself that if she was not unbelievably beautiful someone would surely have accosted her in a rather rough fashion.

"I've got to dash off briefly," he told me. "Do me a favor and keep Faith here company. She's special to me, brother."

"The honor is mine, and you know that."

He gave me a wink and hurried away.

"How do you do, Taneba?" she said to me as we shook hands.

"Fine, now. You must really be special."

"Thanks. You know Tamuno really likes you?"

"What do you mean?"

"Oh, he talks about you often. Sometimes, I wonder if he wishes he could be like you, not that I know what you're all about. Are you really a genius?"

"Tamuno is very kind, even with his language. You're the genius here. Anyone who can be so original in her fashion sense must be one," I said, matching the words with a frank stare.

She regarded me with a bit more attention. "Tamuno must be right then. That's a rather original way of ogling me."

We both started laughing at the same time. And that made conversation easier, until Alonzo came and whispered to her. She fluttered her fingers in farewell, asked me to take care, and left.

I presented myself at Chief Stephens's office a few days later with the resolution that at the first suggestion of anything remotely resembling a "run" I would excuse myself and return to my poverty. But it was a different experience. The office of Stephens Holdings was in one of five contiguous buildings, with a huge signpost announcing businesses that were apparently legitimate. His own office, in the center of the cluster, had probably been translated from an interior design catalog.

"I do not know you," he told me. "But I have known Tamuno since our days at Government College. He went on to the university, and I went into business – real estate, transportation, import, export. And now I am about to go into the courier business, Stephens Speed. I trust Tamuno, I trust his judgment, so I am going to give you a job as the manager of Stephens Speed – if indeed you are a genius. Hold it! You do not have to speak now. I have made some inquiries about you. I am told you know your job but that you left the post office under a cloud. So, I am going to tell you this only one time. Take a very good look at me, and I tell you: do not ever monkey with me. If you monkey with me, I will gorilla you."

Quite an appropriate choice of imagery for a man like Chief Stephens.

I wondered then what deity in the pantheon of supernatural intercessors was watching over me. A job as the manager of a courier firm – for a discredited fraud like me! Just like that? But then in Tamuno's world, things often happened like that or not at all. Chief Stephens even told me as much: "Everything is simple in Nigeria, depending on whom you know."

Stephens Speed shot me up significantly. I was offered a salary that promised to make my days – and nights especially – easy. And a car that I was told would automatically become mine if I met my target for the first year of operation. I regarded it as mine already because, except for the unpleasantness occasioned by the Mairo project, I had always exceeded my annual targets easily. Stephens Speed it was that took me out of House 18 up to The Penthouse – a three-bedroom apartment on the top floor of a five-floor building. Stephens Speed it was that sped me to my lambada with Toshiba, whose universe was one for one and all for one.

I met her at the birthday party of the manager of a small insurance firm I was trying to win over to the speed and security of Stephens Speed. She was the external relations manager of Assured Insurance and, as far as I could tell, the coordinator of the party. The first thing that struck me about her was her multiracial appearance. She had a light complexion and an aquiline nose, but the fullness of her lips, the texture of her hair, and the shape of her eyes indicated genetic sources that included Africa and Asia. She was very appealing to look at, with a face that could have been the exquisitely carved mask of the female spirit of beauty, although her height could only be generously described as average.

She went up and down as if making everyone else happy amounted to her own enjoyment. Was she trying to please her boss? He would have to be cast in stone not to be pleased already.

"Why don't you have some fun, dance with me?" I asked her, with my best smile, when I could.

"Excuse me?"

"I'd like to dance with you. It'd be an experience for me to treasure, to dance with someone so unambiguously fascinating."

"I'll be right with you." And she was off again.

She had given that night a purpose beyond the mostly insincere backslapping and business-class smiles. When she eventually did dance with me, because I kept after her, she danced with a working-class girl's sense of respectability. But it was also not difficult to tell that she was enamored of the pop icons of the day, with the manner she hummed their songs. I asked her out on a date afterward.

"Because we had a dance together? Sorry, I don't go on dates with strange men."

"I'm not strange. I manage Stephens Speed, and I believe our two companies are going to be doing a lot of business together very soon. More important, it shouldn't take a lifetime for two people to meet and know each other."

"I know, but I just met you today. I don't rush into these things."

"None of us has forever to live, you know. If we did, it'd probably be fine to spend ten years or so on pre-dating acquaintanceship. I probably don't have more than five years more to live, or you. Who knows?"

She gave me a sour look. "I don't like people who wish themselves evil, and then that on other people too. If that was meant to impress me or make me change my mind, it had quite the opposite effect. Excuse me."

I stood there watching her hurry away, looking like a fool. Why did I have a talent for bungling these things? But I was too smitten already to give up. And, mercifully, she was on her best behavior that night.

"Sorry about that," I told her when I could. "It's probably a good sign that we're clarifying ourselves right from the beginning. What I was merely trying to say is that we live under such intense pressure these days that it's not uncommon to age early or die young. Which is where we the courier firms come in. The whole world is in a race against time."

"And what do you do with the time you save?"

Was she that kind of girl?

"Anyway," she went on, "what do you want from me?"

"Experience. Friendship. The best of you."

"You're not sure which?"

I laughed then, thinking I had softened her. All I got from her that night, however, was her name and office telephone number – after circling around her like a bodyguard.

In the next two months, I called her every day at work – sometimes two or three times a day. It was an unusual situation for me. In those two months, I told her everything there was to recount about myself – except my fondness for nightlife – and inevitably some other stories I had to invent just to keep the conversation going. I also learned much about her. Her father was Ijaw and had named her Tongha. Her paternal grandmother was Chinese and named her after the city where she was born: Shanghai. Her mother's mother was from the Philippines and had named her Imelda. Her English mother had named her Barbara. It was from these four names – the first one or two words – that she had pieced together the name she answered: To-sh-i-ba. She had grown up in Shanghai and gone to elementary school there, then moved to England for her high school and college, and finally returned to Nigeria with her father.

"You know, you're the world," I told her, "the new world of racial hyphenations."

"You always know the right thing to say. You're really very nice to talk to."

"Most people are, if you listen to them."

"No, that's not true. Most people are boring to talk to, wrapped up only in their self-interest."

At that point there was no longer any point in postponements. I took her to dinner in an exotic restaurant where we tried out buttered rice and ostrich stew. It was a grand setting, with the tables laid as if for a royal banquet. Later, we retired to

The Penthouse and made such pleasurable love that I was convinced she was worth all the effort. She told me she had finally been won over by my table manners. It was something I needed to be reminded about and even then did not really remember.

Then followed three heady months in which we existed only for each other. We spent a lot of time shuttered in at The Penthouse, as if we had been sex-starved since creation day. We also spent some time in her room at the two-bedroom apartment she shared with a female colleague in the office. Next to lovemaking, she loved cooking – three-course meals – and I believe I added weight because of overindulgence. On weekends, however, neither The Penthouse nor Number 33, her residence, was enough for us. We went from nightspot to nightspot – especially on the Island – from resort to resort, and even a couple of city destinations outside Lagos. It was new love, and we were supremely intoxicated. There were no complications because we viewed ourselves and the world through lenses tinted with a romance yet to become dusty or tasked by travel.

She loved flowers and cards and letters so much that, in the third month, I finally consented to write her a letter expressing my feelings for her. It was the time for the truth of the time – with fanfare.

"You are, in God's name, one of the great loves of my life. I love you with such passionate intensity that just a tiny furrow on your face is enough to bring tears to my eyes. For me, it's all and everything for love. Sometimes, I ask myself: am I seeking in love, or through you, something that may not even be there? All my life, I've been searching for something just beyond the edge of my consciousness, just a little above my comprehension. I doubt if I'll ever find it, and that thought continually saddens me. It devalues the simple adventures of existence, although it deepens the mystic aura of being. But through you, life sprang a pleasant surprise on me. When you came along, it was as if I returned to the tabernacle of meaning. It's as if I'm onto the last great love of my life. Everything without you is like a tablet of ash.

"In three short months, we've lived through many ages, many worlds, and many loves. The aura glistens in my soul. That walk in the drizzle, with the doorman providing umbrella cover, at The Tavern; that glorious weekend at Virgin Island; those magical nights wrapped into each other at The Penthouse; those surfing crests at Lakeside; the musical ascensions at Music Temple; the fish regattas at Number 33... The litany lengthens. I remember them all, moment by moment, and I grow heads. I'll always remember them until the day I die.

"'What do you want from me?' you asked me that first night. 'Experience,' I said. You have given me experiences rich in bliss. Memories, each one shining like a gold coin. It's the depth and scope of these remembered moments, and the hunger for more, that strengthen my conviction that if I lose you I lose a great part of myself. I've done very many spins in this brief life. I've turned in four directions, into alphabet streets filled with smoke and alabaster, but you're an experience above experiences. You have given me memories, by simple signs of affection and paradisial conjugations, that spiral me into giddy heights.

"I loved you yesterday. I love you today. I'll always love you. We are what happens to us. And you happened to me – like a rainbow, like a homing song. And I know I'll never be the same again. And now, in search of meaning, words almost suffocate me. You're my destiny, I believe. You're what happened to me. You have made me, wearied by a million journeys into myself, feel the sacramental power of love. And your love has uplifted me. May we stay high forever."

That letter fetched me a recorded cassette, which she did herself, of ecstatic love songs. And a written response that even if we became so poor – "God forbid!" – that we had to live in a grass shack and cover ourselves with newspapers in order to keep warm, she would always love me.

I had a great time with Toshiba. No doubt at all about it. But her assertive nature was evident right from the beginning. She blew through The Penthouse like a benevolent tornado, if there is such a thing, and rearranged everything to suit her taste and convenience. My protest? She kissed that away.

She wondered about my friends and proceeded to give me what could pass as coaching lessons on how to make "decent" friends. I had told her I was the only child of a couple who had been the only children of their parents. She desired to meet anyone who could pass as my relative because she believed it was important to her marriage plan. She warned me that she was a jealous lover and usually teased me or even sulked if I held a long conversation with Jessica, her colleague and housemate. She decided where we should go, how we would dress, and even how I should bathe. She loved fish so much that I was practically sentenced to it, although I was a hearty lover of beef.

I believe I would have married her, regardless. Despite her rather domineering nature, I found in her a matching lover of pleasure and we applied ourselves to lapping up every molecule. But whenever we disagreed on any subject, she had a way of slipping in the remark "What do you know about the world?" that truly irritated me. Was it because I had only been to Liberia, and what a trip, whereas she had lived in many countries?

"What do you mean by that?" I demanded one day. "You think because I've not been to the Philippines or any of the countries you've been to..."

She shushed me up with a kiss. "Cool your temper, darling," she cooed in my ear. "Don't you know you're a blessing to me? I was only teasing you."

Nevertheless, she soon initiated a plan for us to travel to England so I could "see a bit of the world." It was then that I began to take stock of my financial situation. Although I had a well-paying job, I often found myself broke. Toshiba said again and again that money did not have anything to do with whom or how she loved, but she was in reality like a goddess of pleasure requiring constant and lavish sacrifices. She was fond of presents, from love notes to house furniture. And there was the constant traveling – with the costly accommodation and flight arrangements, because she would have nothing but the best. As far as I could see, I was on a journey that was leading me to no other destination than the fulfillment of Chief Stephens's threat: "I will gorilla you."

So, I contrived an absence that truly pained me because it denied me Toshiba's fountain of pleasure. I began to invent reasons, usually related to the office, why we could not go out so much or why I could not get a particular present for her within a certain period. Sometimes, I pretended I was traveling out of town on official business only to oscillate between my office and Seventh Heaven. She apparently knew what I was doing, sometimes, and actually called me "Taneba the Liar" once. Before I could seize on that as the reason for an extended absence, she sent me a tape-recorded apology of doubtful originality – against the background of her favorite love song.

"I want to say once more that I truly love you – from the depths of my being and in totality. You don't have to stay away from me when things are a bit rough. I think I am old enough to know that no condition is permanent and that the purpose of life is not to 'stay high' – be happy – all the time, but to learn. And our world is a perfect learning environment because it's filled with vicissitudes. We expect everything to be smooth, but friction is what we get and that's what we learn from. I also know that we can't have adventures all the time because life itself is inherently problematic and hurtful, which most probably is why most people prefer to live in a world of fantasy – if only to escape from their hurt and fears.

"I also know that falling in love is totally narcissistic. Most times, we fall in love with a fantasy of the other person, which is in fact our fantasy of ourselves. Real love begins when we realize that the other isn't 'I' but 'you.' It's a good thing we have the fantasy to bring us together, or no one would get married. But the work of true love begins when illusion is over, and we no longer hang on to it. What am I saying? I may not be your wife, and perhaps may never be, but that's left for the future to decide. For now, I am your girlfriend and I deeply love and care about you. I will always have you back, no matter the situation. It pains me when you stay away.

After all, what is love all about? A good relationship is all about balance and complementing each other. Love, kindness, intimacy and warmth are those things that make good relationship. Money doesn't come into it.

"Sometimes, society is to blame for some of the problems we face. We have a culture of rugged individualism and people can't be real when life is like that. I know in the face of any problem between a couple, the woman is supposed to valiantly bridge the gap, to assuage her partner's guilt and resentment and to bear the brunt of disapproval from friends and family. I may have disappointed you in my handling of the situation so far, and I am truly sorry for that. Maybe somewhere in the middle of trying to do all that, I may have collapsed under the strain. I am very sorry. No matter the names I must have called you, please overlook them. I didn't mean any of them and you know it."

It was meant to call back my spirit. It succeeded. I hurried back to the shrine of Toshiba and the worship of her excesses. I was just in time to take over arrangements for her birthday party. She was a student of astrology and was fascinated by birthdays.

"Everyone's day of birth is her first country," she told me. "We are, first, citizens of fire or air or water or earth before we become citizens of the common geography of this planet. Even then, we remain citizens of the elements."

She was a citizen of fire, with its fiery combustion. If I had any doubt about that, her bursts of temper annulled that. As breathtakingly beautiful as she was, she could also be insufferably ugly.

She was going to be twenty-seven, and she had characteristically drawn up a program: dinner at Foods of the Earth, a restaurant I had not heard of before then; song and dance at Music Temple, her favorite karaoke bar and nightclub; and bed – for two of us – at The Tavern. In all, she wanted six other dinner guests: Jessica and her married boyfriend; a distant cousin of hers, Eunice, and her Italian husband, Antonio; two of her friends: Sandra and Rita; and at least one friend of mine. I did not know whom to invite, but I eventually asked my assistant, Ubanwa, with whom I sometimes passed the time of the day during the lunch hour. So, there were eight of us that set out that night from Number 33. Every financial detail, it was understood without discussion, would be taken care of by me.

The moment we arrived at Foods of the Earth, I knew I was in trouble. It looked like what it was: one of these places that charge an arm or a leg without even an anesthetic "Thank you." Since tables could only be had by reservation, Toshiba had called earlier to reserve one – a gaudy affair, with birthday balloons strewn all over. We were ushered to our seats and presented with menus that could have been signposts. Even the simple act of making a choice was made difficult by the exotic, indeterminate labels. I was the only one worrying about the prices.

To make matters worse, the dishes were mostly experimental conjunctions meant to appeal more to the eye than to the palate or the stomach. The result was that by the time we arrived at Music Temple, even Toshiba was complaining that she was still hungry. So, once more, we settled down to eat – before Toshiba went on stage to mime a love song she said she was dedicating to me. I hardly heard it. I was in a different world – one in which my head was possessed by the demons of arithmetic because already I was spending money meant for my office.

"Wow!" Ubanwa whispered to me, affecting my concentration. "Do you grow money on a tree?"

"I don't believe this. There are two unaccompanied girls here, and you still have the time to wonder about me?"

"Thanks, but I don't want to go back to my village with only a plastic bag."

I managed to go through the other motions of that night, including dancing with Toshiba and her friends, and making the long toast with which we closed that chapter of the celebration. But at The Tavern, my mood became very evident to her.

"What's the matter, Taneba? Aren't you happy with me?"

I reckoned my money would not be returned even if I

cried, so why not put a fine face on the situation – as I had bravely been doing?

"I'm fine, just a bit tired. It's been a full day – and night."

"Thanks, darling. It was great. We all had fun. My friends said I'm blessed among women to have you."

And me, I asked myself, am I blessed among men?

"Your friend, Jessica, and her boyfriend: is that the way they normally drink?" I asked her. "Perhaps it's not altogether too late for them to get married. They deserve each other." I probably would not have noticed but for the fact that the two – displaying a stunning capacity for extravagant cocktails – had seemingly taken an oath to completely empty my pockets that night.

"It was a dinner party, darling, was it not? Was that why Sandra was making eyes at you and Rita almost thrusting her breasts into your face? You think I didn't notice? If they come any closer to you, I'll deal with them!"

I burst into laughter, because that night I had been so busy with my mental calculations that I had taken poor notice of the other guests, except those at the fore of trying to translate my calculations into a minefield. Had she not noticed my mental state, or had she insisted on not doing so?

From that night, we went back to our old ways. Habits have a strong pull. I managed to make up the office money I had spent before it became an issue.

"This place called Seventh Heaven, why haven't we ever gone there?" she asked me one day. "I hear it's quite a place."

The more I tried to keep Toshiba away from Seventh Heaven, the more she was determined to go there, convinced that I was trying to dissuade her because I was hiding something. So, on a clear Saturday night, we set out for Seventh Heaven. The moment Tamuno saw me, his smile grew as wide as the universe. He enfolded me in his characteristic embrace.

"Taneba! Where have you been, brother? It's great you decided to come home after all. And who's the queen with you?" He turned to Toshiba: "The name is Tamuno, Don. How're you doing? I trust you'll take good care of my friend. He'll take good care of you too, I'm sure. Welcome to my world. Have fun."

"So, you know that character?" Toshiba asked me when we were inside. "He's air, sly air."

That was another way she had, describing people as one of the elements – usually, the lower or sinister aspect.

"You don't even know him, yet you're already putting him in a bracket. We were classmates at the university, and he's a very nice person."

"What else would you say? And after the university, here has been your home since?"

"In another world, before I met you."

"That's why you didn't want us to come here. I'm sure you've been sleeping around with all these prostitutes."

"Toshiba! We came here to have fun, not for you to become like an archaeologist digging up old worlds."

"My God! And I've been making love to you without a condom!"

"I didn't say I've been sleeping around. I only told you to quit acting like an archaeologist. Don't you trust me?"

The incomplete peace that followed was soon shattered. On my way to the toilet, I ran into Esther. She had transferred her service from The Owl. She beamed when she saw me, put down the tray she was carrying and embraced me.

"Ah, Taneba, your eye! How you dey? Na you carry that mermaid come? Taneba, you and better women!"

"Esther, I didn't know you work here now. You look even more tempting without all your clothes on."

"Comot *jo*!" she said playfully.

"How's Sam?"

"Im dey. E dey always ask after you, but e don reach one month when I comot there. A-beg, make I dey go first. We go see later. E be like say your mermaid no happy at all as I dey greet you."

Toshiba was in a state when I got back. With her face

congealed the way it was then, I wondered how she could ever have been beautiful.

"Is this what you brought me here for – to watch you cuddling these loose girls, to humiliate me?"

"You were the one who suggested we should come here. And I've known Esther..."

"Taneba!"

It was Faith, looking otherworldly in a gown that hymned her features. I shook hands with her without any comment. Toshiba ignored her when she turned in her direction and extended a hand. Instead, she got up so violently that she upset the table as she strode out of the club. I went after her.

"Don't you dare come near me!" she thundered at me before she got into a taxi.

"Tomorrow, robins will sing, brother. It really is no big deal." Who else but Tamuno?

I returned to the table and found Faith tidying up.

"I'm sorry," she said. "She thinks I'm your girlfriend or what?"

"Never mind. These things still happen."

"Anyway, God is kind, which is why evil comes in small quantities. Hey, before you kill me, I'm just quoting from somewhere."

"She's not a bad person, not at all. She's just in a bad mood tonight. It's my fault, really."

"What's your problem? Is this the way geniuses behave? Everything is smoke, Taneba. It comes and goes, comes and goes."

I contemplated her.

"There's a friend of mine," she went on, "the one in red back there. Isn't she a fine girl? She's fallen for you all at once, says she likes everything about you. There must be something magical about you. Her name is Tricia."

Under any other circumstance, I would have been thrilled. "Don't you understand?" I asked her instead.

"I understand, or I'm trying to. I'll ask her to call you

instead – or, better still, she could pay you a visit at the office."

I neither accepted nor rejected. My mind was on Toshiba. Her other reaction came the next day – a letter that had neither a beginning nor an end.

"What's the use of this relationship anyway if I cannot trust you? For now everything seems distorted and unreal. It's as though a great bell of glass has descended around me, and life reaches me through its warp. A sense of unreality cloaks everything. Even the most insignificant gestures seem false and formal. All my actions are conscious and mannered, focused outward, but my mind wanders inexorably back to the thought that one day you'll be gone to them. Never before have I experienced such a commingling of dread and expectation.

"But, you see, my mind also wanders to how my life was before I met you. There have been some good times, I know, but after comparing everything, I know I was happier then than I am now. I was freer with my thoughts and actions. Life, for me, then was much more fun. But I had to change all that, although you never asked me to, because I thought we could have something together. I did it myself so as to give us a chance."

This time, I did not hurry back. In my mind, I began to punctuate the relationship. I too had been freer, so much freer, before I met her. How could one blessed with so much beauty be so niggardly in her appreciation of other people? Why could she not be happy with her charmed and sometimes charming life without denigrating others? What was it I had done that had so much riled her – my knowledge of Tamuno, or of Esther, or of Tamuno's girlfriend? With her fierce tantrums, was I even safe with her? How much sacrifice or appeasement would ever be enough for her? Why was it that those who told me the robins would sing another day or that life is smoke appear to be happier than me in my season of bonding?

One week passed, during which Toshiba and I kept to ourselves. Tricia called. I told my secretary I did not want to speak with her. Then Jessica called.

"Taneba? What have you done to Toshiba?"

"I know you live together and work together, but shouldn't you be asking me what happened between us instead?"

"You sound testy. I'm sorry. What happened?"

"Ask her why she walked out on me the way she did. I greeted a classmate and friend of mine who runs a nightclub. Was that it? I greeted a waitress I used to know, as a waitress, before I met her. I was supposed to shove her and her good-natured greeting aside? I greeted my friend's girlfriend, who also came to greet Toshiba. I was supposed to tell her off?"

"Was that what happened? You don't understand, Taneba. You're the core of Toshiba's life, so you should understand if and when she gets jealous. She's not been herself since. She's been crying every day, and now she's talking of buying a tanning machine."

"What for?"

"She believes it's a color thing, that you're especially attracted to dark-skinned girls. So, she wants to do some deep tanning."

"That's an identity crisis she has to resolve herself. I love her the way she is, and I've always told her so. But I wish she wouldn't throw such mighty tantrums over nothing. I can't live the rest of my life pacifying her for a guilt I neither feel nor deserve."

"You two had such a great thing going. Please, don't let it die. Why don't you come and..."

"I'd rather not. She walked out on me. If she walks right back, then we can move on."

"What about lunch tomorrow?"

"Jessica, Toshiba doesn't require an appointment to see me. Everyone here knows her."

"At two o'clock then. And, please, Taneba, try and understand Toshiba a bit more. You're her roots now."

Two things arrived in my office at about half past two o'clock the next day – no, one thing and one person. A card from Tricia. It contained only a telephone number and the message "Call me anytime." The white card bore a lipstick trace. I was still studying it, wonderingly, when Toshiba walked in unannounced – with outstretched hands. That was the way we normally made up – with a reconciliatory embrace. The only reason I could surmise for my not being forewarned about her arrival was that she had connived with my secretary to surprise me.

"You naughty, naughty Taneba!" she cooed in my ears. "Did you think I would ever let you go? I'm sorry, my darling."

We were still locked in that embrace when she saw the card I had hastily tried to hide. A swift metamorphosis took place. She wriggled away, picked up the card and studied it, with her face congealing.

"Look, Toshiba, it's not what you may be thinking. I swear. I have nothing to do with this girl. She's taken a fancy to me, and she's been up to all kinds..."

"Who do you think you're talking to?" she hissed at me. "Damn you, you cheap water!" It was a reference to my zodiac sign.

I felt very bad after she stormed out of my office. I tore up the card, chastised my secretary, and decided I would go and see Toshiba after work – to apologize. But her letter arrived that same afternoon, the one that finally turned me against her.

"*We are what we are, no matter what happens. I only did my best to make you what you didn't want to be. You can take a man out of a gutter but you can never take the gutter out of the man. That saying is very true. You are a dog, and you belong to the streets!*"

Instead of Number 33, I ended up at Seventh Heaven. Tamuno, I was told, was out on "other business." Faith was nowhere in sight. But Tricia was there, wriggling her waist on the dance floor. The song was about a fellow who lived next door, for twenty-four years, to a girl called Alice – waiting for a chance to tell her he loved her. At climatic moments, the disc jockey would fade out the sound and the dancers would roar the chorus – with almost all the girls wriggling their waists and the men snapping their fingers.

Alice!

Who the hell is Alice?

I went straight to where Tricia was and led her away to a table. She came with me without hesitation or protest.

"Taneba, it's good to see you!"

"Now, tell me: what exactly are you up to? You called me on the phone. I didn't answer. The next thing you did was to send me a scandalous card."

Her face was not exactly anything to hallelujah about, but she had a figure worth a hosanna. Was it in me to find something appealing in every girl? She was the first girl to spiritedly make a pass at me. And, face to face with her, my anger began to dangerously abate.

"What's the matter? You don't like the card?"

"That's not the point. Why are you doing this?"

"What do you even think I am? I don't hustle, mind you. You can ask around. I saw you and I liked you, so what? I'm sorry if that has offended you. It's something I've never done before, and I doubt I would even have gone that far if not for the way your companion treated you that night. Excuse me."

I found myself in the situation of encouraging her to calm down, wondering what I had ever intended to achieve by coming there that night to see her. I bought her a drink, we danced together to a few songs, and I took her to The Penthouse. There the smooth transitions ended. She wanted the very thing that I was becoming terrified of – a "relationship."

"I don't sleep around," she protested. "I don't want any man to just use me and dump me."

How would Toshiba have classified her – sly air or schizophrenic water? What was the meaning of this girl's meaning? I took her home on my way to work – she worked somewhere, she told me, as an advert canvasser – and told her I would call her or visit her as soon as I was able. On the streets, I reminded myself, very many things are not at all what they seem.

That afternoon, I received another letter from Toshiba –

this time, a verse-like arrangement lifted from a song about being saved from "a relationship that just wasn't fated."

It certainly did not help that I was still smarting from her calling me a dog. Yes, I was very much attracted to the streets, especially at night, very much attracted to nightlife and its easy invitations. Still, hers was in my view an offensive reaction to a matter that could have been resolved with a bit of calm and understanding. Being the material girl that she was, I considered, would she probably not have been part of that nightlife if she had not been fortunate to be under the care of a father who worked in a multinational company?

Despite my anger, I finally convinced myself to go and see her that evening before she sent me another riot of a letter. Upon my arrival, however, Jessica informed me that Toshiba would not come home until much later. She and some others in the office had gone for a dinnertime presentation. I left a message that I would return the next day. I did not want her to return and find me waiting forever for her – like a dog.

"Don't be in such a hurry, Taneba. I'm very concerned about you and Toshiba. Before this latest quarrel, she was even talking of taking you to see her father in Port Harcourt. I'm sure she must have told you that."

I made no response.

"Please, I'm not even asking what the matter is. These things happen and will happen. You're the man in this relationship. You have to angle it away from the rocks. Don't judge Toshiba by anything she does in anger. She needs you. I know. Both of you need each other. You had such a wonderful relationship, the toast of everyone around you. I'm sure you know the saying: the quarrel between two lovers is the renewal of love. Please, don't let this misunderstanding stretch out into something serious. Every relationship has its peculiarities, and the more people stay together..."

"Do you ever talk to Toshiba?"

"Of course, we talk. I know she's sorry about what

happened."

"Honestly, I don't believe that. I think you're just trying to be a good friend. Yesterday, she sent me a letter calling me a dog. Today, she sent me another thanking God for saving her from me. Are these the sort of things that teem in her multinational soul?"

"You should know how to read a woman's heart by now, especially Toshiba's."

"If she really wants to save this relationship, she has to try harder. Both of us have to. Anyway, I'll be here to see her tomorrow evening and we'll settle this matter, one way or the other."

I was therefore shocked when Toshiba called me in the morning to demand: "What were you doing in my apartment last night, you and Jessica?"

"Have you gone out of your mind?"

It was the harshest thing I had ever said to her, and it must have gripped her by the throat because I heard her catch her breath.

"What did you just say?" she asked at last.

"I said: have you completely taken leave of your senses?" I told her slowly, for emphasis. "I resent Jessica when she is trying to ruin me by drinking like her boyfriend, or the other way around, but she's probably the only true friend that you have."

"You wanted to see me and you chose to come when I would not be at home?"

"Take my advice, Toshiba: go and see a psychiatrist."

"You low..."

"Don't you dare! Let me tell you something: if you want to fight with Jessica, go ahead, but the only enemies we have are the ones we make or the ones we keep."

"I should have known better than to trust a Nigerian male."

Why couldn't she simply have said "Nigerian man"? I believe I would have felt a bit better.

Both of us dropped the phone receiver at about the same time. She did call later to say she was sorry – about her accusation. I could almost hear her lips rebelling. We then fixed to meet at

Number 33 that evening because I told her: "We need to talk this over once for all."

But it was not to be. My thoughts about Toshiba were eclipsed by an incident that day that remapped my world in a circumscribing manner: the brutal slaying of Tamuno, Don of the night of the streets – the refuge, mainly, of the dislocated.

The cowards never left? The weak died on the way? Do you still think so, brother? I am trying to make meaning of meaning itself. And it is evident to me now that it is not only the weak that die on the way. Everything passes, sometimes even the road itself.

Yellow

The news on the radio was like a verdict: "Suspected Drug Baron and Nightclub Manager Murdered in Gang Feud." Acting on a tip-off, the police had arrived too late at the scene of a shooting in a hotel suite. They had discovered the body of Tamuno, "riddled with bullets." The body had since been taken away and police detectives were continuing their investigation, working on the theory that the murder was the consequence of "a gang feud over territorial control." It was a report that provoked many questions. In which hotel had the shooting taken place? Where had the body been taken? Who else had been with Tamuno at the time? Who were the main suspects? What sort of "gang feud" was it this time that had claimed the life of someone like Tamuno?

I did not know when I started screaming. And kept on screaming. Was it even a scream or an irrepressible wail? The next thing I knew, my office started filling with people – preceded by my secretary. With all the people wondering what the matter was, I ran into the street. I felt a powerful need to breathe. I took great gulps of air, like a man who had run a great race. No one's death had ever affected me as much as Tamuno's. No one's passage had ever made my world seem so much smaller, seem so much robbed of its charm and foliage. I simply turned in one direction and started walking, wondering why there were so many people about and why they all looked so alive or without a care in the world. "Tomorrow, robins will sing," Tamuno always chanted. Yesterday and yesterday, speeding into the day before.

When I returned to the office, I was told that the police had come for Chief Stephens. Into my mind leapt the image of a meeting between two species of gorillas.

"Why?"

"They didn't say, but I think it's in connection with the murder of Mr Tamuno," my secretary told me. "They...also asked for you, sir."

Really?

"They left a message that you should come down to the station as soon as you return."

An invitation to the police station was a summons to the perimeter of death and decay. In their blustering search for clues, it was possible that if I went down to the police station I would be shoved into one of the notoriously overpopulated cells. Not to answer the summons could mean their coming back the next day or even that night to give me the beating of my life before carting me off. We lived in a country policed by demons in uniform who often solved crimes – or stampeded about in the name of doing so – by dismembering the lives of persons even tangentially connected to the victim or the geography of the incident.

"In that case, I'll go there immediately," I told my secretary.

"Wouldn't it be better to wait until tomorrow, sir? You can then go with the lawyer."

"Call the lawyer right now and tell him to meet me there, if you can get hold of him."

Ubanwa had reported sick, so I could not ask him to accompany me. I felt very alone and vulnerable. At the police station, I was told Chief Stephens had left. The station officer, acting like a god in an empire of putrefaction, asked me to write a statement.

"In respect of what?" I asked.

"You want to teach me my job? Look here, young man, when I say write statement, you write statement. Otherwise, I put you behind the counter – under detention."

"In respect of what?"

"Put him behind the counter," he ordered a police corporal. "Charge him for...for refusal to cooperate."

The overenthusiastic corporal gave me a violent shove in the chest that sent me behind the counter in a dizzying translation of comprehension. Behind me, in the infamous police cells, cries for blood went up. "Bring am inside," several rough voices solicited. "We go take am do pepper soup." Was I still in the world I had always lived in, I wondered, or was I suddenly in a space and time warp?

"Comot your shirt and your trouser!" the bully of a corporal ordered.

"In respect of what?" That inquiry, now a mechanical quest for meaning, was the only action I was capable of at that moment.

"Look here, my craze pass your own-o! If you no remove that *yeye* shirt and trouser now, I go bastard you!"

"In respect of what?"

Even the corporal, who had been all ready to strike me, paused. I had offered no resistance, just perhaps an unanswerable question for clarification nagging at the root of my being.

"Bring him here, corporal," the station officer now ordered.

I was catapulted with a vigorous shove to the front of the counter. Already, my shirt was soiled and I was beginning to look disheveled. It occurred to me that, with all the bullying and blackmail, it was difficult to arrive at the police station only as a suspect and depart as one. It was very tempting, if only to stop the very brutal treatment, to proclaim: "I confess...to everything." Only that that would mean a torture furnace that would make the rough handling so far seem like petting.

"You're ready to cooperate now?" queried the station officer, who had a way of asking questions as statements.

I took the proffered paper and began to write: "In respect of the murder of Tamuno, I was in my office..."

"Look this man," the station officer complained, wrenching the paper away. "You don't know how to write statement? Anyway, we do interrogation first. You ran away from your office when we came for common courtesy call, why?"

"I didn't run away. I went outside to clear my head, after hearing the news on the radio."

"Your head needs regular clearing, yes?"

"No, but I was shattered by the news."

"Tamuno is your brother, no?"

"No, he was my classmate at the university, and he was my

friend."

"You know his other business, and you help him, yes?"

"I know he ran a nightclub. I was not part of the management or personnel."

"But you go there often, yes?"

"Yes."

"You have much money to spend then?"

"He gave me free access to everything there."

A triumphant glint came into his eyes. "He gave you free access, for what reason if not for payment?"

I told him the story of the thesis.

"You write paper for him, and he give you free access to everything. You make sense to yourself, no? Anyway, we come back to that. You were where about five o'clock this morning?"

"In my apartment, sleeping."

"You were seen by whom?"

"No one, but I believe my landlord can confirm when I came back and when I left for work this morning."

"Your house is where?"

I told him.

"Sergeant! Corporal! Get ready, we go for search right now," he ordered in a state of excitement that was puzzling to me.

"In respect of..."

"Look here," he addressed me with a very severe look. "If I hear any 'in respect of' anything from your mouth again, thunder will strike you dead. Corporal, bring suspect along."

As the corporal seized me as if there was a longstanding feud between us, Chief Stephens walked in. The corporal quickly let go of me – to salute him, as did the station officer and all the other police personnel present. He had been told about my mission to the police station on returning to the office, and he had thoughtfully come back for me.

"He's your boy, yes? He should have told us so, sir," the station officer said lamely.

I named him Officer Yes-and-No as I hurried out of that

station of horrors. I thanked my equally sorrowful employer, exchanged views about the news of the day, then I made my way to Seventh Heaven. It was like a muted gathering of the tribe. Even at that early hour, it was a full house. There was no service. It was more like a wake. People sat around the tables and talked in low tones. A lamentation song played in the background. Never had I thought I would see Seventh Heaven play the role of a funeral home.

What happens when the lights go out at night?

The Faith that I saw that night was not of the world at all. She sat in the midst of a stream of sympathizers, rocking herself like someone unhinged. When she spoke at all, it was to wail a dirge. Her sorrowful voice and general discomposure made my eyes mist.

Tricia was there too, but she could do nothing more than study me.

"Which kin' world be this?" wondered a tearful Esther when I saw her, out of uniform. "Which kin' world be this wey they want kill all the better people finish?"

To some questions, there are no answers and no need to answer.

Alonzo was also beside himself. He and André sat right in the middle of the dance floor, like incapacitated actors before a bewildered audience. There was something about them that night that spelt this out for me: these men – for all their courtesy toward me – were no strangers to danger.

"Oga Taneba, you see as they just kill Don," Alonzo said to me. "Just like that."

"What really happened?"

"Na the world. Na so this *yeye* world be."

"I mean: why would anyone want to kill Tamuno?"

"Nothing simple like ABC for this world. But Don no die for nothing, not at all."

I did not know how to respond, because I suspected I did not properly understand him.

"Something wey I want ask you, Oga Taneba. You know

say Don no mix business with family. Im get any brother?"

"Not that I know of. Why do you ask?"

"Because before e die, e leave message for im brother."

"How could that be? According to the report I heard, the police found him riddled with bullets..."

"No be say they no shoot am, but na for hospital e later die. And before e die, im talk something like 'You know...my brother Norman? Tell him...game.' Something like that."

I did not make the connection immediately, but I later remembered the song Tamuno had played the day he told me the story of his life, "Norman the Gambler." Had he, in his final moments, gone back to his first moments of rebelling into the fast lane and adopting a song-hero as the brother he never had? Had his death been related to his propensity for gambling? Had he simply been reiterating his philosophy of life as a gamble?

According to Alonzo, Tamuno had retired alone to his hotel suite because Faith had gone to her mother's for a family reunion and because Tamuno himself had been feeling a bit low in spirit. His killers had tampered with the lock on his door and let themselves in, then shot him severally and left him for dead. Curiously, they had placed a copy of his thesis, not the one in the club, on his chest. Tamuno himself must have managed to get off a few shots because there was a trail of blood out of the suite. Alonzo and André, returning from the club, had been just in time to accompany the ambulance to the hospital.

It was evident that Alonzo knew or suspected why the murder took place, but he would not discuss that. On the streets, there were several theories. The most popular was that, by locating Seventh Heaven in the same area as The Owl, Tamuno had sounded the death knell for the latter. Because both places were said to be subterranean drug outlets, it was like eating into the territory of St Notorious. So, his former partner had bided his time.

There was also the speculation that the killing had to do with a struggle over a girl, Her Majesty. Tamuno was said to have lured her away from the character called Zanda and, by association, from the camp of his former partner. Some others claimed that, no, the girl that had been poached from that camp was Faith, whom they said had once been called Hope. I do not recollect ever seeing Faith with St Notorious, but then what did I really know about these people?

There was yet another story: that Tamuno had paid the price for a gambling debt he had neglected. He was said to have uncharacteristically gambled with shares in Seventh Heaven. He had lost. He could not pay because he had offered to give that which he could not since his shares were nontransferable. In a bid to pay in cash instead, he had started skimming off the earnings at the club. And Chief Stephens had put an irrevocable end to that.

The lattermost theory sounded preposterous to me. I could not believe that Chief Stephens had any hand in Tamuno's murder. The man was overwhelmed by grief. He called me into his office the next day, looking very subdued and aged.

"You see what they did to my friend?" he said to me in a voice without its usual thunder. "How they killed him as if they were killing the resurrection. Fourteen bullets. Why would any man shoot fourteen bullets into another? Every bullet went into him, and he was still alive. Tamuno, he was the last of the strong breed. There is no doubt about it. But did he have to die in that manner? I have money now, but in school it was Tamuno that taught me everything I knew outside the class – the important things like how to chase a girl, how to dress, how to be strong. If it was money alone, I would have paid him to leave that other business, but there was something more that I still do not understand. Excitement? Danger? Attitude? Laughter at the society and its conventions? There was something more, but we may never understand it. You are my link with Tamuno now. I want us to work closer than before. May his soul rest in peace."

"Amen."

Was this the "gorilla" speaking? In that season of grief, he changed the name of Seventh Heaven. It became Tamuno's Heaven. On the streets, it became known mostly as Fourteen Bullets or, simply, 14.

Chief Stephens saw to the burial, a fitting nocturnal event that was like another gathering of the tribe. St Notorious and his group were there, in their immaculate button suits, looking as grieved as water. That same night, an armed gang laid siege to his January 15, despite its vaunted fortification. He escaped, but the attacking gang left a trail of blood in its wake. No one saw him for some time after that night. It was said he had fled abroad. When he reappeared, he had more than a dozen policemen as his bodyguards – led by Officer Yes-and-No himself. He renamed January 15. It became June 1. Another puzzle for my former neighborhood. Not for me. June 1 was Tamuno's birthday.

He had been abandoned at birth, dumped outside an orphanage. There was no way of knowing who he was, but he had been named Tamuno: the name for God in the superintendent's language. She was a woman of prodigious energy whom they all called Auntie, and she was a disciplinarian. As he grew older, Tamuno began to take note of the constant "invasion" of the orphanage by people he would later describe as "gamblers."

"They were couples looking for a child to adopt. Despite all their inquiries and examinations, they had no sure way of telling which child would turn out well. It was a gamble, mostly, like many things in life. Because they themselves had to be seen to be upright and disciplined to get the chance to adopt anyone, they usually arrived at the orphanage looking stiff and forbidding. Life at the orphanage was already too stiff as it was, brother, so I never fancied these strangers. I was presented for several of these examinations. I failed them all. So, I stayed on in the orphanage, and it was there I got an elementary education."

Growing up, Tamuno soon found a way to run a bit loose on the streets, although he still remained in awe of Auntie and her belief in the wisdom of the cane. From hanging around a local eccentric called "Mad Matthew," who tried to induct him into the fraternity of smokers, he progressed to stealing chicken – more for the excitement than the dietary supplement. On the day Auntie caught him with a dead chicken under his shirt, she was so mortified that she organized his shipment to a juvenile center. The place was a breeding ground for future criminals.

"I'll tell you this, brother: it was a good thing, a very good thing I had spent the most important years of my life at the orphanage, otherwise I would probably have followed that trail. In that juvenile center, there were characters like Joking Gentle, Peter Thunderbolt, One Thousand Pieces, Jeff Instant – all of whom later ended up at the stakes as convicted armed robbers. The great thing at the center was the secret beer parties. It was also there that I fell in love with a popular song, 'Norman the Gambler.' It filled my head with pictures of the 'outlaw' whose only 'crime' was that he insisted on pleasing himself. He did not fight with knives and draw other people's blood, as Joking Gentle was wont to do, or shoot other people and terminate their lives as Jeff Instant boasted he had done. No, Norman was a gambler, ranging around in a rambler. Life was a game to him, his game.

"With Auntie still looking out for me, I had a chance to sit for the common entrance examination. I had never had a problem with doing well in school – that is, when I actually study at all. I passed the common entrance examination so well that I received a scholarship to Government College. I didn't have to worry about the fees, but then I still needed pocket money. And there were the holidays when I was forcefully reminded that I was homeless. It was hard, brother, very hard. I hung around the markets, the world of confidence men you'll find around any big market. In those days, it was easy to get a catalog and order whatever you wanted – cameras, wristwatches, toys, clothes, even bicycles – from overseas companies ever ready to send samples and trial offers. It was quite a racket. When the companies got wise and started insisting on pre-payments, we moved on to other things. Everyone was already telling fortunes the regular way – by palm or card reading or even with the aid of mobile oracles. I had to invent a new line for myself. What could be better than eye reading?

"You'll be amazed at the number of people hungry to know

what the future holds for them. I promised this multitude that the clearest way to see their future was by verifying it in their own eyes. I knew nothing about eyes or futures. But if you adopt a certain attitude, it isn't that difficult to tell the future or do almost anything. There is always the gambit: 'There is someone who doesn't wish you well.' People are always scared that others are plotting against them. That's our world, brother. If you're lucky, your client will supply you the details with which to tell him about himself. If you're not, you could always try another approach, with your legs properly positioned for easy flight if the situation began to get too tricky. But the damnedest thing always happens. Gradually, I tell you, I actually began to see and interpret the future in people's eyes. It was then I had to stop because I always saw too much pain.

"By the time I arrived at the university, I had already been recruited into the drug trade. I actually went to the university because I wanted to win a bet. On the day Auntie caught me with that dead chicken, she had told me: 'I bet you will never amount to much, never get as far as the university.' I had made no response, but in my heart I took her bet. And I never forget a bet, brother. Upon graduation, I went looking for her. She had retired, but she still remembered me. She had my picture on the wall, among many others. But she played a fast one on me, telling me she had only thrown a challenge at me with that statement. She was so very happy to see me that that was enough anyway. I wonder how she would have felt if she had known that all I really want is to stay high until I die. The great gamble. I believe that's the life God Himself put me in. Which was why I never wasted my energy crying for my parents. They didn't want me. I don't need them. Every thunder charts its own course and makes its own meaning. One day, perhaps when and if I ever become very particular about any girl, I just might reconsider."

He had met Faith and become very particular about her, but he had not stopped. What would Tamuno have been like without being like the Tamuno everyone already knew? Did he become a victim of his own image? At what point did the rhythm change – from a mastery of the song to being mastered by it?

I was so wrapped up in my grief that I had almost forgotten about Toshiba, about our quarrel. She must have waited for me to come to her before finally deciding to call me.

"Taneba, why haven't I seen you since?" It was typical, since I was the one who usually hurried back to her every time we had a disagreement. She must have become used to my apologies, even when she was in the wrong.

"Didn't you hear about the death of my friend, Tamuno?"

"The suspected drug baron?"

"He could have been a suspected Lucifer for all I care now. He was my friend, and he was dear to me."

"So, hasn't he finished dying? Am I always supposed to wait..."

"The problem with you, Toshiba, is that you're terribly insensitive."

"Excuse me?"

"Excuse yourself." Had she chosen another moment or person to disparage, I probably would not have gored her the way I did.

"Are you talking to me like that?"

"What do you think you are anyway? There are very many like you, and many too who can trace their ancestry to four countries or more if they apply themselves to it. So, why is your head in the clouds? How dare you scoff at my feelings in that manner? What makes you think you're half as significant as Tamuno? In the final analysis, what do you and your sort mean? You're just a greedy consumer of other people's creative ideas and their translations. What's the big deal about your so-called morality or decency anyway? Yours is a material universe like that of those you condemn, and the difference between you and those other girls is just attitudinal, mere atmospherics."

"You're insane!"

"Yes, I am. I'm crazy, but no longer about you."

"You'll be sorry!"

"That is beyond your power, you immaculate angel of sin."

When Jessica called me later in the day to get me to come over to their apartment that evening, I declined.

"I think Toshiba and I know in our hearts that it's over. It's very sad that someone blessed with so much beauty could also be very mean-spirited. I'll never let anyone bend my mind, and Toshiba will never let it be as it is, so what's the use?"

"But two of you were getting on very well…"

"Because I always played the fool. Which shouldn't have been difficult still if she had found it in her to be a bit kind to my sensibilities."

"Love will find a way, Taneba."

"Beyond a certain point, love alone is not enough. Perhaps one day both of us – myself and Toshiba – will realize that we came close to paradise, but we couldn't find our way in."

I did not miss Toshiba sorely, or rather I missed the magical crests she was capable of but without hankering for her. I believe I took everything she had to offer, the best things, and I left just in time. But who could ever have experienced Toshiba, in bed, and be entirely free from desire? Even her pelvic plateau and skin texture seemed to have been especially sculpted and tenderized for unforgettable pleasures. Women like her come to the very lucky man once in a lifetime. She was truly special, and that was what went into her head.

As that sun set, another sort appeared in the sky. Bantu reappeared. He arrived at The Penthouse, having got my address from one person or the other, in the early hours of the night – without notice, the same way he had vanished. He looked robust and wore the look of a man satisfied with himself. This time, he did not even have a bag at all.

"Bantu!" I exclaimed, pleasantly surprised. "Bantu, where have you been?"

"To find the heart of the ocean, man."

"Talk to me, like Bantu to Taneba."

He laughed merrily.

"I'm sorry, man, the way I took off the other time. I simply went to the port to look around, and I ran into this fella who had captained a ship I once sailed with to Toulouse. He wanted more hands on deck. My spirit said: 'Go!' To New York, New York? Still, my spirit said 'Go!' There was no time to lose, so I sailed on that ship."

"To New York?"

"All the way."

"Without a passport?"

"That's detail, man. First, you rhyme with your spirit."

"So?"

"All that way, I was thinking that the earth doesn't like the sea much. Both are locked in mortal combat. There were islands that I had never seen before on that route. Maybe the sea is losing the battle, or maybe when you sail around so much you're no longer so struck by the vastness and the roar of the sea. Anyway, I was in low spirit when we docked. But I got off that ship and I went looking for my family. I had arrived with the right address but on the wrong side of time. You know where I finally located them? Lefrak City. El Diablito was gone, like a thief in the night, probably off to steal another woman's heart with them crazy lines of his. You should see my kids, man. They're great, just like me. And Naomi? She just kept circling around me like I was a ghost from the sea, full of repentance like the Vatican. Oh, how she lost her head that time, how she turned El Diablito out because she realized she still loved me, how the kids need their father, and oh and ah. I told her she doesn't need any forgiveness from me because the day I had the revelation I perpetually forgave everybody and everything. It sounds like it's hard, man, but not when you live in the spirit. Anyway, I'm never going back to live in New York, New York. It's a wasteland. I'm going right into the desert, and she's coming with me if she's truly repented."

"You're taking your wife and kids to live in the desert?"

"She's my friend and ex-wife now. La Mundo: the world. I renamed her. For the kids, there are boarding schools. For two of us, a desert home for two flawed lives beckoning to others."

"And she agreed to come?"

"Sure, but first I have to go up to the desert and sort out a few things."

"You won a lottery, or what are you going to use for money?"

"Trust you to remind me. That's something I have to figure out, man. But you know I'm not much for property. I've got enough mental luggage already, and I think the problem of the world is the amount of baggage the devil took with him the day he was evicted from heaven."

"What are you talking about?"

"Don't tell me that with you in them religious fogs you don't know these things. The devil just wouldn't surrender, until they let him go with loads of gold, frankincense, and myrrh. Are you surprised? Anyway, let's not dwell on that right now. Something happened to me on the way back, the main thing. I heard the meridian song, man. I was standing on deck pondering the heaving motion of the waves. Then I heard – clearly – the sound of gunshots, fourteen shots in all. Fourteen. Then I heard a powerful voice chanting them lines that made me giddy:

> I dream in the intimate semi-darkness of an
>> afternoon.
> I am visited by the fatigues of the day,
> The deceased of the year, the souvenirs of the
>> decade,
> Like the procession of the dead in the village on the
>> horizon of the shallow sea.
> It is the same sun bedewed with illusions,
> The same sky unnerved by hidden presences,
> The same sky feared by those who have a
>> reckoning with the dead.
> And suddenly my dead draw near to me...

"Look, Bantu, I took a course in African poetry at the university. You're simply quoting Senghor."

"Senghor? That's strange, man. He must have been in the spirit then, for those were the very words I heard the voice chanting. The vision and the voice. You see how they go together?"

"Don't give me that, Bantu. You must have lifted those lines from Senghor. I remember I had quoted some of his lines before:

> I saw them preparing the festival of night for escape
> from the day.

> I proclaim night more truthful than day."

"I never ever heard them lines before. But why don't you come out of them academic fogs, man, and hear me out? The voice – or the shots and the voice – filled me with new power. I lifted a hand, and I said to the waves: 'Cease!' The riot stopped immediately. And because I have conquered the waves, I'm *Om* Bantu now. But never mind, I don't insist on the title. I know what I know."

I regarded him for some time. The Bantu I used to know had apparently been lost in the desert long ago, and I was faced with a new phenomenon.

"You've heard that Tamuno was shot fourteen times?" I asked him.

"I learned that only today. I didn't even know they had wasted a great brother like Don until I arrived today. It's the saddest thing, man. May his soul soar into higher heavens." His voice was unusually sad.

"Bantu, you're mixing up the way Tamuno died with whatever mood you were in after reconciling with your former wife."

"You're becoming altogether too predictable, man. How come a fella like you who's able to navigate all them fogs find it difficult to understand that everything in the world makes meaning beyond our comprehension? Everything is one."

What was there to say to this new Bantu? "Well, are you still one with the night?"

"Always."

We went off to the clubs. In all, he stayed with me for a

month, during which time he nearly struck me deaf either whistling his alpha song or chanting his meridian song. But he was still a jolly good fellow, even jollier, especially when we were not in "them fogs." The day I brought out the bag he had left in my former apartment, he looked at it as if he had never seen such a thing before.

"It's your bag," I told him.

"Are you kidding me? I don't remember anything like that."

"Look, Bantu, I'm going to put this in the garbage if you don't take it with you."

"To the garbage then, because I don't rhyme with them things."

When he left to go back to the desert town where we had once run a poor nightclub, he left the way he had arrived – without a bag.

Once more on my own, I began to frequent the recently reopened Tamuno's Heaven. Chief Stephens had marked a month-long mourning period for Tamuno by having the club closed for business. When it reopened, he took the inspired decision of engaging Faith to manage the place. It was then I learned she had an MBA and knew about such things. Having her in that stead also suited the sensibilities of the regular patrons. It was like a continuation of Tamuno's legacy.

The only thing that stopped, from what I heard, was the drug trade, which in any case had been such an underground thing that I never really noticed it in Tamuno's time. Faith herself still spoke of Tamuno as if he were still alive and for a long time used to ward off advances from her numerous admirers with the statement: "I've been loved by the best." She was still very kindly disposed toward me, but we never discussed my credit. In any case, I was comfortable enough not to need the favor any longer.

Tricia still came in often. Although I had not believed her, she had indeed told me the truth about where she worked. She still wanted that which I was not ready for.

"I don't sleep around. I just come here to have fun," she told me.

"I respect your feelings enough not to lie to you. The last relationship I was in has spun cobwebs in my brain. I know I'll get over it, eventually."

"No, you don't want to lie to me because you know I'll check whatever you tell me. Anyway, have you never heard the saying that nature abhors vacuums?"

"So, why does it keep creating them?"

We remained friends, up until the time she gave up on me and began dating a man who would not let her roam at night.

Esther was still my closest friend there, but she had been reassigned to the gaming tables. I hardly ever ventured there. Lucas still managed the figures. Both Alonzo and André were now in charge of the floor operations, which in reality made them Faith's assistants and personal bodyguards. Both of them, and six others, had spent some time in police detention in connection with the siege on January 15. Among the eight detainees, I did not know the other five anyway, the person whose alleged involvement surprised me was Yellow.

"How did you get into this matter?" I asked him.

"Na police. Them no like Yellow."

"You know what I mean."

"Bad thing no good. Simple."

"Did you know Tamuno personally?"

"Na street I dey, almost ten years now. Nobody wey no know Don. Nobody wey no know Yellow."

"I mean: did you ever work for Tamuno?"

"Na survival we dey, nothing less. Oga Taneba, you don dey work for police now?"

That was the worst thing to be branded on the streets: a police informant. And I was no longer deceived by these people's courtesy toward me, probably because of my association with Tamuno. The streets were mean, and there was little doubt that people like Yellow who had survived for so long were capable of responding accordingly. Since his release, he had transferred his presence to the vicinity of Tamuno's Heaven, and he usually greeted me as if he had known me right from his hometown. Better to keep things that way, I counseled myself.

"Well, let's talk about something else," I said to him. "Have you started sleeping now?"

"Ah, that na the only better thing wey the police don ever do for me. Them beat me, beat me until I pass out. I come enter wetin them dey call *coma*. Na since that time I come begin sleep again."

I gave him cash handouts every time I saw him. That drew me closer to him – and to his story.

He had grown up in a place called Uzi Quarters, a settlement with a generous allocation of cranks. There was Yaro, a lanky, bald, and bearded fellow who was fond of cooking at night when everyone else had gone to bed. At past fifty, he was still single and preferred to do his cooking himself, something he chose to do at odd hours. Those who claimed to have seen him said he "worked" in the motor park in the city, usually dancing to a song he sang himself:

> *Asampete nwanyi oma*
> *Gosim ife iji eme nganga*
> *Gosim-u!*
> *Tinye tinye*
> *Wepu ya mama anatago*
> *Oga abaram mba*
> Shut up*: Mechie onu!*

This lewd song was said to be something he had picked up from his frequent, unexplained travels, a reference to a woman he had loved but never possessed. His harsher critics called him "Shut Up!"

There was Mr Goldsmith, who in reality was a blacksmith. Why a man who worked in a forge – and in such a forge! – would insist on wearing a white overcoat was a puzzle to everyone. But Mr Goldsmith had scant interest in people's perception of him. He had a passion for brandy, which he would usually measure out in a teaspoon – insisting on an exactness that only he understood. Because these exact measurements were frequent, Mr Goldsmith, in an exact state of inebriation, was often to be heard in the forge excoriating his tools and attempting a raucous symphony with a one-man orchestra. Not unexpectedly, his products were such that drew angry expressions from his customers, who either requested an explanation or demanded a refund. Mr Goldsmith would regard the calmer ones like a priest at a confessional and undertake to attempt another "masterpiece-in-progress." Confronted with violent demands, it was not unusual to see the bulky Mr Goldsmith in a very spirited flight, straight as an arrow despite his exact measurements, his white overcoat flapping in the breeze like a parachute. But he had a rule: he never ran from the same person twice.

Dr All-is-well, the local quack, boasted of curative powers that covered all forms of illness – from cough to cancer. "You have come to me; all is well," he would assure all those who consulted him. He claimed such a vast comprehension of symptoms that he would often diagnose the illness by merely contemplating his patients. He had some modest successes, although there was the general complaint that he attached almost impossible conditions to his drugs, as if to ensure that he would be free from blame should anything go wrong. He would issue a cough medicine, for instance, with the instruction that it should be taken just before coughing or even advise his patients to forego water altogether. His career ended ingloriously when he had to be taken to hospital in a delirium because he was down with a fever that had defied his vaunted power. When he returned, he gave a noisy testimony of how his enemies had attacked him with witchcraft. No one contradicted him publicly, but no one consulted him afterward. He finally took up a job as a gateman at the local dispensary.

Auntie Martha owned the most important restaurant, a one-story affair called Martha's Kitchen. It was reputed to serve such excellent dishes that it convoked very many people from outside

Uzi Quarters, enhancing Auntie Martha's social and financial stature. She had been in a convent but, so the story went, had been disrobed because she had developed a fondness for pornographic magazines. Those who peddled this story pointed to the lavish murals inside Martha's Kitchen as evidence of Auntie Martha's inclination in that regard. When she reacted to these stories at all, it was simply to remark: "Business is business." Martha's Kitchen was a phenomenon of sorts because although it was raided by the police several times, with the claim that it was a meeting place for criminals, it was never closed down. The story went abroad that the raids only occurred when there was a lovers' tiff between Auntie Martha and the police chief. Auntie Martha was represented as the super mistress of many power brokers, hence her invincibility in the face of all trials.

Another remarkable figure was Oyibo, who was so called because he had spent a long time abroad. He had gone to America when doing so was seen as an event worthy of the most boisterous celebration. The day he left, the community had brimmed and thundered until daybreak. He was supposed to study medicine. Instead, he played around as much as he could and suffered as much as he had to in the strange streets of America for nine years. He returned with only a strange accent and an easy proliferation of Americanisms such as "wanna," "gonna," "doggone," "catcha." Still, the community clapped and thundered. He was entertained wherever he went. Unfortunately for him, it was not long before economic hardship began to drive scores of people abroad. Many returned or visited with tangible signs of success. Oyibo suddenly found doors being shut in his face where he had once been everyone's darling. He disappeared for some time and returned as the scout of a business ring on the lookout for young girls to send abroad for prostitution. The doors that had been shut in his face were thrown open once more.

But by far the most interesting character in Uzi Quarters was Papa Real, who sold reality. He was forever sixty because he refused to reckon his age beyond that point. And he did actually look sixty, despite the passage of time. Soon, as his relatives died off, people started saying that he was sacrificing them in exchange for his own life. Although he did no work, he lived in the best house in the settlement, in upper-class comfort. People came to consult him, laden with gifts, and he proportionately doled out promises – a good harvest, a job change, an income swing, a lawsuit victory, whatever. If his promises turned awry, which was unusual, he would tell his clients to blame themselves for neglecting a detail he had asked them to attend to. Not to consult him at all was an almost certain way to ensure that problems would arise.

Papa Real was the character that particularly intrigued Yellow. He could not fathom how Papa Real transformed the promises he sold to his teeming clients into reality, but he believed he knew how he cut the others down. His explanation: Papa Real must be using thugs to accomplish the instances of arson, theft, and even illness that befell those who refused to consult him. Yellow had been rejected at birth because his father could not believe he had fathered an albino. Tossing about in search of stability, he saw in Papa Real an opportunity for regular, profitable employment. So, he presented himself to the man.

"Yes, what can I do for you, boy?" Papa Real asked with the easy air of one used to being consulted by all sorts.

"I have come to serve you, master. Anything at all you want me to do, I'll do it as you wish."

"What are you talking about, boy? I'm not looking for servants."

"I want to serve you, master."

"As what? How?"

"Against your enemies."

"Who are they?"

"Anyone who doesn't come to you, I'll do anything you tell me to do against him."

"Like what?"

This was not the way Yellow had envisioned that the conversation would go. He decided to be blunt. "I want to join your army, master."

"Me, an army? I'm not a soldier."

"I can steal, burn, loot, do anything at all you want me to do."

"Why do you confess your crimes to me? I am neither a priest nor the police. Clear off, boy, and let me have some peace."

Yellow kept wondering: why was Papa Real bluffing? Gradually, the thought took hold of him that he was being subjected to a test. Of course, did he expect the man to accept just anybody into his service without ascertaining the person's trustworthiness? He then decided to conduct himself in a way that would assure his intended master that he was indeed capable. He took to preceding or following Papa Real, acting as his unsolicited herald or bodyguard. But where were the others in the man's service? He was unpleasantly surprised the night Papa Real arrived at his mother's residence and pronounced the sentence on him: "There is a boy here who will not let Papa Real rest. If that boy does not leave Uzi within three days, he will disappear. I, Papa Real, have said this."

Yellow fled the next day, to Lagos, wondering how he could possibly have failed the test. He hung around the streets for six years, some of which he spent in a psychiatric hospital and in prison, before he ventured to go back. Papa Real was still there, still looking sixty and still emperor of Uzi Quarters – without even an army, not any that Yellow could see. On the very night that he returned, Papa Real gave him two days to leave. Once more, Yellow took flight, questioning himself whether he would spend the rest of his life running from his hometown. He then decided to go to a famous medicine man that was reputed to have the secret of all the earth in his pouch. It was this medicine man that instructed him how to steal into Papa Real's dream, that it was there he would discover the man's secret.

That night, Yellow dreamed of finding himself in a coven, with Papa Real at the head. The others were Auntie Martha, Oyibo, Yaro, Mr Goldsmith, Dr All-is-well, and some people he did not recognize.

"You, again?" Papa Real said to him. "Interrupting our meeting? Your eyes will not know sleep again for a long time to come."

"Na so the whole thing happen, Oga Taneba. Na so sleep no dey 'gree enter my eye, until those police bastards beat me enter coma. I hear say Papa Real still dey Uzi, still dey do like God. If you count him age well, the man go don dey head toward eighty, but e still dey like person wey never pass sixty. You don see that kin' thing before?"

His was one of the most fantastic stories I heard on the streets. With his history of mental illness, I was inclined to disbelieve it. But he had actually given me an easy way to verify the story. If I so wished, I could make the four-hour journey to Uzi Quarters and ask around for Papa Real. If there had been an Ada Eke and a Mama Rekia, was it so difficult to envision a Papa Real? What other sort of person would a desperado like Yellow be afraid of?

"So, you're in exile in Lagos – banished from your hometown?"

"I no go tell you lie, as I come this Lagos e good. E good well well. But I don enter one powerful church. When I don strong inside, I go go back go face that man."

"You, church?"

"Strong one. Maybe sef all these medicine men dey the same gang with all those people, so na church I go take fight them. And, Oga Taneba, e go good make you follow me go there. No, no be Uzi. Na the church I dey talk."

"Me, why?"

"As you just dey waka about for night without protection, e no good. Anything fit happen."

"Look, Yellow, I've been around and about on the streets at night the past six years or so."

"Look you, you no know say na Don dey protect you since? Im understand as the night be."

"And they killed him like that?"

"No be death them dey take know strong person. That na

another matter."

I nodded thoughtfully.

"No be say Don no use you-o..."

"What are you talking about?"

"Plenty things dey wey you no understand. Don use you clean for business, but im dey take care of you because im like you well well. Now when im no dey again, na you get to look out for yourself."

I took a hard look at Yellow. I was tempted to smash my fist in his face, but I suspected his reaction would have disastrous consequences for me. I reckoned if he was not "stoned" or insane, neither of which he appeared to be at the time, then he was either talking nonsense or indeed he knew more about Tamuno – his other side – than I did. But even the thought that Tamuno might have used me, in a way I still could not fathom, to further his drug trade, did not diminish my fondness for him and the immensity of my sense of loss.

I accepted to go with Yellow to his church not for the door of protection it would open but the window of experience it promised. I was in a dry season and more intrigued by the character called Yellow – and his portrayal of Papa Real – with each new day. Besides, I had never been to the beach at night. For that was where the 'church' was located – a late night assembly around the boulders used to restrain the sometimes-intemperate rush of the Atlantic Ocean into Victoria Island. Everywhere around, there was a carnival-like procession of people in and out of the many bars in the area. There were musical bands at some spots, the mixed smell of alcohol and pepper soup and marijuana in the air, and numberless women around and about obviously waiting for like-minded men. This section of the beach struck me as definitely more interesting than the dangerous perimeter of the boulders that was our destination.

"I think we better have a drink before we continue," I invited Yellow.

"Ah, I no dey drink before I go church."

"Well, you'll have to hang around and wait for me then."

I had my drink, and pepper soup, and our journey continued – up to the waterfront. The 'church' was marked by a huge red candle in a transparent glass cage and a gathering of a few people like Yellow and some other forlorn-looking individuals who appeared as if they had spent the better part of their lives trudging from shrine to shrine. Everyone was barefooted, including the prophetess in an ankle-length robe who introduced herself as Mama Zi. All around us was the gurgle of water.

"Welcome to the Beach Kingdom," she told me, revealing a gap tooth as she smiled sweetly. "Today, all your problems are solved."

"Oga Taneba," Yellow said, after they whispered together, "you never comot your shoe?"

I removed my pair of shoes.

"You no bring something wey she go take do sacrifice?"

"Like what?'

"Just put hand well for pocket."

I did, brought out some high denomination naira notes and put them inside a pot beside the cage. The prophetess whirled among the boulders, which was remarkable for someone so corpulent. She then led me away from the other members of the assembly, many of whom were engaged in rather worrisome spasms of prayer. When we were alone, shielded by a heavy boulder, she invited me to wash my feet in the water to commence my "cleansing."

"I'd rather not," I said, wary of being initiated into the unknown ways of this rather questionable church through such a seemingly innocent ritual. I had heard about such things.

"You don't trust me." It was a statement, or so I let it become – spoken with a pitiful shake of the head. "You don't believe in my powers. I will show you a bit of what I can do. Do you have a piece of paper?"

I gave her a naira note. She squeezed it into a ball in the palm of her right hand, spat into it and threw it on the ground.

There was a crackle, then I saw the paper catch fire right there by the edge of the water. She then gathered as much of the wet ash as she could and cupped it in her left hand. The ash became a strip of paper filled with astrological signs. All these she did without looking at me, as if it was beneath her to stage such a demonstration for my benefit.

"You will have woman trouble," she suddenly addressed me, as if throwing my fate at me.

"I've had it."

"No, you *will* have it."

I was almost on the verge of considering her specially gifted when I remembered Tamuno's revealed techniques of divination. Telling a young man like me that he would have "woman trouble" suddenly did not strike me as noteworthy. What else would I have if not woman trouble? Snake trouble?

"You will have water or sea trouble."

"Me?" Was this woman mistaking me for someone like Bantu?

All around us, water continued to gurgle.

"So, what should I do?" I asked, humoring her.

"You have to read the Seventh Book of Moses. You have to read it from beginning to end, front and back, back to front. When you finish it, you will know what to do."

I thanked her, parted with a fair sum of money, and promised to return.

"You call that a church?" I asked Yellow on our way out.

"Strong one."

"Your prophetess strikes me as the sort that will cure a headache by chopping the head off."

"Ah, she get power-o. She don promise me say she go prepare me well well make I go deal with that Papa Real."

"Well, a drink before we go?"

"Ah, I no dey drink when I dey come from church."

We parted company there because I wanted to hang around the beach – its fun spots, not the grottos of people like

Mama Zi.

A couple of weeks after that night, Yellow announced to me that he was "fit" to go back to Uzi Quarters. I had a bad feeling about the impending confrontation.

He was gone for more than one week. On the day he showed up outside Tamuno's Heaven, he was apparently no longer of this world. Only his stark walking stick was the same. He looked as haggard as if he had made the long journey on foot. His eyes shone with an intense energy that appeared to be above recognizing mere mortals, although I believe I once heard him say something that sounded like my name: "Taneb." His speech was rather unintelligible, almost as if he were reciting the Seventh Book of Moses backwards. Apart from "Taneb," the only other word we could make out was "Real," which was repeated a number of times. He answered no questions, perhaps did not even hear them, but kept on with his recitation – or narration or whatever – at such a frenetic pace that it was unsettling. He stopped once in a while to point a finger at the sky as if issuing a personal threat, but he seemed to consider any other stoppage or gesture superfluous. This specter of Yellow gave me a very low feeling. What had I done to prevent this from happening, after he had entrusted his story to me? What had I ever done to successfully save anyone?

Faith arranged his movement to a psychiatric hospital. He went without a struggle – in fact, with an equanimity that would have been unusual before his journey to Uzi Quarters. And the gates of reality, as we know it, closed on Yellow.

Beware of water, my daughter; beware of the depths of water. In the beginning, a great mist went up the face of the earth. It has not subsided. Not air, not fire, no other element is like a mirror of the earth – a rippling testimony of its hollowness. In its revelations, water maps the ironies of man and his onshore existence. Beneath its surface world is a cavernous universe that transforms whatever it sucks in or whatever navigates its depths with only the compass of the earth. Great things come from water, including terrible images. In almost every history, there is a water crossing. In almost all geographies, there is water mapping. Everything, virtually every mystery of man, comes from the water or is related to it – the larger mystery of wine, of blood, of the foreshadowing of thunder. Wherever there is life, there is water. Beware, my daughter, beware of the depths of water.

Abedie

I visited Yellow a couple of times at the psychiatric hospital. He was still lost in another world and still largely unintelligible. However, he appeared to have substituted "Real" with "Papa"; his "Taneb" remained the same.

Each visit was a troubling experience for me.

"You know, Yellow told me his story, the story that explains why he's in this situation now," I said to Faith after one such visit.

"When?"

"Before he made that last trip home. He even took me to his church a couple of weeks before the journey."

"Church, Yellow?"

"Well, the Beach Kingdom of a prophetess who promises magic and miracles."

"That's rich. What's his story?"

I recounted Yellow's narration about Uzi Quarters and his battle with Papa Real.

"You believe that?" she asked me.

"I'm inclined to believe more now than I did then. He keeps mentioning Papa Real in his almost unintelligible speech. I would probably have made a trip to Uzi Quarters to confirm or remove all doubt, but the story and Yellow's present condition don't exactly encourage that."

"Besides, it's not your fight. If a fight doesn't directly choose you, then it gives you the room to decide whether it's worthy of your choice. This Papa Real – maybe, maybe not. Someone like Yellow who's been around for so long has probably made enough enemies right here in Lagos to send him to several psychiatric hospitals, if that's what his enemies are wont to do to him."

"Why are you taking care of his bills then?"

"He's my people, regardless, because he hung in there with Tamuno."

"He did? I never saw them together."

"There are a lot of things that are not seen together that are together all the same. Like Tamuno and I, we actually go farther back than many people realize. But let's not go into all that."

"Why not? You've brightened up a lot..."

"I still miss him. I still miss him very very much." At that point, the brightness dimmed, but she regained it. "They didn't just kill him. They killed a part of me. And in the more-dead-than-alive world I was in for quite some time, I never believed I was not a heartbeat away from death. You're a genius, so I'm sure you know about these things. Tamuno always used to say the robins will sing tomorrow. He was right. It's all smoke, this life."

Not long afterwards, she began dating a young fellow who reminded me of Tamuno's dazzle but without his air of a conquest of the spheres. His nickname was Fernando, because he cried over love songs. It was also about this time that she had Tamuno's thesis reinstalled at the bar. She had had it removed after his murder. The affair with Fernando was like a prologue. She blew through two such affairs before she finally maintained a steady relationship with a pilot who was called Planet because he often talked about world unity. When she arrived at this stage, she started wearing a long necklace with twin pendants reminiscent of Tamuno's. I called them Tamuno's Twins or TT, depending on the company. She started calling me "my genius."

Meanwhile, my maternal uncle sent for me. The invitation gave me a guilty feeling because, since I moved out of his home, I had never visited. He had moved out of the apartment in my former neighborhood to a house in the highbrow Victoria Island area of Lagos. He had been promoted to the rank of a deputy postmaster general for the entire country.

He and his wife, and the children and the maids, welcomed me as if I was a co-inhabitant who had only been away on a long journey.

"How are you, Taneba? Are you well?" his wife, who was on her way to a Sunday meeting, asked me.

"I'm fine."

"You don't look well to me. Your eyes have receded."

"Really, I'm fine."

"Well, take good care of yourself – only that when a man gets to a certain age he also needs someone to take care of him, and for him to take care of."

My suspicion about the reason for the invitation was confirmed. My uncle himself was brisk in addressing the issue. "I've sent for you, Taneba, because we don't see you anymore. Is there any matter between us that prevents you from coming here as my sister's son?"

"Not at all," I answered truthfully. I had since finished paying the money I misappropriated from the post office, and I never looked back on the incident without thankfully recognizing that he had stuck out his neck to save me.

"Well, then, let's get to the matter at hand. A man gets to a certain age and he begins, or should begin, to look around for a wife. It's the way of our people, and it's a good way of life. Completely. You're even going past that age. What are you still waiting for?"

"I haven't seen the girl I'll love to marry, uncle, a girl that understands me."

"A girl that completely understands you? My heart goes out to you. Do you think romance is at the root of marriage? It may well be. It's a very good thing. But our people favor marriage so much because it ensures the continuity of the tradition of family that sustains and shapes society. Anyway, I've taken the liberty of helping you look for a suitable girl, and I think I may have found her. The final decision, of course, is yours."

I offered no response during this break. I would have been surprised if he had not gone that far.

"She has a university degree and a good job. She's a very well-trained girl and is in fact the leader of the Ave Maria Committee in our church. I've questioned her. She's a virgin, completely."

He delivered the last bit almost like an actor expecting an

ovation afterward.

"How old is this girl?" I asked.

"Twenty-six. Just the right age for you."

If he had not been my maternal uncle, with his severity of humor and penchant for the completeness of things, I would have burst out laughing. A virgin, at twenty-six, in Lagos? Well, it was a possibility, I reconsidered. But I reasoned that a girl who was still a virgin at twenty-six, after going through the university, was more suited for a psychoanalyst's couch than my bedroom. And why was my maternal uncle beaming with satisfaction? Virginity had never seemed to me enough proof of character or compatibility or anything upon which to build a marriage. I wanted experience from my women as much as I wanted to experience them, because the more one knows the more one often understands. In the case of this twenty-six-year-old virgin, she was also a church leader – someone who would probably draw up a calendar for lovemaking according to the feast days of the saints. Good old old Mr Ebenebe, my maternal uncle.

"I'll arrange for you to meet her then," he said. If he was not such a modest man, I believe he would have congratulated himself.

"I'll think about it first, uncle."

"Think about getting married, or think about meeting this girl?" Did I detect disbelief in his voice?

"Think about it generally."

"I don't see any problem. You can meet her while you're thinking. That should help the thought process. She won't bite you, if that's what women have been doing to you. She's a decent girl."

I repeated that I wanted to "think about it generally" and avoided his eyes.

"While you're about it then, you had better think everything over completely. Don't you think it's time you returned to your father's home? Your mother's home is also your home, yes, and we regard you as our blood. But your father's home is even more your home. Even if his people still say they don't want you, that village is as much yours as theirs. It's time you started going home, there, so you'll begin to know people and they'll begin to know you too. As your father's eldest son, you can initiate a process of healing. You can invite everyone together – his other wives and your brothers and sisters – and chart a new course for the entire family. That's why you're a man, and the eldest son. I can help you reach out. It shouldn't be difficult, once you demonstrate the will."

"I've buried the ghost of my father, uncle. I don't want to resurrect it. I have no stepmother, no stepbrother, no stepsister."

"You're deluding yourself if you think you can ever deny the blood flowing in your veins."

"The blood itself denied me, and I've been getting along very well without acknowledging it."

"Where are you going to tell your children you come from – the streets of Lagos, a fugitive from his own self? Every sort of life that we live eventually catches up with us. It cannot but be so. The day you see what you're looking for among the sort of people whose company you keep and the sort of dens you favor, at night, then you will rest – if you can still rest. Time is of the essence, Taneba, because if we don't seize it while we can it eventually seizes us. Do you completely understand me?"

I thanked him for his "words of wisdom," promised to reflect soberly on them, made a few polite inquiries and departed – like an apparition returning to its other world. I did reflect on the meeting, but I was still inclined toward letting my father haunt himself, if he still could. If my father himself had treated me like a bastard, what was the worth of his fatherhood to me? Why should I recognize him by accepting his village, which in any case was earth and water like everywhere else? There were many people like me on the streets who had made the best of a life that could always be better, made their sort of meaning and departed from a world where treachery was the king of all its spheres. So, what was the big deal about my father and his village? On the subject of marriage, I remained convinced that one day I would meet a girl who would so possess me with both her presence and mystique that I would duly make the transition from admiration to marriage.

It was the season of apparitions. A few days later, my secretary brought in a visitor's form, which informed me that someone called Mary Ann, from Race Automobiles, was waiting to see me. The purpose of visit? "Official." It was not unusual for me to receive visitors whom I did not previously know, but I always preferred to know in advance the identity of my female visitors.

"Who's this?" I asked her.

"She's a young lady."

"I can discern that. Have you ever heard of Race Automobiles?"

"I have no previous knowledge of it, sir."

"Have you seen this young lady before?"

"No, sir, but if I may say so, she's a decent young lady, and very friendly." Suddenly, the word "decent" was threatening to suffocate me. Whatever made everyone else appear to merit this description? But such a description from my secretary, who could as well have been the twenty-six-year-old virgin and church leader my maternal uncle was talking about, was unusual.

"Ask her to come in, but next time I want a better explanation of the purpose of visit than this word 'official.' I believe I've told you this before."

"Sorry, sir."

I did not know who I expected, but it was certainly not Mairo – in a skirt suit, shining like the sun, her feet advertising a simple black shoe. The transformation was so electrifying that the currents jerked me up, open-mouthed in wonder. Beaming like a mid-noon miracle, she came around my desk, embraced me, gave me a peck and then settled into a chair. I finally sat down, very pleased to see her – in that form.

"Mairo! My God! And I almost considered not seeing this unknown person called Mary Ann from an unknown company called Race Automobiles!"

"Those are my creations. I wasn't sure you would agree to see Mairo," she said with a winning smile that made me tingle all over. My God, had she always been this beautiful, this immaculate?

"Those were the bad days, Mairo. I'm sorry. We live and learn."

"It wasn't entirely your fault. You did the bestest you could. I needed the cold turkey treatment."

"Where have you been, Mairo? And what do you do now?"

"I'm studying Sociology, like you did. I'm in my second year now."

It was my turn to beam. So, the Mairo project had not been a failure after all?

"Two or three things happened to change my life. There was the incident that tore us apart, that single terrible error. It was the worstest thing that ever happened to me. I was so so in love with you. In short, you broke my heart. But it also made me take a hard look at my life and challenge myself. Then, another disaster happened to me. I was gang-raped."

"What?"

"It happens. Once in a while, the police sweep through the streets hunting for free sex. Woe unto the girl who is caught alone at such a time, like I was. I had to 'service' six of those bastards. You see, when the girls on the streets fight heedlessly for their money, it's not just because of the money itself. There's also the principle of the thing, for the expositoriest form of labor. I had always detested group sex. There are girls who never minded going in a group of two or three others with one man. I never liked it. I never did it. There are also girls who never minded going alone to sleep with two or three men. I never did it. I never liked it. So, you can imagine the horror the police inflicted on me, apart from the physical torture. It was the terriblest thing to happen."

Was Mairo, channeling her restless energy into language, deliberately stretching her superlatives?

"After that police horror, I banished myself from the streets. Fortunately, I had the money you had given me, and there was my landlord who became like a father to me pointing me in the right direction. He even started vetting my visitors, insisting that Jovita could not come and see me there."

"Where's she now, by the way?"

"It's the saddest thing. She's dead."

"How?"

"I think she was killed for ritual sacrifice. They found her body, with the breasts slashed off and the eyes gouged out."

I had heard about such things, but I could still not stop myself from shuddering.

"One of the hazards of the profession. It's the very saddest thing. May God have mercy on all of us. I finished my high school education with a good grade. I went home, and what do you know? I got married."

"You're...married?" It was then that I noticed the ring on her finger. My heart fell. Despite her history, I had begun to look on her sudden reappearance as a manifestation of the presence and mystique that I had been hoping for.

"You're not happy for me?"

"Of course, I am," I said, with a smile.

"What else could I do? You refused to marry me, even to see me after that single error. I went to the village, and I caught the eye of the chief's son. Of course, there were problems. There was the rubbish about my mother being implicated in the death of my father. And there was the matter of making the appropriate sacrifice to obtain a divorce from my river husband. But we eventually got married, and I went to live with him in Kaduna. I took the university entrance examination, the rest you know."

"Do you have any child?"

"Not yet."

"Do you love this man?"

"He's my husband. I need him, and he needs me. These days, life is that simple for me. He doesn't know about my life in Lagos. He doesn't have to know. I learned that from what happened between us."

"You don't consider love an important foundation for

marriage?"

"It could be, but need is more important to me."

"So, what are you doing in Lagos?"

"I came from school – to see you. My bag is outside. A part of my heart has always remained with you."

"So, you've come for recovery?"

"As much as possible."

We both laughed. In all, she stayed with me at The Penthouse for two weeks. She put away her wedding ring – she insisted on doing so – and became like my wife. I thought I would take her on a triumphal tour of the main nightspots in Lagos, but she wanted only a bit of that. She was contented, she said, with just keeping house and being with me – in my arms. She made love to me with such energy that I sometimes wondered if there was more to her visit than I understood. Those were glorious days. And I found myself pleading with her to remain with me.

"I wish too that we could go back in time, Taneba, but I'm no longer a baby."

"You and this thing about not being a baby. You're just twenty-two or so."

"Every day is a lifetime. So much has passed between us that will probably always follow us. I think we're enjoying this reunion so much because these are stolen moments."

"Don't blame me so much, Mairo. I believed you were entirely addicted to the streets."

"I was. It's the most addictive addiction, and I think there are very few who ever kick it. But what you call addiction is also a long story."

"You finally shortened it."

"Circumstances drive people to the streets. Show me the street-life of any city or country and I can tell you its history or politics. And once you arrive on the streets, it's the stupidest thing not to imbibe a bit of its madness, if you want to survive. The triumphalism of this madness becomes an addiction or a habit that draws you deeper and deeper. I'm simplifying, of course."

"You sound like a professor."

"Shouldn't I be? I was there."

"I was there too, and I'm still there."

"What do you know about the streets at night?"

"Me? I should think I'm an encyclopedia now."

"You're just a familiar outsider. One simple question: do you know Abedie?"

"Who's he: a new baron?"

"Don't worry, the day you get to know Abedie, you'll understand a few more things."

"Who is he, and how come I've never heard of him?'

"Some things are better whispered. Many bad things that happen on the streets happen if Abedie wishes them to."

Another Papa Real?

"Anyway, don't worry about Abedie. Let's make the mostest of our time together."

The fact that you are alive and well, and still care about me, has brought a breath of fresh air into my dusty old life.

When Mairo left, with her ring back in place, I sank into a valley of depression. She had made a husband of me, in a time short enough for the memory to be long and rich. Mairo. I dreamed her, wished for her, longed for her. The knowledge that I could not have her to keep and behold battered my soul the way the desert wind tortures the traveler. She had promised she would return soon. Instead, what arrived ten months later was the news of her transition to motherhood. She sent me a picture of the baby, whom she said she had named after me.

I looked at that picture a few times, then I went and bought a microscope for further scrutiny. The more I conducted the examination, the more I asked myself: had Mairo come to me for something more than recovering her heart? She made no clarification. I made no claim. But deep in my heart, the belief is forever strong that Mairo came to take a fundamental part of me, and that she did take it.

Was she the "woman trouble" Mama Zi had prophesied for

me? But that would mean that she understood pleasure as a problem. Or had she been prophesying about the consequence of my sleeping with a married woman, even if that woman was Mairo? It was something I had previously been vociferous in denouncing. But Mairo – whether as an innocent-looking, confused girl or as a radiant, single-minded woman – appeared able to break all my barriers.

After her departure, my depression was complemented by a series of physical incidents that unruffled me. I was returning home from work one evening when I ran into an uprising. A sculpture of the latest military ruler had been put up earlier in the day at one of the major roundabouts. Considering the nasty dictatorship that this tyrant represented, it should not have been difficult to predict that the sculpture would outrage the repressed and pauperized masses. The story of the sculpture spread like the bad news that it was, and by evening an angry crowd had massed around it. After smearing it with rotten and rotting things, the crowd – angrier as its number swelled – then progressed to the job of pulling it down. But the collective anger had risen to such heights that simply pulling down the sculpture was no longer enough to assuage it.

It was this mob that I ran into. It was too late to turn back. I was not very worried, because I was fully in accord with the violation of that violating sculpture. Besides, my presence on the streets had acquainted me with many of the characters that were usually at the fore of such uprisings. Many people knew me in different ways – as Taneba One Man or Gentle or Oga Taneba. But the important thing was that they knew me, or so I thought. When that mob surrounded my car, I was reassured because the most vocal people in the crowd were faces I knew: Lefty, who sold marijuana as if it was chocolate; All Correct, who was a pimp; Sugarcane Boy, who was said to be a robber and had spent as much time in prison as he had outside; Major, who was both a pickpocket and an audacious beggar.

I brought the car to a halt and began to extol the uprising.

"Come down, one time!" ordered Sugarcane Boy, like the highway robber I felt certain then that he was.

I alighted from the car. "What's the matter, Sugarcane Boy? You don't know me again?" I said to him.

"Why not? I know you, but today get as e be."

"Na your boys dey for road," chipped in Major. "You go show cause?"

Both Lefty and All Correct tried to intervene on my behalf.

"Sharrap!" bellowed Sugarcane Boy. "Wetin concern una inside?"

"No mind them, Sugar," encouraged Major.

"No problem. You're my people," I assured them.

I would gladly have "shown cause" at that time by giving them all the money I had. But they were not entirely in control of the situation. From outside their circle, a vicious looking man queried me: "Wetin you dey work sef wey you get this kin' car? No be our money wey una dey thief?"

Before I even got through the thought that that was hardly the place to begin to reel out my employment history, two things happened: a stone hurled from within the mob smashed my windscreen, and I noticed one or two characters dart in and out from under the car. Then, there was a hissing sound, and an explosion. Everyone sprinted away as the car went up in flames. In the commotion, someone stole my wallet, and the mob moved on to living things.

When I regained a shadow of life, I simply began ambling toward The Penthouse – singed and all. I cursed the military dictator seventy times seven. I cursed the mob seventy times seventy. I wished then that the car had not been transferred to me. Perhaps it would have been easy to explain my situation to Chief Stephens and get another official car. As it was, I was at the mercy of the insurance company, which could not understand fools like me who could not stop themselves from running into a mob, or when they did could not levitate their vehicles above the range of destruction.

"You have no case, Mr Taneba," the insurance agent told me gravely, as if in a great wonder at my presumptuousness for ever thinking otherwise.

Without a car, I found my nightlife cut short. I had always been wary of relying on taxicabs and motorcycle taxis to move about at night. And I particularly did not like lounging around after three o'clock waiting for the first sign of daybreak to catch the early morning bus. All these I had done in those early days at The Owl. Having become used to the comfort and privilege of having a car at my disposal, I looked upon going back to the old ways with disfavor. So, I was marooned at The Penthouse at night, pretending to enjoy the drab programs on television and feeling as restless as I always felt on those nights after the not-irregular coup d'état when a curfew extinguished for a time the joy of the night.

Eventually, I secured an office loan – after a long session with a business-like Chief Stephens. I bought another car and I returned to the night. And I almost became an obituary notice. This time, I was coming back at about three o'clock at night from Sundown! As I descended a flyover, only the superb reflex of someone used to the pitch-dark streets of some parts of Lagos prevented me from ramming the car into a boulder right in the middle of the road. I stopped and got out of the car, shaken. I had only one thought: the object could be a basket, and I had almost killed myself avoiding it. It was a lonely road at that hour. To remove all doubt, I hurried back to verify the nature of the object. Rock, every bit of it. That confirmation sent me racing back to my car and away from that scene.

I slept very little. I returned to that same spot at daybreak. The boulder was gone, and people were already up and about as if I had not very recently escaped what I considered a murder attempt. Was I becoming paranoid? But I assured myself that boulders did not appear and disappear from the middle of the road without evil being intended. I went around telling my story and asking questions.

It was the boulder that finally took me to Abedie. Alonzo

led me there, showed me the place and left. It was a simple bungalow in a part of Lagos where only fools and saints felt safe. With a ram's head mounted on its frontage, it could have passed for an eatery offering a ram's head specialty – except for the smell of marijuana where six young men sat on benches outside. I walked up to them.

"Please, I'm looking for Abedie," I said to none in particular.

They neither looked at nor spoke to me.

"Excuse me, please I'm looking for Abedie."

It was obvious then that they would neither look at nor speak to me. As far as I could see, they neither looked at nor spoke even to one another. I climbed the short flight of stairs and knocked on the door. No one questioned me from outside. No one answered me from inside, although I could hear voices from within. I knocked again. Still, no one questioned and no one answered. I tried the door. It opened outward. I walked into a spacious living room in which a number of people sat expectantly on the rich rug. Apart from the rug, there was no other furniture in that room besides a ram's head mounted on the wall facing the door.

"Please, I'm looking for Abedie," I said to the gathering.

A few people studied me again. No one answered.

"Hello! Can anyone here please answer me? I'm looking for Abedie."

"Sit down," the man nearest to me said curtly.

I sat down and waited for further enlightenment, wondering what the place was all about. Soon, a man came out of a doorway, steered himself across the room and left. Another man went in.

"Do you know whether Abedie is in?" I asked the man who had spoken to me.

"I don't know."

"Do you know whether he's been here today?"

"I don't know."

"Do you know whether he was here yesterday then?"

"I don't know."

"Do you know whether he will come tomorrow?"

"I don't know."

"Who are you waiting for then?"

"Shh!"

The going and coming continued, according to the time of arrival, until it was my turn. I went through the doorway into another room, in which an elderly, clean-shaven man – with a pouch around his neck – sat on the same rich rug, with his back against a wall on which was another mounted ram's head. I was struck once more by the skill of the taxidermist. I sat down, facing the old man and the ram's head.

"I've come to see Abedie."

"Speak."

"You're Abedie?"

"No," he said, as if I had uttered a blasphemy.

"I'd prefer to see Abedie."

"Go."

"Excuse me, I don't mean to offend. I want to see Abedie in connection...no, over...you see, I nearly had an accident at night. There was a boulder in the middle of the road. I asked around and I was told that Abedie might be calling me."

"You're still alive, so what is your problem?"

"I just want to make sure I've not offended Abedie, and if I've done so in any way to make my peace with him."

"Go now."

I left, no wiser than I had been when I arrived and still not assured that I would not have another boulder waiting for me in the middle of the road at three o'clock – the hour of saints and demons.

I kept coming to that bungalow with mounted ram's heads, hoping to see Abedie. I would sit in the waiting room, and when it was my turn to go in and see the old man, I would yield that opportunity to the person who had come in after me and leave. No one questioned me. No one spoke to me. Were these people, whoever they were, that sure of themselves?

I began to understand who they were the more I visited there. Once a month, they superintended a cult for prostitutes. A stunning number of street girls would arrive, in sober processions, bearing packages. In the backyard, they would deposit the packages in baskets that looked like shrine artifacts, then the old man – bearing a clay pot – would rub an ashen substance on their foreheads as they knelt before him. Later, some chosen ones would set out, with the old man bearing that clay pot, in a dance procession through the streets. The procession, I was told, terminated at a stream where the dipping of feet in water completed the ritual. It was said to be a strong guarantee of safety for at least the next month. The girls were free to arrive in any manner of dress they chose, but the procession dress was a white wrapper. The girls were encouraged to prettify themselves then as if for their wedding feast. It was quite a spectacle.

And a revelation. I realized that my knowledge of street-life at night was truly incomplete. Had Mairo been part of such a procession? Had her friend, Jovita, also been part of it?

If the girls came once a month, there were other people who came every day or every other day. These were well-dressed men – politicians, traditional rulers, professionals, and all sorts – who arrived in purring cars. They would go in to see the old man, heaving bags that I had the impression contained money. Midway, one or two of the young men would be summoned, and the bungalow would come alive in its secret corners. Afterward, the men would hurry out without the heavy bags but bearing well-wrapped packages. There was certainly the smell of blood and death about that place. Once in a while, police officers themselves would pay a visit, greet the young men, go in to see the old man and then come out heaving heavy bags and beaming.

The number of young men on those benches kept changing. Sometimes, there would be six of them – as there had been the day Alonzo took me there. Sometimes, there would be up to twelve, sometimes only three. Where they went to and what they did, I had no idea, but I had the feeling that they sometimes traveled outside Lagos.

Gradually, by keeping track of the going and coming of those young men, I came to a summation. The probability was high that any night more than three of them disappeared to wherever they went, a corpse would be discovered the next morning somewhere in Lagos with its body mutilated – the penis or the breast or the tongue or even the head chopped off.

I refused to reach any conclusion, because the only one possible was terrifying. But I did make one more spirited attempt to see Abedie. I went in to see the old man once more.

"Please, let me see Abedie. I've been waiting almost three months, sometimes very far into the night, to see him."

"I know. You've been watching us."

"Oh no, it's not that at all. I've only been waiting to see Abedie."

"You have waited long, and you have seen much. But I know you, Taneba. I have always known you." I had not told anyone there my name. "You may now go into the other room and see Abedie."

I went through the curtained doorway on his right. There was nothing there, except the rich rug and a mounted larger-than-life ram's head facing me. Was this a joke? I perished the thought. That old man did not look as if he still knew what a joke was. What was I supposed to do – start talking to the ram's head? Would that not convince even me that I belonged in a mental home? I tarried there awhile, then I returned to the room where the old man was. He said nothing to me, only looked piercingly at me. I said nothing to him, only left his presence.

I left that bungalow that night determined to forget all about it – that is, to forget about Abedie in the same way a man wills himself to forget a dark secret. Why had I even persisted in seeing Abedie, hanging around that bungalow smelling of ash, money, blood, and death? Everyone had counseled me to so persist, that it was only then I could rest easy that Abedie was not after me. And why had they let me take note of all the comings and goings? Well, evil finds its kind, I hoped, so why should I worry so much about Abedie?

I tried to return to the peace of my old life, but it was at this time that I began to have the serial dream that I was certain could have only one conclusion: my brutal death. It was not even a dream as such. It was a series of nocturnal experiences projected into me, or into which I was projected, in the previously secure sphere of my bed. On the first night, I saw myself in a vast space spreading from infinity to infinity. I was alone, very alone, in this limitless universe. Then, one of my gray hairs fell off. It fluttered in the air, evoking my father's face, before finally falling a short distance from where I stood. First, it became a ram's head; the ram's head became a boulder; the boulder became the night masquerade from my village world of moonlight tales. Its feet were evidently positioned for a quick charge. In its hand, it held an evil-looking spear. It is impossible to describe the menace that possessed the air with this latest transformation. No language was possible, no flight probable because I appeared to have lost both my ability to speak and the capacity to flee.

Nothing of that magnitude of terror had ever confronted me before. When I awoke, I was thoroughly soaked in my own sweat and almost breathless with fright. I pondered that dream for a long time, a very long time, then I went into the bathroom and painstakingly counted all my gray hairs. There were twenty-five in all. What was this new danger that appeared to be so closely related to my gray hairs?

The next night, I returned to the very same dream world. The masquerade was still there, ready to charge. I lost another gray hair. Its final transformation – from my father's face to ram's head to boulder – was into an unknown masquerade, a stout warrior also bearing a spear and positioned beside the night masquerade. I nearly lost my loosening hold on sanity altogether when I awoke and counted my gray hairs, four times over, and discovered there were only twenty-four left. I had actually lost one in that dream world. This was way beyond anything I had ever heard or known.

This was madness!

I could not imagine who to tell this story to without getting a knowing look about the state of my sanity. Perhaps the new Bantu would understand, but then he was so very far away – at an unknown place in the region of the desert town where I had discovered my first gray hair. In the unequal battle into which I had been thrown, I had no arsenal or counterstrategy of any sort. But I went to a barber's shop and had every hair on my head scraped off. After that, I bought hair dye, which I rubbed into every part of my head as if I was shielding it with an oily helmet. Still, that night I was once more transported into that battlefield. The next appearance was another unknown masquerade, which looked into me as if conducting a prefatory investigation before thrusting its spear into the exact location of my heart.

Why, in God's name, was this army massing against me?

I reported sick at the office and took to sleeping only during the day. I would spend the entire night, right until daybreak, dancing in the club like a freshly oiled twirling machine, and then I would return at dawn to sleep. In the afternoon, I would begin going the rounds, consulting all sorts of medical personnel.

The nearest I came to a solution was a neurologist who examined me. "As far as I can tell," he said, "you should be in order. However, it may be that you have problems related to personality coordination. You should see a psychiatrist."

"Me, see a psychiatrist? I'm not mad. Look, I have dreams or experiences in which I lose a gray hair on this side of my reality and it turns into a battle foe against me on the other. I know exactly what I'm talking about. I'm not mad."

"You have a simplistic notion of what psychiatry is all about."

"Look, I don't have much time. It's clear to me, very clear, that the only aim of this gathering army is to strike me dead. Please, believe me."

I was on the verge of kneeling down to plead for understanding, but I felt that that would strengthen his belief that I was of unsound mind. The burden of language and gesture!

"I strongly recommend that you see a psychiatrist," he restated firmly.

I went off to the psychiatric hospital. I was referred to a young fellow who was fresh out of school and had read too much of Sigmund Freud. He asked me all sorts of questions that kept me wondering if he understood the gravity of my situation. Had anyone ever sexually molested me? Had the horns on the ram's head reminded me in an exaggerated manner of erect nipples? Had I had ever fantasized about masquerades or the masquerade cult?

"Excuse me," I cut him short. "I think you mean well, but I'm in danger of my life. Do you understand that?"

"I'm a psychoanalyst."

"There must have been a mistake then. I need someone who understands how the brain works, the connection between the different spheres of reality."

"That's exactly why you were sent to me. You said you needed someone who understands the mind, dream associations."

"No, no, I must have made a mistake then. I don't need any association in dreams. I need intervention."

I calmed down a bit when I noticed him regarding me warily as if expecting me to go berserk the next minute. I simply walked out of the consulting room. I went in search of Yellow, whose sort of madness was suddenly appealing. I was told he had been discharged two days earlier. That was surprising. I had not seen him on the streets, and I was not aware that anyone had. I returned to The Penthouse a defeated man considering his manner of surrender. My secretary had been and left my letters that had been addressed to the office, as I had instructed her to do every evening. Among the lot was one in an unforgettable handwriting. It was an invitation from Toshiba to her wedding. I could imagine Toshiba addressing the card to me as if sticking her tongue out: "See what you lost, you dog of the streets!" I did not for a moment consider attending the wedding. But that card gave me an idea that sent me racing back into the streets. Perhaps I had actually entered the first stage of madness, what with the twinkle of mischief and cunning in my brain.

I bought two Bibles, one for Toshiba and one for myself. The one for her I sent off by night express with a note that simply said: "Congratulations on your wedding." The one for me I took home and read far into the night. When I felt sleep coming, I took a rope and fastened the Bible, opened, on my head before I dozed off. I had heard so much about the Bible and its power. Not for me in that case. The next materialization in my nocturnal experience was another unknown masquerade, as if the night masquerade was convoking its entire fraternity. When I woke up, the weight on my head gave me an added jolt before I realized what it was. I searched all the crevices of my brain for a solution. I had never been to church since I left my maternal uncle's house. Except that shrine superintended by Mama Zi. I had never been to a medicine man all my life. Was this the time to start?

The Bible I had sent to Toshiba returned shortly. She also sent me another wedding invitation – with the date highlighted. I had not taken note of it previously. The event was still four weeks away. I might be dead by then. A section of the Bible had also been highlighted for my attention:

"Hold not thy peace, O God of my praise; For the mouth of the wicked and the deceitful are opened against me: they have spoken against me with a lying tongue. They compassed me about also with words of hatred; and fought against me without a cause. For my love they are my adversaries: but I give myself unto prayer. And they have rewarded me evil for good, and hatred for my love. Set thou a wicked man over him: and let Satan stand at his right hand. When he shall be judged, let him be condemned: and let his prayer become sin. Let his days be few; and let another take his office."

You used to be my friend, but now you are a foe in my heart.

In some circumstances, levity answers gravity. I understood then why some men would face a firing squad with laughter. My reaction to Toshiba's Bible was to wonder: had this most complete prayer of damnation come out of the very book that I had hoped would save me? And what was it I had done to Toshiba that even a few weeks to her wedding she could still invoke this comprehensive curse on me? How is it that some people never forgive, even when they should be waltzing? Or did she think I was mocking her by sending her the Bible gift four weeks before her wedding?

I reviewed the relationship again, and my levity transformed to rage. Was she the continuing "woman trouble" Mama Zi had prophesied for me, assuming that she knew the difference between dancing among the boulders and divining the future? I began to wish I had not lived such a lonely existence. I experienced a finally devastating loneliness of the spirit. If I had my time all over again, I mused, oh how I would rush about and make friends with every man and woman I met.

The next materialization was what I supposed was a female masquerade, with its spear firmly clasped as if to assure against any error. Its eyes bore into mine like liquid fire, as if my eyes – complete with their sockets – were its chosen prize. A tiny hope flared up in my heart, without any clarity of logic on my part then, that I might just survive.

"Taneba! What's the matter with you?" I spoke to myself crossly. In the heat of everything, I had developed the habit of speaking aloud to myself. "If you don't want to die in this unnatural and gory manner, then you must do everything, everything, to guard against falling asleep at night. Do you understand, completely?"

I prepared for my outing the next night like a man going for a vigil. I met Yellow outside Tamuno's Heaven. When I embraced him, he was surprised. He looked gaunt, but he was still his sprightly self – like his ageless walking stick. He did not think that spending some time in a psychiatric hospital was anything to worry about. If anything, as he told me, it was a better place to spend some time in than the maximum-security prison, where he had been in more than once.

"But where have you been since you came out of the hospital?" I asked him.

"I go for special prayer."

"You mean you still go to Mama Zi's so-called church, after what happened?"

"No be there. This one na correct church where them dey use Bible and holy water. I even give testimony."

"Yellow!"

"Forget all those ones first. Something don happen. S-o-m-e-t-h-i-n-g happen! You see say the man don die?" He brought out a newspaper obituary notice announcing "the passage of Chief A. A. Uzi, of Uzi Quarters, aged 60 years." More than three-quarters of the page was filled with the picture of a bright-eyed, well-dressed man who indeed looked sixty.

"Where did you get this? And how did you read it?" Yellow, I knew, had only an elementary school education.

"I pick am. When I see the picture like that, na im I know say e don happen. No be say I no know better English at all, but the matter simple: when person picture appear for paper big like that, na die be that."

I could not help laughing. "So, will you consider going back now?"

"God forbid! As this one die so, them go promote another one like am to replace am. I don comot from Uzi final."

I took him aside and told him the story of my dream experiences.

"You serious?" he asked me.

"Very serious."

"Oga Taneba, that kin' thing no suppose happen to better people like you. Na your mind e dey, inside your mind."

I was disappointed. "Look, I'm actually losing my gray hairs. That's a physical experience."

"If no be say you don bald your head like sacrifice, I for help you count your hair correct. Na your mind e dey. But the thing wey I go tell you be say make you go back to psychia. Them go give you drug wey go cool your brain. That one dey very important."

"Look, I've been given tranquilizers and all that."

"I no know the names, but I know say if them give you the kin' drugs wey them give me, all those masquerades wey dey worry your sleep go pick serious race."

The very person I had been longing to see most woke me up the next day: Bantu! Just seeing him gave me a major lift. I hugged him and dragged him about the room in a mock war dance. He did his best to get into the rhythm of whatever it was I was doing, but I could see he was puzzled.

"Bantu! It's great to see you. If I knew exactly where you were, I would have come there."

"I would go right back to the desert and come back again and again if that's the kind of welcome I'd get every time. How are you, man? I've never seen your head like this before, like an egg, and you've got worry lines all around your eyes. What's eating you?"

"I'll tell you soon enough. How's Naomi's?"

"Are you kidding me? I bet they've broken the signpost for firewood since. The place is called something like Limbo these days. I didn't even stop there long enough to squint. I've got this great place by the edge of the desert, with a few fellows as neighbors. It's just right. Now, we're going to commune with the sea of sand."

"Have you got money now?"

"Not much, but it'll come. Have you heard of The Desert Fund?"

"Not until now."

"I'm it. I got into this NGO riot all over again. Just give me your money and entrust the desert to me. How's that, man?"

"A scam?"

"I don't think people mind scams so much, so far as you don't make them look especially foolish. You have to push a lot of important-looking papers around, and if anyone as much as mentions the letter *s*, you have to push up your eyebrows right into your hairline and trot out a little sermon on how much you've already accomplished without anybody's money because you're in it for the principle of the thing. Never forget that expression: 'the principle of the thing.' It has a vigorous way of worrying the mind of your audience."

"Bantu!" I was laughing hard enough to burst.

"It's not me, man. There are a lot of them fellas out there with their rich dramatics and costumes of respectability that are shaming all of us. I never ever took anyone's money without earning it – or trying to."

"How are you going to bring your family over?"

"I'll go right away and check the port situation, but I'm going to be in town for a week or two. I'm hoping to hear the omega song before I travel. I can feel it coming.
Maybe I need some elevation this time."

"You want to travel from the valley to the mountaintop?"

"Something like that. You can laugh if you want, but I tell you..."

"I'm not laughing at all. Look, Bantu, something extraordinary has been happening to me." I told him the story then.

"Hurrah for the revelation!" he shouted after he had heard me. "Your time has come."

"Is that what you have to tell me? My time has come – to die?"

"Not at all, man. You will not die. You will live your life."

That was very good to hear, although I was well aware that hearing it was not enough.

"What you've got to deal with now is to translate your revelation and make it work for you," he told me. "It's not that difficult to get the revelation. Everything, properly interpreted, can even be a revelation. What is not as easy is to claim it and remain steadfast to its tenor. Have you ever witnessed a burial at sea?"

"Look, Bantu, you're beginning to get into a sea fog. My

problem is immediate."

"And what do you think is not immediate in a temporal universe?" He moved toward me and laid his hands, in a cross fashion, on my forehead. "Believe, man, believe! When you return to that dream-experience, you will take control of your life once more, and those masked soldiers banding against you will retreat to wherever they came from. I, *Om* Bantu, I have said so."

"What was that all about?" I asked when he took his hands away.

"I have banished them rioters."

"You think this is a joke?"

"You're the one who thinks so, man. I have told you: believe! The laying of hands is also the pooling of forces."

After Bantu left, I dressed up for work. If the experience persisted, I told myself, I would present myself at the psychiatric hospital and insist on being admitted – under the care of an experienced psychiatrist. If salvation was not forthcoming within a week, I would then seek out either a "healing church" or a medicine man and bind myself to the protection of supernatural forces.

That night, after having defied sleep for about forty-eight hours, I found myself again in that vast universe where I was up, alone, against five obvious assassins. Once more, a gray hair detached itself from my head. It began an evocative free-fall until it became a ram's head. Then there were five unexpected gunshots that nearly deafened me. Everything went blank. I sprang up in bed, frightened out of my wits. Were those shots part of the dream sequence or did they signal an invasion by armed robbers? My stealthy survey informed me that neither was the case. The story was almost anticlimactic. The national soccer team was playing a qualifying match for one tournament or the other in a country with a time zone that made our night their afternoon. Our team had looked into the tunnel of defeat, then hurried back to win in an unbelievable triumph of the will. My soccer-crazy neighbor had been so jubilant that he had fired five times into the air. And I had been snatched away from that nightmarish experience.

After that night, I regained my ability to sleep and dream without being waylaid by any of those homicidal foot soldiers. I considered it such a major salvation and redefinition of being that it was at this time that I cast away my first name, Taneba. After all, was it not my father who had given me that name? I renamed myself Baneta: Baneta Baneta. But, like Bantu, I did not insist on the name.

Bantu. He had still not returned to The Penthouse, contrary to his assurance. I went in search of him. It is difficult to believe that there was no one among the very many people I interviewed – on the streets, in and around the port – that could give any account of his movement. In desperation, I wrote to his former wife. Bantu seemed to have become one with the air or the water. I never saw him again. I never heard from him again. The abrupt parting of kindred spirits is among the most saddening experiences in life. Many were the days and nights I thought long and cried hard for Bantu.

Tamuno. Bantu. I had been so enriched and warmed by their friendship that their absence widened that void in me which we all carry in us, widened it so much that I believed nothing could ever fill it. Bantu. I remember him, that revving presence that he had, as if it were yesterday. I still miss him. I still mourn him. Certain things are forever.

And everything goes to sea.

Angel

Sometimes, change steals in on us even with our eyes open. We sense it before we firmly remark its pattern. The passage of Tamuno had been like a signal that my class in the school of the night was graduating. Bantu's disappearance was like a strong reminder that very soon I might become like an old man who refuses to yield his place on the dance floor after all his mates had departed. Gradually, I began to notice that Tamuno's Heaven was changing. I began to see more new faces and less of the familiar ones. Nightlife is also the sphere of drifters, who often gravitate toward new experiences. So, the old clubs frayed or died out and new ones came into being or reckoning.

While the going and coming among the patrons continued, the personnel remained more or less the same. Eventually, some of the key workers began to leave. I arrived at Tamuno's Heaven one night, after a brief absence, and I was told that Esther had left. She had been transferred back to the bar and had seemed contented the last time I saw her.

"What happened?" I asked Faith.

"The world must roll."

"Do you know where she is now?"

"You think I should know, my genius? You've got your eyes on her for other things?" She gave me a wink to underline her meaning.

"Do I look like the stutterer who lived twenty-four years next door to Alice? I've become used to seeing her around."

"I understand, don't mind me. But you've got to get used to everything and nothing. That's the way it happens."

"You didn't ask her to leave or squeeze her out?"

"What for? She was one of the best I had."

I could think of no special reason why I was upset about Esther's departure. Had I expected her to remain in the service of Tamuno's Heaven forever, eternally fighting off men who thought that because she worked in a nightclub she was fair game? Was it merely nostalgia or was there still a part of me that called to a part of her? I had started out by taking a fancy to her but had converted her into the liaison between my desires and my difficult conquests. But that had still not stopped me from looking her over thoughtfully in her erotic uniform at Tamuno's Heaven. She had such a frankly sensual appearance that she did not have to be beautiful.

It was the night that bound us together, but I did eventually see her during the day – a few months after her departure. I drove into a filling station to fill up the tank of my car, and there she was in a bus that had also pulled up for the same purpose. Her face brightened when she saw me, and she came down from the bus.

"Taneba, na you be this? How now?"

I had always seen her in the club at night, so she seemed rather overdressed to me in the daytime.

"Esther! Good to see you, but you look like the lunch break."

"You and your mouth, you never change?"

"How are you?"

"Nothing spoil."

"I've been asking around for you. You couldn't even tell me you were leaving?"

"Sorry, but e get as e take happen."

"Where are you going now?"

"Home – for Victoria Island."

I had no business on the Island, which was quite some distance, but I invited her in – to take her home.

"You must be richer than I thought," I told her. "How come you're able to live on the Island – the same as politicians, expatriates, and government officials?"

"Taneba, you wan' laugh me? No be that side at all, na for shanty town I dey squat."

"And you've been coming from there to work on the mainland all this while?"

"How person go do? This na Lagos. Every person for

herself."

She had run away from her forgotten village after completing her junior high school education, because it offered her no other opportunity. Besides, her stepfather had thrown her out after she tried to denounce him to her disbelieving mother for violating her. Lagos was the place to go to, the magical city of instant self-enlargement. On arrival, she had gone to stay with her mother's brother. His wife barely tolerated her. So, when she got a job as a waitress at The Owl, she was jubilant. The employment enabled her to move into a shared space with a "Lagos friend" – a stranger in Lagos brought together by the same sort of need – in one of the shanty towns that ringed the Victoria Island of affluence like accusations.

The fact that she was a waitress did not stop some of the male patrons from taking an interest in her and trying to draw her into intimate one-night embraces. Initially, she saw this as a way to boost her income. But two things stopped her: her bitter experiences and the realization that the club girls were using every resource available to them, even the invocation of supernatural forces, to outdo one another. Besides, her experience with her stepfather had also functioned, in her own case, to deepen the dignity of choice. Both at The Owl and Tamuno's Heaven, she had always been on the lookout for an opportunity for the sort of job that would in reality widen the latitude of that dignity of choice. She left when she had the opportunity to work as a receptionist in a packaging company.

"Na one man wey dey come Tamuno's Heaven sometimes na im give me the job. He say im don dey look me as I dey behave. Na for im brother company I dey work."

"So, you had your boyfriend looking out for you all the time?"

"You think say everybody be like you? Nothing connect me and the man at all. I just dey greet am when e come, that's all."

"Why did you have to leave like that, in that sort of hurry?"

"They say make I start work immediately. I never try? Eight

years na im I don work as waitress. And I don look everything. Nothing dey inside that life. You still dey waka for night?"

"Of course."

"Nothing dey inside that life, Taneba. You no go stop? Wetin you still dey find? You don carry all the better women finish."

"Except you."

She looked at me strangely, before she started laughing. "Me? Me and you? Ah-ah, Taneba, you be like my brother now. You be better man, proper person. God dey inside your heart, but no be only for you Im create this world. I don get serious boyfriend now. My life don change. At least, I dey fit sleep well now. And no be say man go dey talk to me anyhow."

"Was that why you left, the male attention and perhaps the uniform?"

"Ah, if man no look woman, wetin e go look? But at least respect go dey inside, no be like say I be tomato wey them dey price. The uniform, that one na show, e no comot hair for my body."

"You're not trying to tell me off because of all those girls..."

"Comot *jo*, you no dey ever serious! You no go try marry before all those girls pieces you? No take them play-o! As their eyes dey hot, na so their mind strong."

I changed the subject – to previewing her plans for life outside the ambit of the night. She would soon be moving into the junior staff quarters of her company, she told me – a "proper house" in a medium-class neighborhood. She planned to enroll for evening lessons and complete her high school education in that manner. And if everything worked out, the way she envisaged, she would marry her "serious boyfriend" and settle down to family life. She was so sure of her plans, so proud of her vision that I envied her.

By the time we got to her residence, after negotiating several potholes, my envy had become admiration. I could never have spent one night in that place, which looked like just salvaged zinc and rotting wood hurriedly thrown together, without grumbling my head off. Yet she had lived there for years, and in all the time I had known her she had always radiated the warmth of someone who lived in a palace. My heart went out to her. I gave her all the money I had on me, gave her my business card and asked her to call me if she ever needed any assistance. She oh-ahed over the money, gave me a vigorous embrace and thanked me profusely. I believe there were tears in her eyes when I left. I was sure then that I had broken her defense mechanism and that it would not take long before she called me. She never did.

Hers was a quiet departure. André's was not. When he stopped showing up at Tamuno's Heaven, the story soon spread that he had gone back to work at The Owl as a general-purpose man, which was interpreted to mean his defection to the camp of St Notorious.

"Is it true, the story about André?" I asked Alonzo.

"Oga Taneba, no be everyone understand this world," he said as if that was ample information for my enlightenment.

There was no point interviewing him further. Soon, people like Yellow who claimed to know everything that happened on the streets announced that André had also disappeared from The Owl, killed on the say-so of St Notorious because he was a "saboteur," killed and dumped in the Lagos Lagoon.

There the story would have ended. But if he was ever killed, André resurrected a few months later. He was shot dead by the police when an armed gang, which he was part of, engaged a special police squad in a gun battle in an attempt to flee a robbery scene. It was then I learned that his real name was Andrew. All these were stories to me. I had no reason to disbelieve them, but I never saw any confirmatory report.

What was lavishly reported was the fall of St Notorious. It appeared that he had "staged" the wrong American "bull." A series of media salvoes ensued, both in Nigeria and abroad, during which time the man at the center of the storm still paraded himself about like a local festival, boasting that he was a "notorious survivor." The story changed notoriously. He was captured at home, then flown to America in a cage. The home media and government raised an outcry, in which a phrase like "violation of national integrity" was thrown around like a bomb refusing to detonate, then they fell notoriously silent. St Notorious was tried for advance fee fraud and money laundering, sentenced to a long jail term and was eclipsed.

Without St Notorious, his group fell apart. The Owl was soon put up for sale. Whoever bought it – many names were thrown around, including the local government and even Chief Stephens – chose to turn the place into an insect museum. On the streets, some people spoke of the section where the colorful insects were kept as the Tamuno section and the area that housed the fattened ones as the St Notorious section. There was also talk of a new gang leader called Cappuccino, or something like that, rising to fill the vacuum. I did not stop to listen to such stories.

What stopped me, in a sense, was Faith's announcement that she too was leaving. It detonated in the world of Tamuno's Heaven like a bomb, with the workers scurrying to various observatories.

"What's this talk about you leaving?" I asked her.

"I'm sorry you had to hear it from someone else, but you know how it is. Even our thoughts get peddled on the streets as facts. You're like my brother here, Taneba. I am, indeed, leaving."

"But that's abandoning ship."

"Not at all. There's nothing wrong with this ship. I'm the captain. I should know."

"Should I say like stopping the music then?"

"You and I know there's no stopping the music. It will go on and on. Even when God decides to end the world, if Armageddon is not a fable, the water or whatever will make music on the bodies of the dead."

"Look, Faith, you know what I mean. Your departure will rock this monument, maybe even create some sort of panic."

"Don't dwell on it. Tamuno left, and the world didn't stop. I'm just moving on with my life. It's a personal thing. I've done everything within my power to keep the faith, but I can't live forever in a tomb."

"Is that what this place makes you feel?"

"Sometimes. But that's not what I'm talking about. When anyone makes the future a slave to the past, or simply refuses to explore the possibilities of the present, then it's like entombing oneself alive. You're my genius, and surely you know these things. Do you realize how much I'll miss this place and all the beautiful people I've met here? Surely, I'm the one who should be in mourning."

"Are you forewarning me that it is this place, only, that connects us?"

"There are some things that distance cannot change. You may never realize how much you've helped me brave everything. I can tell you this straightaway because it's a thing of the spirit. Ours is a fabulous way of life, Taneba, but everything comes and goes – like smoke."

The way she spoke the last word, like a balloon puncturing, made both of us laugh.

Her boyfriend was going on accumulated leave to his hometown in Greece. His next posting was not likely to be in Africa. She had decided to relocate with him. Why didn't she wait for him to marry her, if he was serious about her? They had decided to do that in Athens, she told me, and in any case she believed in unconditional love. She did not require marriage as a precondition for loving or living with anyone. I wished her well immensely, feeling like an undertaker moving from farewell to farewell. Was it the time for me to quit? And do what with myself, with my nights?

The news of Faith's intention upset Chief Stephens.

"You've heard the terrible news?" he asked me in his office, downcast. "Terrible. Disastrous. Where am I going to get another wonderworker like Faith? I've talked to her myself, offered to double everything. She is determined to leave. Do you think you can talk to her? I've seen both of you giving each other the eye."

This man was a marvel, the way he heard and saw everything.

"We're too close for that sort of thing," I assured him. "I

have already spoken with her. She's leaving."

"Don't misunderstand me. I've nothing against the way she wants to organize her life, nothing personal. She deserves her happiness, I have no doubt about that. But this is business. Business! It's only you that is left now, Taneba, only you from that old school."

I believe he wanted to say something more, but he did not. Nevertheless, the story was soon on the streets that I had been recruited to take over from Faith as the manager of Tamuno's Heaven. It was a story that made me pause. If that offer had been made to me, how would I have responded?

"Congratulations, my brother," Faith hailed me. "I've heard the great news. Now, I know two things: Chief Stephens is a first-class businessman, and I'm leaving Tamuno's Heaven in very good hands."

"It's all a rumor. I had a meeting with Chief Stephens. He proposed no such thing. He made some suggestive remarks, but that was all."

"He's taking his time. You and I have to sit down for a long time, so I can pass on the lessons I've learned on the job, give you a head start."

"Faith, it won't happen. Chief Stephens realizes how much more valuable I am to him at the courier firm."

"A great pity then. I think he missed it this time, because you're a natural."

Chief Stephens gave a rousing farewell party for Faith. It brought the heavens down. First, Faith danced with all the girls – quite a clamor – then she danced with all the men – quite a riot. Thereafter, she took the longest bow I had ever seen because the ovation would simply not abate. There she stood, in the middle of the dance floor, in that sensational dress she had won on the opening night, gloriously highlighted by a hundred points of light. Watching her being spun round and round by the revolving stage, like a never-ending farewell, gave me a great feeling.

To manage the club after her was a fellow called Fedora

because of his fondness for that sort of cap. He came as the head of a new team, because both Alonzo and Lucas left about the same time as Faith – Alonzo to become the personal bodyguard of a government minister who had recruited him from Seventh Heaven, Lucas to work in an accounting firm. One of the first signs of Fedora's captainship was the change in the appearance of the waitresses. The sombreros came off. The high boots became plain shoes and socks. The leather bra and pant transformed into short-sleeved shirt and short. Perhaps he felt he had to create a personal style, but to the habitués accustomed to seeing the girls as they were they suddenly looked like members of a choir.

I did not stay much longer to note the other transformations. There were too many ghosts haunting me there. And I often tended to see things as they used to be. So, since I would not quit the night, I went in search of another spot to plant my flag in.

My search took me to a club called Kabila. The freshly painted, walled exterior was very promising, although its location was in a neighborhood where a robbery incident or a broken head at night was nothing to panic the residents unduly. But the interior was as empty as a void, except for a bandstand and chairs arranged around it in a semicircle. The special fare was Makossa music, the Central African dance music that had swept into Lagos – as in other parts of the world, I was told – like a gale. Makossa was everywhere – in the song of babies on the streets, in the dance-gyrations of working-class women, in the sexy appearance of street girls, even in the breast language of old women who no longer felt any need for the convenience – or inconvenience – called the bra.

At Kabila that night, I witnessed the sustained erotic provocation called the Makossa dance. I did not understand a word of the lyrics being belted out by the band, but I neither needed to nor was I particularly interested. My interest was wholly seized by the three dancers in tight dresses that I first wondrously mistook for their skin. There was so much sexiness in their dance motions that I was exhilarated. There was so much vitality about them –

translated into acrobatic buttocks, suggestive hip swings, body spins, knee jerks, breast thrusts, and every other convertible physiological detail – that when the dance stopped, the entranced audience jerked into consciousness like voyeurs caught in the act.

I found the experience tingling, even if bawdy. I told myself I would most likely visit there from time to time, but it was not the sort of place that I wanted to plant a flag. Apart from the fact that I tended to find live shows progressively boring, I also preferred to frequent places where I did not have to keep fidgeting about my safety. However, it was Kabila that led me to The Red Hat through an overheard conversation between two half-dressed girls behind me. One wanted the other to come with her to this "exclusive" place called The Red Hat the next day, where there were "plenty of whites."

When I finally located the place, my pride in my knowledge of the streets was somewhat deflated. How could this sort of place have been there all along, on the mainland, without my knowledge of it? There was no signpost of any sort, just a dancing restaurant with a garden ensconced within a fascinating stone wall. The parking space was right inside, and there were no hangers-on outside as in many other clubs. So, it was easy to drive past and mistake the place for someone's residence.

The gate was opened when my car pulled up. I drove inside and parked. My entrance to the club proper, from where I could hear the sound of music and laughter, was however barred by a bouncer whose biceps rippled with every movement. Did these fellows nurture these professional muscles in the gymnasium or was there more to it than that?

"What's the matter?" I asked him calmly.

"Members only."

"That's strange. This place is for members only, always?"

"Tonight."

I went back to my car and drove away, calmly. I was not satisfied. What sort of respectable place would have those two girls at Kabila as members? The next day, I dressed myself like

Christmas and went to The Red Hat once more. If this club was truly for members only, why then did they let me into the premises at all? Did I look like someone's driver, assuming that they did not know the identity of their members' drivers?

"How are you today?" I said to the bouncer familiarly.

"Fine. Members only."

"I thought that was yesterday only."

"Tonight."

"Tomorrow?"

"Every night."

"Why didn't you say so yesterday? Okay, I want to become a member."

"You come back in the day and see the manager."

Fair enough, I thought. I would have left at that point, but then I saw two chattering girls approach. They walked up to the door and were allowed in casually. They could as well have been the two from Kabila. I then decided that the "members only" claim was humbug. "There's only one thing to it," Bantu would have said. I started walking toward the bouncer, believing he would then make way. Instead, he put his hand on my chest and gave me a muscular shove. It was the first time I would receive that sort of treatment and I was not about to accept it at night. I walked back a few paces, dug my feet into the ground in readiness for a massive charge that I hoped would perforate that bouncer. I had never had to resort to violence in all my years of running with the night. But then I had never been provocatively denied admission into any club.

My charge was stopped by the appearance of a flamboyantly dressed man who could have passed for a local chief. He took one look at the scene and correctly interpreted it.

"What's the matter?" he asked the bouncer.

"He want force his way in, after I tell him it's members only."

"Did you take a good look at this gentleman? He's not the type you were asked to keep out, DG. It's okay."

I did not know this flamboyant fellow vouching for me. I had first taken him for an overdressed club manager, but it was evident then that he was a respected member.

"Colonel Briggs, EC," he said and patted me on the back.

"Baneta."

He patted me once more, said something about having other matters to attend to that night and departed.

"You're welcome, sir," DG – short for Douglas, I later learned – told me as he ushered me in. The good thing about him was that he accepted the annulment of his judgment graciously and even became close to me – as close as we could be, considering – in my nights at The Red Hat.

It was a white and black club – white men, black girls – owned and run by a Dutch character called Jan. For the whites, it was free entry. For the black girls, a monthly "membership" fee was required. According to Douglas, his error was an over-interpretation of this rule. But in all the time I hung around there, I hardly saw any black men – apart from Colonel Briggs, who was a regular, and a few others who drifted in and out. In the main, it was a place where black girls came to prospect white expatriates resident in that part of Lagos.

Even if the management had so wanted, it would have been impossible to bar black men. Not only would that have provoked a public outcry, it would have led to charges of discrimination. It was the girls themselves who perpetuated this discrimination, because they had eyes only for whites. It was clear that this was the structural adjustment of our national economy at work. These girls knew that with its constant devaluation the naira had become relatively worthless, so they lusted for stronger currencies. Besides, although I considered my annual salary impressive, it was about as much as a less qualified expatriate earned in a month in "hard currency." So, they were freer with the relatively worthless naira than I could afford to be. The result was that black men were mostly like islands unto themselves or color orphans at The Red Hat.

The interior was such that there was a dance floor at the

center, and dining tables all around – with a bar and the disc jockey's cubicle in different corners. It was especially interesting to watch these girls dance irresistibly for their white prospects. The whites themselves hardly ever danced. They derived their pleasure mainly from watching the Kabila-style dances promising bedroom excesses. There was so much more pinching, teasing, kissing, and exploratory fingers under miniskirts in that place than in all the other places I had been to.

Usually, I favored the tables near the dance floor. Often, I sat there alone plotting how to go about the business of properly integrating myself into the flow of the place. One night, however, a portly Lebanese man smoking a fat cigar sat beside me. Quite unexpectedly, a conversation developed between us. It was made up of so many suspended and recalled words because every other minute or so one of the girls would come and fondle his hair or sit on his lap or kiss him on the cheek or even rub his crotch. There was so much of this going and coming that I considered leaving and not returning. But my motto in such matters had always been: never ever quit. In this black and white situation, I was particularly determined not to.

"These girls," the cigar-smoking Lebanese said to me, "they think every white man is rich. Maybe, you're richer than me. They don't even know."

"They do. These girls can smell money, real money."

So they could. In Colonel Briggs. The discrimination against blacks excluded him. The girls flocked around him as much as they did the expatriates, although he did not always have an interest in them. When he was in the mood for debauchery, he sometimes left with up to three or four of them. It was said that his sexual energy at such times was activated by the smell of a special perfume he bathed the girls with. He also bathed them with money, obviously, because any night he was in such a mood there was a scramble among the girls – even the hints of a fight. An actual fight was always unlikely because that would mean immediate revocation of membership.

More often than not, however, Colonel Briggs's interest was vocalizing the future, his. A retired military officer, he had an active interest in politics. But his own EC meant Ex Cathedra. He did not expect any disputation on his views.

"When we get to power," he would say, "the first thing we will do is to set up a Ministry of the Night. Yes, a ministry for night affairs. When we get to power, soon. You see, the problem is that those in power don't realize there is a powerful army of the night constantly being enlarged by the policies of the day. It's a dangerous army, and the first thing any government in power that wants to survive should do is to convert danger to its service. I can tell you now that all the changes of government that have taken place in this country were initiated or perfected at night. All the major coups. All the major electoral victories. All the major oil contracts. All the major everything. The night, hmm! But I'm not talking about these obvious instances. I'm talking about the army that decides that you cannot go to sleep at night because it's hungry, that you cannot park your car safely because there is a fuel crisis and the members of this army have had a punishing day moving from anywhere to anywhere, that you cannot take your girlfriends out because this army is sex-starved. That's an army to beware of. Every government in power without a Ministry of the Night is a government soon out of power. I'm sure they have such a ministry anywhere that's anywhere."

Why he would choose such an incongruous setting and such an uninterested audience was a puzzle to me. Perhaps he realized that if he said as much anywhere else, he ran the risk of being dragged in chains before a special tribunal and tried for coup plotting. Who were the "we" he always talked about – an enlargement of himself, or was he truly in league with some other retired officers as indiscreet as himself? Amidst all the twirling and pinching and fingering, no one listened to Colonel Briggs, except the people he sometimes came with. On some nights, I would be the sole member of his audience because I had not contrived how to be part of anything else.

"I see you know the future," he told me. "When we get to power, you'll be my ADC."

"Will it be a military government?"

"Every government in Africa is always military."

I was on the verge of commencing a disputation, but I checked myself. Colonel Briggs's ego was so monstrous that if I dared prick it the thunder of its explosion would sweep me off The Red Hat in bits and pieces.

"Anyway, don't worry, we can always call you 'Special Assistant' or something. We can even make a special decree or constitutional amendment to customize your title. I'm not talking to you about money. I'm not talking to you about credentials. I'm not talking to you about citizenship. I'm talking to you about power. It doeth all things."

Colonel Briggs talked and exuded power. Very many people there treated him like an emperor-in-waiting and would rather ignore than challenge him. Even Jan, who was sometimes as erratic as a club proprietor made power-drunk by his success, treated him with obvious respect.

It was through Colonel Briggs, sort of, that I finally broke into the almost cultic world of the girls at The Red Hat. On that night, he was in the mood for what he called "bed politics." Initially, he selected four girls. After he had made his choice, he then talked and drank far into the night. When he was ready to leave, however, he changed his mind and departed with only three. Unlike places like Tamuno's Heaven, which opened at about midnight, The Red Hat was an eight to twelve sort of place. And Colonel Briggs was often one of the last people to leave. Although he compensated the rejected girl, she had a bit of a problem with regard to getting herself from The Red Hat to anywhere else.

Ironically, if I had had to choose from the four, my first choice would have been the girl rejected. She was boyish, a look accentuated by her hairstyle. But she had a carriage that I found intriguing – like a leopard about to pounce, as if her heels never touched the ground. And when she danced, she did so both with skill and a certain suppleness of the joints.

"Why don't you come with me?" I invited her.

"I no dey follow black."

"Is it my color you want?"

"I don tell you: I no dey follow black. Na by force?"

I gave her more money than she was worth, according to my estimation of the flesh market there, without another word. She came with me without enthusiasm. Her name was Jacqueline, she told me without warmth.

"I no dey follow you go your house," she warned me inside my car before I drove off.

According to her, the girls preferred not to go with blacks not only because of money-related considerations but also because they were the ones most likely to use them for ritual purposes.

"Do I look to you like that sort of person?"

"Na today?" Whatever that meant was still translatable into a rejection of the idea of going to my house.

"So, where do you want us to go? I don't intend to go to any guesthouse." I had never liked that option, what with the room attendants studying the clock and the room door with too much agility.

"Wetin do your car?"

That was a new proposition to me. But the arithmetic was inequitable.

"What about the money?"

"If you want make we sleep inside the car till morning, no problem." She smiled then, a smile as old as trickery.

We then commenced the search for a quiet, dark corner on a quiet, dark street. I was amazed when I slid my hand under her flimsy miniskirt and my fingers snaked, unrestricted, into a moist forest of hair. Who was this girl, and where was she from?

"You mean, even in this skirt, you're not wearing anything underneath and you've been prancing about, dancing like that?"

"I no send anybody message."

Was this what The Red Hat was all about then, why there

were so many itching fingers under miniskirts?

It threatened to turn into a bad night. At the first place we parked, in a blind alley, we had hardly transferred ourselves to the back of the car when all sorts of things – old buckets, sand, tin cups – came flying at us over the wall of a house that had looked deserted. We scrambled back to the front seats and bolted. At the second spot, beside a well-built house, we were already on the back seat when the light of a car suddenly lit up the darkness. It was the owner of the house, whom I had supposed was then already sleep, being driven home. He came down from the car and walked toward us with a bit of trepidation.

We moved to the front seat and left. We had not gone very far before the lights of a car appeared behind us and stuck to us. I made way for the car to pass. What I saw, instead, were armed policemen coming toward us.

"Wetin dey happen?" demanded one, searching out the details of our faces with his torchlight.

"Nothing, officer."

"Where you dey go?"

"Home."

"With this girl?"

He made it sound like an offense. I declined to answer.

"Who you be anyway?"

I gave him my identity card. He studied it elaborately before he returned it. "Make you no dey waka anyhow, you hear?" he said.

"I no dey do again," Jacqueline said, almost petulantly, as I reversed my car. "Next time," she added, softly, after she waited for an answer from me that never came.

I simply drove to The Penthouse, with her in the car. I suppose she accepted the situation as inevitable.

Inevitability was also what figured in the disappearance of Bantu shortly after. I finally received a reply to my letter from his former wife several months after I had sent it. I had since come to the conclusion that either my letter did not get to her or that, for whatever reason, she had chosen not to answer.

"Dear Taneba,

"By now, you have probably given up on my response to your letter. It's no fault of mine. Your letter incredibly arrived only yesterday, four months after it was first postmarked. The envelope deserves a place in the museum of postal errors. It bears a history of blunders: 'Missent to Bangkok.' 'Missent to Niagara Falls.' 'Missent to Auckland.' 'Missent to York.' The content is even more alarming. When Bantu left here, he said that he would be back within three months. The months have since stretched endlessly. I have wondered over and over again whether he had a change of heart, and I would have written to you myself if I had any proper address. Is he back now? I can only hope that it is so. This letter then is a profound appeal that he should forgive the past, even if he still can't forget, and return to his loving family. I know that there are some errors that are grievous, but I believe there is no compassion that is so. We still love him, and we still miss him every day of our lives.

"La Mundo."

What had ever happened to this woman with such a tidy handwriting when the fellow Bantu called El Diablito came along? I sent her a reply, detailing the unsuccessful attempt to find Bantu. A prompt response came, in one sentence: *"So, it is my fate then to bear this burden all the days of my life?"*

Something about that letter made me initiate another vigorous search for Bantu, this time with the aid of the police. Suddenly, Bantu sightings were reported all over the country. One person had seen him climbing a tall tree by the edge of the Cowrie Creek, another had seen him on top of a cargo lorry on the way to Maiduguri, and another on the elevator of the tallest building in Ibadan. Within a week, Bantu was reported seen – sometimes at the same time – in more than fourteen places. The police decided to suspend the search. I had nothing uplifting to report to La Mundo, so I decided not to write to her again.

But I did sit down, for several nights, to carefully prepare a document entitled "Forwarding Errors in the Postal Service: A Control Manual." Everything I had learned in all my working years went into that document. I dispatched it to my maternal uncle. He actually came to my apartment, the first time ever, to congratulate me with unusual effusion on "the single most important thing you've done in your life" and "the single most insightful study that has been undertaken in the postal service in a long time." His gratitude that I chose to forward the document directly to him was equally profound. On that occasion, he did not mention my marital status or comment on the fact that my apartment smelt like a den.

Meanwhile, at The Red Hat, my acquaintance with Jacqueline remained no more than so. Although her "bed politics" was "as good as an electoral victory," as Colonel Briggs would sometimes say, she was the sort of girl whose sweetness was no longer strongly desired once tasted. Everything she had to give she possessed only in a single dose.

My interest had been seized by a slender, light-skinned girl whom I found even more intriguing. She did not have Jacqueline's leopard walk, but she had something more. She was slightly bowlegged. In her, this was a blessing. With her braided hair almost threatening to touch the floor, she had a fascinating lilt that was a personal dance-walk. Inebriated. Inebriating. It was a statement: "I am." It was a question: "Who you?" She was called Nameless because she gave a different name to whoever asked her for that information. I called her Angel because that was the name she told me. She was the live-in mistress of a French man who had left his family behind in Paris to come and work in Lagos.

They usually came to The Red Hat together and left together. Why such a toast to vibrancy would choose to live with such a man was a thought that usually disturbed me. Of course, I understood the "money politics," but surely there were younger men who would only be too happy to oblige her. Colonel Briggs, I knew, would very happily have done that. But Angel – Venus to him – was one of the very few girls, in our time at The Red Hat together, that was impervious to his power. Watching that pretty girl pulsing with so much energy, I was convinced her French lover, whom we called Pourquoi, could not be enough for her.

I decided to relay messages to her through Douglas. I gave him my business card to give to her and told him to ask her to either call or visit me. In all, I gave him five such cards. She neither called nor came. Douglas insisted she had taken all five cards and had promised to honor my request. I regarded him thoughtfully. Maybe he was simply putting my cards in one of his pockets and my money in the other, hoping I would not exhaust myself too soon.

One night, when Pourquoi appeared – as was often the case – to have been too generous to himself with wine and was croaking what he said were romantic French songs to his circle of friends, I followed Angel on one of her restless jaunts – to the garden. At first, she looked askance at me. Did she know she was a sincerely pretty girl with a charming dance-walk? Did she know how much I admired her? Did she get my cards?

"Yes, DG gave me."

"And?"

"Who are you?"

"I know we can't talk much here, so here's my card again. Why don't you come and see me and let's talk? It's simple: if you don't like what I have to say, you're under no obligation certainly. But I feel we're going to have a great time together and do great things."

Before she took the card, she wanted to know how old I was, whether I was married or had children, whether I was a "night crawler," whether I had my own office, whether I had ever been in love.

She came the next afternoon. I was pleasantly surprised because she had given me no firm commitment. In any case, I was used to assurances of consequent contact that remained only so. In my ecstatic mood, I took her to a late lunch. There was no coy "I don't eat much, thank you" about her. Despite her enticing slender shape, she ate and drank heartily. And talked as much.

She was from a middle-class family, but she had felt

hemmed in by her family's way of life. She felt she was missing out on the great adventures of life. After she received a diploma from a catering school, she had gone with some other girls recruited by a "modeling agency" to Paris for "big modeling jobs" on the other side of the globe. She had believed that there would be better prospects there and that life would be freer. The jobs made available to her entailed intimately modeling her body. She had run into trouble and had been deported.

Back home, some other people told her that she had made a mistake by going to France. Spain was the setting for the great new adventure of a great new age, they said. She set off with some others, across the desert, to Spain. Once they arrived in Morocco, they believed, they could buy their crossing into Malaga or any other convenient entry point into Spain, and then it would be a brand-new day. Her journey terminated in Algiers, where she was stranded. She was then sucked into the underworld of prostitution and drug-peddling, a life of mind-boggling suffering in which many others had found themselves thrown into or threw themselves into – suffering and perishing, like the story of Africa. Once more, she was caught in a raid.

"They caught me in only a flimsy wrapper. I was deported like that, with everyone staring at me in a certain manner. What a disgrace! I could not even take a pin with me. Can you imagine?"

Still, she was determined to go back, across the desert, until she made her way into Spain.

"That doesn't make much sense to me. Why would you do that?"

"You're already comfortable in Lagos, I think, so what else would you say?"

"You're not doing poorly, from what I can see. Besides, you said your parents are not poor."

She was through with the sort of life her parents lived and wanted her to live. And the sort of income they had only ensured that no one starved. She wanted to move into "the big league" and not have to depend on any man's generosity.

"I know the road now, not like the last time. This time, I'll surely make it."

"Why not go by air, if you must go back?"

"If I manage to get a visa, why not?"

"Why would anyone even dare the desert only to..."

"Because of what is there at the end of the desert," she cut in. "It's a hard journey, very hard. Ilella. Algadir. Tamanrasset. Algiers. All these are terrible passages. Do you know how many girls are raped by foreign guards or are forced to sleep with men for only a loaf of bread? Many drink only water – if they can find it – to stay alive, and many are emptied forever into the high sea on the crossing into Spain. Still, there are many who have taken the oath rather to die on the route than to return."

"Why?"

"Because we know we are nobodies, as good as dead at home. Who cares if we die on the way? To stay is madness. To leave is madness."

"A female sensation like you shouldn't be talking about madness and death. Let's leave the desert to cross itself. Let's talk about the two of us. Every meeting promises new life."

"What are you promising?"

"Is that why you were asking me all those questions last night?"

She smiled then, her eyes blinking.

"Is that how you check people out?"

"Of course, there are other ways."

"How come someone like Colonel Briggs..."

"A-beg, I'm not looking for death or madness yet."

"What has any of that got to do with him?"

"Do you know how many of those girls that hang around him have buried effigies of him in the Lagos Lagoon or the Yaba cemetery in attempts to bind him to them?"

"But the man doesn't appear to be bound to anyone."

"So, they keep burying him. Only God knows how many clay pots at the bottom of the lagoon contain effigies of Colonel

Briggs. I don't want anyone to bury me too in a bid to deplete the competition. Besides, the man talks too much. I don't want my story all over The Red Hat."

"I'm a regular there too, remember?"

"I know, but it's just you to you – except your on-and-off girlfriend, Yemisi. You think I don't know?"

"Who?"

"The one that calls herself Jacqueline. Her name is Yemisi."

"Look, Jacqueline or whatever was just something that happened."

"That's the same way you'll talk about me: 'Angel was something that just happened, nothing more than that.' You men! Anyway, it's good; enjoy your life."

"With you."

We began a whirlwind affair. It appeared that Pourquoi turned a blind eye to whatever Angel did during the day, as long as she was there for him at night. Or, maybe during the day when he was at work, he preferred not to be encumbered by thoughts of what his mistress was up to. So, Angel became my regular lunch guest – only that we ate less food and made more love, because I unusually started going home during the lunch break. She had an appealing feline grace. I was certainly happy, even contented, to have her. But the more I wanted, the less I could have. On weekends, I hardly saw her at all. At The Red Hat, we had to pretend we did not know each other, except for hurried conversations in the garden or relays of messages through Douglas. Occasionally, she would steal out and spend a night or two with me, after telling Pourquoi one tale or the other. It was not a situation I particularly liked.

"I don't even know how I got into an affair at all," she told me. "When I saw you, something just took over me."

"If you really mean that, then it's simple. Quit staying with Pourquoi so we can spend more time with each other."

"How many men in Lagos will take care of me the way he does? I'm in his house, yet I'm free to go and come as I choose."

I did not exactly want to invite her to come and live with me, so I left the matter hanging. In the interim, I became her daytime financier. She had very little respect for money. She bought almost everything that caught her fancy, and there were very many. She took me to Treasures, a shop that sold "party wear" and was like the daytime headquarters of the girls on the streets. If there was any treasure there, as far as I could tell, it was for the owner. She also made me an occasional presence at a fast-food restaurant called Variety Taste, where the long line – of mostly young girls – sometimes caused a traffic jam. I could see the variety all right, but I never experienced any taste worth queuing for. But Angel lapped it all up and twinkled. There was not much depth to our relationship, but there was plenty of energy and pleasure – enough to make up for her excesses. Unfortunately, the opportunity for expression was infrequent.

"You have to make up your mind about leaving Pourquoi," I told her. "We can get more out of this relationship than we're doing."

"You really want me to break up with my guy?" She never called him Pourquoi.

"You'll surely break up with him or he'll break up with you one day, so why not now that we have each other?"

"I know Lagos. I had told myself I would never go out with a black man again, but DG kept telling me how exceptionally nice you are. So, I decided to take a chance. I don't want to leave my guy and then become a laughingstock. I know many of the girls have their eyes on him, never mind what they say."

"You have to think this matter through, Angel. You have to make a choice."

"He's even beginning to suspect I have a boyfriend. I think some of those girls at the Red Hat are beginning to talk."

"How would they know?"

"Do you think there's anything they don't know? Besides, I called out your name once when we were in bed and he was very angry. I think I'm beginning to fall in love with you. Do you know that?"

There was, indeed, a mellowness toward me in her behavior that had not been there before. It was that, and one night at 24, that finally decided me. She called my attention to the lyrics of the song we were dancing to – about being in a love affair "with one foot outside the door." I felt I should be the one asking her to take note, but I did not press the point.

"You hear that?" she said. "If you really want me, Baneta, take me."

"Taking her" was not as simple as it sounded. She wanted at least an apartment and a regular income. With Lagos landlords demanding two years rent all at once, this was a capital undertaking. But I convinced myself that once paid it was all paid for a long time. I decided to take her.

Shortly afterward, she arrived in my office one afternoon teary-eyed.

"What's the matter?" I asked her.

"My brother is in town."

"Did he beat you?" I said lightheartedly.

"I'm serious."

"Where's he?"

"My guy's place."

"I still don't see what the problem is. You should be happy you have a brother with whom you're in harmony enough for him to come and see you there."

"They think because I'm living with a white man I must be rich. It's becoming too much. Do they know how this man uses me? Oh, I'm very sorry, but I'm really tired of everything."

"There's something I don't understand. If your parents are what you told me, why should they be coming to you for money?"

She said nothing for some time, then she broke down and wept. I calmed her down as best as I could, telling her not to cry herself out beyond the value of some pocket money for her family.

"It's more than that. I...I just want you to know that I'm sorry."

What could be this girl's problem anyway? Had she been plotting evil against me or was she not who she had told me she was?

"Look, Angel, I don't care who or what you are as long as you love me."

A line from a song. I was tending in that direction.

According to the new story she told me, her name was not Angel. She, like other members of her family, had been named after a shrine. That was the custom in her village. Somewhere deep in history, her father's father's father's father, or beyond, had sacrificed himself to the deity of that shrine. So, her family was regarded as outcasts. She had been able to go to catering school because her father had been a catechist then. He was later "retired" by a new parish priest on the curious grounds of "old age" for a man in his fifties. His "retirement" helped the church win more converts. While in catering school, she had had a daughter for a boy whose affection progressively cooled as her stomach protruded. She had left her daughter with her mother when she traveled to France.

Falsehood and its demons. I was in a very foggy mist, but I gave her as much money as the circumstance demanded and helped her dry her tears. She enfolded me in the longest embrace that had ever been my experience, professed her love for me, and left.

I stayed away from The Red Hat for some time. I felt I needed to clear my head. On the night I returned there, Pourquoi sat at the bar looking morosely at his drink and obviously of no mind to even contemplate any romantic French songs. Angel was missing from his side and from the club. The news soon spread. Angel had, once more, embarked on the very perilous desert crossing into Spain.

But the desert was unable to obliterate her footprints. Many were the nights that Pourquoi and I sat in our different worlds staring morosely at our drinks. My head kept telling me it had been folly to have attempted a relationship, that sort, with Angel. My heart kept going out to her, kept wanting her.

When I told the story to Colonel Briggs, he reproved me. "That's bad politics, my ADC. Never go with the heart to a caucus. You should have asked this girl to move in with you, on a contract. Whenever two of you agreed to disagree, you would simply have liberated yourself from her."

"She would never have done that. I think she's fiercely determined never to have to depend on anyone, especially a black man who might simply throw her out in the middle of the night."

"All these you can straighten out in a contract, the mode of entry and the mode of disengagement."

"In this country?"

"You have to show more militarism, my ADC. No soldier goes to the battlefront with one bullet. No politician puts all his politics in one constituency. That is why the constituency of the night is very important."

I decided then that both comprehension and pain are personal.

Do not cry for me, Leila. Do not fear for me. Remember the fate of the rejected cornerstones? They eventually became the pillars of the mansion. Here, in a federal penitentiary, it is the only thought I allow myself to have. It is not as if I cannot admit others if I open the door a little wider, but I have learned that success is very single-minded. Also: out of the stump of the beheaded banana tree springs a new life. I will return, and I will conquer. I will keep returning until I conquer. I will be my own rainfall in the desert of my own history.

Eve

"I believe if I refuse to grow old I can stay young till I die."
I was thirty-four, and I had been running with the night for nine years. I had expected that by this time I would have been able to unravel the core of the life of the night. Reviewing all those years, however, it was either I had missed that core or there was none interpretable in a definitive manner. I knew the character and clientele of almost every club, the identity and orientation of the armies of the night, the interface between the mystery of the night and its mayhem, and its faithless 'vaganzas. I already knew the smell and sound to expect everywhere I went. Every song I heard occasioned a sense of déjà vu. I had been here before, in the good old days when I had everything before me. I had heard this song before, those nights when it made me feel that I could have a royal high forever. I had smelled this air before, when Tamuno was king. I had heard this story before, when Bantu descanted the seas. I had been a witness to everything when I believed everything was inexhaustible.

I had been in the night for so long, and with such intensity, that it seemed as if I was hunting for maternity signs in the cemetery. I was still alone, but I carried with me a village of memories. And everything kept blurring.

Once more, I properly appreciated the role of the often-unsung heroes of the nightclubs: the disc jockeys. Beyond the razzmatazz, it was often the disc jockey's skill that kept a nightclub alive. If the disc jockey did not set the mood or interpret it well, it was only a matter of time before the crowd thinned out. Setting the mood meant keeping the crowd connected to its familiar "anthems" as well as to emerging trends in the world of pop wonders. It was not exactly an easy thing to do, and there were only a few of them who truly did it well – Oscar at The Owl, who pleased his audience so much that they renamed him Oscar Wonder; Bartholomew at Tamuno's Heaven who was called Bat the Witch, despite his gender, because he had a legendary ability for revving the emotions of his audience; and DD – the Duke of Dance – at 24, so hailed because he always managed to make everyone dance, even "dance floor cripples."

Whichever way it turned out, the disc jockeys had to go on and on because it was as much an occupation as a pleasure. Not in my own case. I woke up one Saturday morning with a head-splitting hangover, and I told myself that I was through with running with the night. If I could stay away for one night, then one week, then one month, I told myself, I would have broken the addiction.

The way to go about it, I reckoned, was to keep myself busy at night with other activities. So, the first week, I traversed the breadth of Lagos trying to find a well-kept cinema. It mattered little to me whether what was on view was the history of a cockroach. I soon canceled the idea, however. The structures were abominable and would in fact still merit that description even if they had been located in abattoirs for the entertainment of animals on their way to the slaughter slabs. Some of the theaters were only a little better. But the main problem with this form of entertainment was that the curtains usually came down early in the night, long before I was seized by my escalating nightclub withdrawal symptoms.

As a last resort, I started attending the night vigils organized by the new-age churches. They sometimes provided better entertainment than some of the theaters – with all the clapping and singing, speaking in tongues and laying of hands, and shivering and prophesying. However, the "crusades" just went on and on and on. And sometimes, with all the "prayer punches" being thrown at the devil in physical-spiritual combats, I felt uneasy. Perhaps because I had not come there looking for God, I did not find Him. Instead, amidst all the chaos, I was sometimes to be seen and heard dozing off. When this persisted, I found myself rudely woken up one night by the "brethren" and "sisters" energetically trying to cast out the demon in me, with the more eager ones going as far as trying to accomplish this with roundhouses thrown at the devil, at me. I fled.

Back at The Penthouse, I considered the matter carefully, and I decided that perhaps the best way to stop was to go on and on until I stopped, one way or the other. So, three weeks after that head-splitting hangover, I returned to my life in the night. What had I been trying to do? The first thing I would do on getting to The Red Hat, I told myself, would be to invite Jacqueline – or Yemisi, or whatever her name was – home. If Angel had decided to take to the desert, must I also live in the wilderness?

When I arrived, it was obvious that time had not stood still. Pourquoi was no longer looking morose. Amidst the sound of music, he was happily croaking his beloved romantic French songs and capering about in an unsteady circle with a girl on each arm. One of them was Jacqueline. When she noticed me, she gave me a look that I interpreted as a question: "My God! Who is this sort of character, and how did he get in here?" I had never seen Pourquoi progress beyond croaking and gesticulating to actually dancing. Besides him, everywhere seemed abuzz. What was I missing?

I went to sit with Colonel Briggs, who was happy to have an audience in me.

"Where have you been, my ADC?" he asked me.

"In the wilderness, fasting and praying."

He put his drink down and observed me closely. "Have you had a bit of malaria, Baneta?"

"Sort of." Any other answer might have led to his raising an alarm in the state he was.

"You must guard yourself strongly against malaria, my ADC. Political malaria. Because there are strong forces at work right now. And never go to the wilderness for fasting and prayer. The best strategy is counterstrategy."

I was a bit tired of the way the man went on and on, and I wished then that the "strong forces" would snatch him away from my presence so I could concentrate on what was germane at that point in place and time.

It almost happened like that. Shortly afterward, the ruling military junta announced a reconstitution of its cabinet. Some of the serving ministers were retained in their ministries. Some were reassigned. Many were kicked out. Among the new appointees was Chief Shendam Briggs, the same man I had always known as Colonel Briggs, EC, at The Red Hat. He was assigned to the Ministry of Youth and Social Development.

The new appointee arrived at his ministry like a conqueror with no recollection of his nights at The Red Hat. He was very vocal in his condemnation of prostitution and even gave notice that he would do everything within his power to see that "this obnoxious trade is stamped out." He warned youths to "beware of the night, for the night is evil." He spoke so much about "saving the soul of youths lost to the habit of the night" that I made sure I kept very far away from the new minister.

Colonel Briggs soon grew tired of giving notices. He reactivated a colonial decree against wandering, which earned anyone out on the streets late at night overnight detention. The police jubilated and quickly set up a special squad known as Night Police. Not only did the nightclubs close down, but night shifts everywhere and emergencies at night requiring movement were endangered. Outcries came from every quarter, including people unlikely to be found out at that time of the night but who would rather not live in a "police state." Colonel Briggs paid no attention. If anything, he spoke of "systematically dismantling the night within one year" as if there was a personal feud between him and the night.

I had never thought Colonel Briggs much of a politician, but I had to concede then that he was as good a Nigerian politician as any other – with the way he seemed to have thoroughly forgotten everything he had stood for before he got into government. Among the habitués of the night, who shivered in their enforced corners of a perpetual daylight, we consoled ourselves that the Briggs disease could not last forever.

It did not. The government was overthrown by another band of military adventurers. They cited as one of their reasons "the re-colonization project being championed by strong forces within the past government." They sounded almost like the infamous

Colonel Briggs himself. Did all these fellows get their ideas and language from the same manual? Meanwhile, Briggs had demonstrated amazing agility by spiriting himself out of the country at the very first sign of a coup. He remained one of the few officials of the deposed government neither assassinated nor arrested. The same police that had been his friend recently put a very tempting price on his head with fanfare. They were too late. Briggs resurfaced in London and took care to stay out of harm's way. I could envision him repairing to a club in Soho or thereabouts at night and once more invoking his "strong forces" while lounging around and probably having to pay dearly for being allowed the space in which to air his peculiar sort of madness.

The new junta first imposed a curfew, then it swiftly invalidated what had become known as the "Briggs Decree." It was hallelujah night. The armies of the night returned to the streets like their own indestructible heroes – themselves. The nightclubs threw open their doors, and the crowds bustled in, including those who usually did not go to such places. For a time, the Briggs disease appeared to have been the best advertisement for the life of the night. For that special celebration, I decided to go to Tamuno's Heaven. He had predicted everything, like a song.

Fedora welcomed me warmly. "Taneba! I've been hoping to see you around one of these nights."

"You know how it is. I've been circling, but this is the place I will always return to."

"I've been thinking, about Don's thesis. I know it was a big thing with him, but one mind keeps telling me it's time to put it away."

"Don't do it. That thesis has become part of the mystique of this place."

"That's what the other mind tells me."

"How has everything been?"

"Like a song, only that Bat's gone. He took with him a number of admirers. But it's a swinging door, you know. There are always departures and arrivals."

"What happened?"

"It's business. There's this new place called Nightingale, on the Island. They offered him shares."

"Is that what they offer DJs too?"

"Not usually, but you know Bat's special."

"You've got a problem on your hands then."

"Well, there's this new revelation called John the Baptist..."

"In Tamuno's Heaven?"

Fedora laughed, in that easy manner that he too had, that many of them had. "He has a bit of religion, but that has nothing to do with his performance. He just has this great idea of himself. He believes there's no one greater than him, unless perhaps Jesus returns as a disc jockey."

"Rhythm plus hype. I like him already."

If Fedora had not told me about the change upstairs – in the disc jockey's cubicle – I doubt that I would have remarked it precisely. John the Baptist was almost as good as Bat the Witch. He did not have that uncanny and timely manner of connecting with his audience that Bat had, but he was an obvious talent that had finally found the space he needed. I decided I would transfer my flag to this new place called Nightingale, but certainly I would keep coming back to Tamuno's Heaven.

The crowd too did not appear to have noted the change, although the mood that night was so jubilant that people fluttered mostly on their own wings. They were celebrating their transition from an enforced perpetual daylight to the unstinting 'vaganza of the night. The corruption of Briggs's name was everywhere evident. "Brigg me a drink," I heard one man say to a waitress. Another requested for "whisky on the briggs." How would any or all of these people react if I told them that I had sat at The Red Hat with the fellow called Briggs many a night, and that before he was seized by that terrible disease he was already in the priesthood of the night?

At the bar, there was a letter waiting for me. From Faith.

"My brother, Taneba,

"I trust that you're keeping well. How are your nights these

days? Have fun, have fun. I still remember the good old days, and the memory always brings a glow into my heart. Sometimes, it brings a sense of loss. It's good to have you to write to. It makes me feel much better, not entirely cut off. I believe that you're a genius, and that there's so much intellectual energy in you that hasn't been applied. You're not one of those who try to go beyond the frontiers of knowledge, only to end up more ignorant than they were before. You're like a revelation in suspense, but I believe your day will come – if it hasn't already. You see, everything has become clearer to me from this distance, don't you think?

"I broke up with Planet after only a few months of marriage. No regrets. The robins always sing. Tamuno. I think about him a lot still. He was the only man I've ever loved enough to abide with through everything. Right now, I'm in Melbourne, Australia. I have a fantastic day job in an international consulting firm. But the night still calls. So, on weekends, I work at this nightclub called Tamarinds, as a DJ. It's something I'd always thought of doing. And for that job, I've adopted a very special name: T14. Everything comes and goes, but the aura often persists.

"I encourage you to think seriously about going abroad. There are, of course, problems. But travel is always good. It widens your experience in very personal terms. And I encourage you to think of Australia, of me. You can stay with me whenever you get here. Give my love to all at Tamuno's Heaven.

"Your sister, Faith."

That letter lifted my spirits greatly. In my reply, I said nothing about traveling, but I could not stop thinking of Australia.

I was not the only one thinking. Chief Stephens sent for me some days later.

"I'm very happy with you, Taneba," he told me. "I'm very pleased with you, and I don't usually tell this to my employees because I thank them enough with their salaries. But you, you're a miracle."

When he had invited me to start Stephens Speed, it had been a dot of an idea. I had transformed that dot into a world of secure speed that had made it the biggest local courier firm, the fastest growing enterprise in Stephens Holdings, and the only company to receive the Standards Bureau award for innovation for two years running. I could have taken a better offer elsewhere, because there was no shortage of corporate suitors after me. But I had never forgotten what an unusual chance Chief Stephens had taken when he employed me – at a time when these new corporate suitors would most likely have sniffed at my record and kicked me back to my valley of despair.

"You know we do a lot of business abroad," he went on, "businesses that pass through other hands because we have no office abroad. It's time to set up that office, and I want you to do so."

"Where?"

"New York. You'll become the international manager of Stephens Holdings, with shareholding after the first year – if you meet your target. You'll have your choice of assistants, full passage for yourself and dependents..."

"What about Stephens Speed?"

"I believe Ubanwa can take care of this end, don't you think so?"

"I believe so too."

I had never been enthusiastic about going abroad – even then, even with the wealth and corporate power that he was offering me. To go and live in New York? With the number of people, even well-to-do people, massing outside the American embassy and braving the horrors of getting an American visa as if it guaranteed bliss, I should have been excited. I was not. I had a date with Lagos, still. There was this new place called Nightingale singing out to me. Surely, there were many other places like that where I could get used to the life I had always been used to in my own native paradise with its robust rituals.

"When do I have to take up this appointment, to decide?"

"It's all up to you. You should spend some time in the other companies and familiarize yourself with their operations, then we'll arrange the other details. Don't be worried about living away from home. The whole world is in New York. You will get used to it, and you will love it. Besides, you'll be entitled to a fully paid annual vacation anywhere in the world – you and your family."

"I'll take it then. Thanks very much."

We shook hands and I departed. I had better lap up as much of the Lagos nightlife as I could. Or perhaps I should think seriously of marriage and not expect to date the night forever like an immortal.

That night, I went to Nightingale. It was a new place with old cunning. There was ample parking space and an interior decor that spoke of new money but old experience. It offered two forms of entertainment. There was a karaoke bar for those who loved to sing. The clientele was mostly young and middle-aged women, some of them evidently there for no other reason than to sing their hearts out. Some left for home when the bar closed. Some others, the children of the deeper night, relocated underground where the nightclub was. I loved the place. It seemed to have everything, both the Toshibas and the Mairos of yore.

Before I took ten paces into the nightclub, I heard my name being announced.

"Ladies and gentlemen, it's my great pleasure to welcome a very special friend in the house tonight – Taneba Taneba, believer in the rhythm of the night."

It was Bat the Witch. I went in search of him. Not only did I not care for such publicity, even though I knew it was an honor, I preferred to be known as Baneta to everyone who did not already know me as Taneba.

"It's all right, man," he told me. "Taneba. Baneta. It's the same sound, almost. Good to see you."

"And you too. How's this place?"

"Great."

So it was. It was not a big place, compared to Tamuno's Heaven, but it had style and spirit. Bat the Witch's rallying anthem was a very affective song. Whenever he played it, as an unfailing buildup, the girls danced with sensational abandon proclamations of their right to live their lives any way they chose.

I planted my flag at Nightingale. I still visited The Red Hat occasionally. There was something about the place I had not got out of me. One night, I arrived there and once more saw Pourquoi dancing. This time, his dancing partner was his new live-in mistress – a skinny girl who spoke with a falsetto and smelt faintly of bath water. But what seized me was the song they were dancing to, the very same one Angel had called my attention to. Was this disc jockey inclined toward a ghost revival when I was almost forgetting the deserts of Angel? Next, he played my promise to her: "I don't care who you are..." I left midway through that song, and I never returned. Red for absence. Hat for memories.

Meanwhile, my life went on without any highs. There were no lows either. I almost had a capital low, however, the day I saw Yellow again – in the uniform of a traffic policeman, flailing his hands like a hyperactive speed machine. I parked and stared at him. He stopped abruptly when he saw me and ran toward me.

"Oga Taneba! You go live long-o. I just dey think of you today. How that your dream?"

"It stopped."

"I no tell you? You go psychia, *abi*?"

"No. I think God intervened."

"You don finally enter church?"

"No, not that."

"How you come take see God?"

"I believe He saw my affliction."

He scrutinized me for some time. "God dey inside psychia too," he said.

"Everywhere, I believe. How did you get this uniform?"

The question startled him a bit. "Ah-ah, you don dey do police now, again?"

"I mean: how did you become a traffic policeman?"

"Oh, that one simple. I go test."

"And *you* were selected?"

"Wetin dey happen? As you dey ask these questions hot hot, e good so, *abi* I do bad thing as I come greet you?"

"You know what I mean, Yellow. You went for an interview, and you told them you didn't go beyond elementary school, that you have been in prison and in a psychiatric hospital, and you were still selected?"

"Na so you dey go your own test? If no be say I dey work now, I for si'down tell you how they dey go test correct. No be as you think am at all."

He sat down all the same, in the front passenger seat, fanning himself occasionally with his beret in the manner of a traffic policeman. He had heard of the recruitment drive in police detention, where he had been hauled in for street brawling. Once out, he had gone to the market for forged documents known as "Oluwole" and obtained what he needed – a school testimonial, character testimonials, and a letter from his traditional ruler certifying his citizenship. A full high school education was not required, only S.75 or evidence that he had completed three quarters of a high school education. For the oral interview, he had traveled to his state capital where the police had no knowledge of him. And he had "brushed up" his "street English," which he said was no worse than that spoken by some of the candidates with high school certificates.

While his manner of expression had raised some eyebrows among his interviewers, his performance in the endurance test had dazzled everyone. He had passed, been sent for "full training," posted to the traffic division of the police force and given living space within the police barracks.

"Oga Taneba, you don go police barracks before?"

"No, why?"

"No wonder police too dey vex. The whole place be like latrine inside latrine."

"How did you get back to Lagos?"

"Na my luck. They post me here. If I know say they go take me, I for even apply to be full police. I go still convert."

"You're not scared they'll find you out?"

"Na only me enter like that? Them ask me some kin' questions wey worry me small – whether I don go prison or psychia. I even swear for them say I never go that kin' place."

"And they'll not find out that you lied?"

"Nothing dey inside. Na sack them go sack me if e come to that. If the thing too spoil, na prison them go send me, no be firing squad."

He was brimming with news, about some of the people I had known. And my past kept drawing near to me.

"You remember Her Majesty, for Owl?"

"How come you know her? I don't remember seeing you there."

"No let my uniform confuse you. Inside uniform, outside uniform, na street I dey."

"What about her?"

"She don marry correct officer. Brigadier. If I see her now, na salute I dey salute her."

"That's nice, for her."

"Na so. You know Bianca, one tall girl wey her cheek go up like this..." His demonstration was that of a caricaturist.

"I know her."

"She don die. She just dry up like chewing stick. Maybe them swear for am."

"Are you serious?"

"I don tell you lie before? Wetin happen?"

"Death is always saddening."

"Na so e be. You hear the thing wey happen for Abedie place?"

My interest shot up. "No, what?"

"Some people carry soldier, two trucks, go there. The *baba* just disappear. Them search the place well well, but them no see anything. But they burn the place, arrest plenty people."

"And?"

"They put the people inside guardroom, but they don

release them. Abedie don get another place, and the *baba* sef don get assistant wey be like am."

"Look, Yellow, have you ever seen Abedie?"

"Ah, I don see am."

"When, where, how..."

"E be like say your question don lose control. Anyway, no be with ordinary eye."

There was not much else that he had to tell me. I invited him to take a break and have a drink with me.

"I no dey drink when I dey work," he told me. "No be like that they teach us this work. You think say me I no like promotion?"

"So, you don't hang out at night anymore?"

"Now when I don get special license to waka anyhow? Now, I dey even si'down inside sometimes when I go club."

Yellow, a representative of the law – in daylight! I mused as I drove away. How everything changes. Chief Stephens had been right. In Nigeria, everything is simple, depending on whom you know. And on what you know – about thwarting the system. How did Yellow feel each time he had to make an arrest, or was he one of those sorts who only arrested what could go into their pocket? Anyway, he had certainly traveled a long way from my old neighborhood where he had been regarded as a smiling bandit to that roundabout where he was the law of the road itself.

So had I too, despite everything. If I had any doubt about it, my workers did not. That night, they sent me a handmade card, the biggest I had ever seen, to congratulate me on my new appointment. How news travels! The card arrived by our "night express," one of my innovations that accounted for the success of Stephens Speed. The message was simple: "Congratulations – to the best boss!"

I mounted the card on my wall and contemplated it for some time. Really, all I had done was to do my job with everything I had and insist that everyone apply himself similarly. Given the poor attitude to work I had met everywhere I had worked, this had meant an insistence on a strict corporate culture of full work for full pay. I needed no education on the sort of grumbling that went on behind my back. But that I regarded as the price I had to pay for insisting on labor when people preferred limbo. Once, one of my assistants had arrived late to work with a story about a romantic engagement gone awry.

"Now, listen, Thomas," I told him. "What you do with your private life is your business. I probably do worse things. But whatever it is you do, never ever let it affect your productivity here. If you must live in two worlds, you have to build a bridge between the two. How you do that is your business. Don't let this matter come up again."

He thanked me and left, probably not believing that I lived in two such worlds. I had tried my best to make a fine distinction between the two, although there had been occasional flux. But the strain of serving two exacting Caesars was beginning to tell on me. I was beginning to require all sorts of alarms to jangle me up after only a few hours of sleep at night. And I was beginning to have monstrous morning and evening headaches that sometimes made me put both hands on my head as if to protect it from being snapped off savagely.

Nevertheless, the night kept calling to me. And I kept answering. After mounting the card and resting awhile – the hour or two during which I sometimes tried to make up in advance for my few hours in bed – I set off for Nightingale. I was becoming a regular presence at its karaoke bar. It was the best I had been to, with the startling talents it often revealed. It was also like a beacon that drew many interesting young women who were not up for grabs by the highest bidder.

From the karaoke bar, my motion was often not homeward but downward to the nightclub. My heart nearly stopped beating there when I saw a dark, stout girl that I immediately believed was Ada Eke. I had never nurtured the notion of seeing her, never seriously considered that possibility. That vision of her froze me for some minutes, then I made my way toward her slowly, with my heart racing. Ada Eke – from faithful mystery into faithless flesh? It was only when I was face to face with this supposed apparition that I realized I was only witnessing a case of uncommon resemblance.

The focus of my interest, already expectant, wondered at my hesitation, then decided to seize the initiative. "Hello, honey, looking for sizzling Suzie?" she said, with a toothy smile.

If only she had kept her mouth shut, I might have succumbed to the temptation of going home with this seeming clone of Ada Eke. That would have been part fulfillment of a boyhood fantasy.

"No. I'm looking for someone called Ada Eke. You look uncommonly like her."

"Na me."

By then, my gaze had discovered more dissimilarities.

She leaned toward me. With the low-neck dress she was wearing, my universe of vision suddenly consisted of only two bulbous breasts. How many times had I witnessed that sort of attempt at seduction? But I was looking for new meanings, not worn-out gestures.

"You like?" she asked me hopefully.

I did not consider an answer necessary. Instead, I went in search of Bat the Witch.

"What sort of place are you fellows running?" I asked. "There's no code down here at all?"

"We start coding from next month."

"I'll see you next month then, before someone kidnaps me here."

I started staying away from that underground. The good thing was that I hung around the upstairs karaoke bar more. And it was partly because I did that I met Eve. She was not a regular there, otherwise I would have noted her previously. She was undeniably pretty but in a reckless sort of way – like a woman who either takes being so for granted or chooses not to celebrate it. In the sleeveless shirt and faded jeans that she wore, she seemed to be casting an insouciant query in the direction of every admirer: "I'm beautiful enough, so what?" And there were many of them, going with hopeful faces to where she sat alone and leaving with thoughtful expressions. When she sang, "a Whitney special," she vibrated with her whole being:

I decided long ago
Never to live in anyone's shadow

The song, her vibration of it, spoke to me in a profoundly personal way. I too set off toward her with a hopeful expression. I half-wished there was a network that could have advised me on where the others who had made that journey before me had erred.

"Thanks for that song. It moved me," I told her honestly. "It also told me a lot about you. What are the personal demons you're trying to exorcise?"

It was either she made meaning out of what I was saying and responded accordingly or she gave me the "Excuse me" look. But I reckoned that this girl who had been wooed unsuccessfully by others would no longer be sitting alone if all that was required was the normal expression of admiration or interest.

"Where're you from?" she asked me.

"That's a strange first question."

"I don't mean your village or that sort of thing, but you're the first person here tonight who has sounded intelligent. Now, if you let that get into your head, that's your problem."

I settled down on the chair opposite her then. It was a good beginning.

"Thanks for the flattery. So, there's indeed something personal about that rendition?"

"Isn't there always?"

"Perhaps that's what made it so touching. Is anyone after you?"

"What do you mean?"

"Someone or some people you're telling: lay off, it's my life."

She laughed. And I knew then without a doubt that it was either her or never. This was the fulfillment of all the rambling and fatherless promise of the night. In all that decade, I never saw anyone laugh like that. It was an all-pleasure meltdown that could not be localized because it came from the entirety of being. What sort of girl was this that could move from suspicion, a hint of hostility even, to bliss so effortlessly?

"No one is after me, or pestering me, except you."

"Do you normally laugh like that, so completely endearing? My God!"

"You want to flatter me?"

"I'm totally in earnest. But let's have a drink. It helps conversation."

"As long as you realize you're only buying me a drink."

I had a beer. She had another Stout. She sang one more song and then decided it was time to go home. I offered her a lift.

"Thanks, but I'll take a cab."

"You're living in the shadow of your fear."

"You think you can blackmail me?"

Whether blackmail or not, I did eventually take her home to a block of residential apartments in nearby southwest Ikoyi.

"Won't you invite me in for the famous nightcap?" I said when she got out of the car and began to bid me farewell.

"You? You don't look to me as if you're about to cap your night."

"If you invite me in, I'll even disown the night."

She laughed. "You're very funny."

"I'm trying to get you to laugh."

"I don't even know your name."

"Baneta."

"Ba-ne-ta. What sort of name is that?"

"Like any other. It gets easier with usage. And you?"

"Eve."

"That's strange. I thought that name went out of currency after the infamous Garden of Eden?"

"I'm not laughing." She did all the same.

The most I got out of her that night was her office address and telephone number. I was very pleased all the same. I was in such high spirits that I simply drove home at that early hour, fantasizing about Eve. Was she my prize for the race I had run with the night? Was she the eventual gathering or restoration of the energy I had dissipated in that decade? She had given me a sense of completeness that I had had once upon a time before I became fatherless at fifteen. I had lived through several ages of the night, even after they had ended or should have ended – wandering and wondering, seeking for a great indefinable essence but finding only small definable pleasures. Now, Eve – the Eve of my Adam.

I did not want the dragged-out Toshiba process all over again, so during the lunch break the next day I went to see her at the art gallery where she worked as the manager. I had planned to take her out to lunch, but she was busy planning an exhibition of great paintings. She believed I knew something about painting, so from time to time she asked my opinion.

"You know something about music, so..."

"More like something about feeling."

"Which is the quintessential evocation of music, of art. What do you think of this, Picasso's 'La Guernica'?"

"This is 'La Guernica'?"

"It's only a copy, but the details are the same."

"This is mayhem. This is the way I saw the world the day a mob burned my car."

"Quit joking."

"I'm serious. This fellow distorts everything in a bid to make his meaning clear, I suppose."

"And you said you know nothing about art? What about this?"

"Is this fellow an artist too? More like an 'area boy' playing jazz."

She burst into laughter. "Jean-Michel Basquiat. He started out as a graffiti artist before he broke into the mainstream, but he always felt that art was some sort of fraud."

"Is it?"

"I think that's an extreme view. What about this?"

"This one I want to own. Who's he?"

"Gani Odutokun."

"This is fascinating, the confident strokes."

"Are you an art critic?"

"I'm almost illiterate about art."

"Not at all."

"It's because of you then. You give me clarity."

Everything kept going flawlessly. I returned that evening and took her to dinner, to the very same restaurant I had first taken Toshiba. To her, it was "too dressed-up." But it was a filling dinner, especially for me. She preferred her cigarettes and Stout to anything more than a few morsels of food. I told her the same edited version of my story I had told Toshiba – no father, no mother, no siblings, no relatives. She had lost her parents and two brothers in a vehicle accident when she was fourteen and had been raised by her father's brother, whom she never really got along with. At the university, where she had studied communication arts, her interest in art and music had been such that she had taken all the electives she could in the two disciplines and audited many of the courses she could not. Upon graduation, she had bid her uncle farewell when she moved to Lagos to take up a job at the National Museum, then a recording company and finally her position then in an art gallery. A simple story without many shadows, like many first stories.

After dinner, I took her home. She had left her car in the office because she did not like driving at night. This time, I invited myself in, mostly. It was as if we had always known each other. Besides the many paintings in the one-bedroom apartment, it could have passed for a music library. There were rows and rows of records and CDs, mostly classical music and jazz. I actually began to feel somewhat inadequate. What was I taking on – a girl who would soon throw me out for being an ignoramus?

"You bought all these?" I asked her in awe.

"I'm a collector. You like classical music?"

"Not until I hear it."

"Many people don't have the patience and understanding,

which is sad. A world without classical music is much diminished."

"A girl who works in an art gallery, loves classical music, and sings pop songs. That's a strange mix."

"I like the feel of the bar once in a while. I love music, all kinds."

"Do you always go out alone, without your boyfriend?"

"Right now, I'm not 'boyfriending.' What else do you want to know?"

"No offense meant."

"None taken."

"Why not a musical nightcap? Some classical music."

"You must treat classical music with a bit more respect. It's the purest kind of music."

She made me recline on the settee and close my eyes, then she played a composition. I was entranced by what I interpreted as the rippling harmony between the waves of the violin and the dense rhythm of the hornpipe.

"What did it make you feel?"

"As if I was floating."

"It does that to me too, especially after the stress of working in Lagos. It's therapeutic. That's Handell's 'Watermusic,' one of the great compositions."

"As great as Mozart or Beethoven?" Those were the names I had heard before.

"It depends on the composition. I'll play you two of my favorites, and you'll tell me what you think – Mozart's 'The Marriage of Figaro' and Beethoven's 'Tempo di Minuetto.'"

So began my education in classical music, which in all my years of running with the night had only been a vague name to me. Eve had a composition for every occasion, sometimes burrowing deep into her collection. That first night in her apartment, we made love to the buoying cadence of Bartholdy's "Dance of the Clowns." In the flesh, her firm, great hips shamed my vaunted knowledge of the night and its offerings. She was more than what I had hoped she would be. She gave me the feeling that I would never be the same again, never whole again without her – as if I had vainly been living life outside life itself.

"This is what you wanted all along, so what now?"

"When I first came toward you, yes. Now, I want everything."

"My soul?"

"Everything."

"You must be God then. I think you should listen to classical music a lot more. It'll tell you a lot about the soul. It's harmonized sound without the burden of words, mostly, because there are spiritual spheres that words can't reach, and words sometimes interfere with possibilities of meaning. Just listen to the organic quality of each sound, the dialogue between the instruments, their motion in concert with one another. They speak to the soul."

"Everything passes, Eve."

"Except the triumph of the spirit. Like Pheidippides running that great race to request aid from Sparta before the battle at Marathon. That's about the only lesson I learned in elementary school that has endured."

"That was a physical thing."

"When he started, not when he arrived. His arrival was powered by his spirit. He gave his message, and he collapsed and died. The flesh had since expired anyway. And that race has become a great paradigm. I think that classical music represents the triumph of the spirit in art, requiring not Pheidippides' stamina as such but the fidelity of his spirit."

It suddenly became clear to me. My race with the night had been that of the flesh and I had been rewarded accordingly. Had all those years truly been anything more than sheer waste of the possibilities of my spirit?

It was very hard to believe that Eve was thirty then. She looked at least five years younger. We talked art and listened to classical music, but that did not stop us from going dancing in the nightclubs. One night, at 24, we ran into "sizzling Suzie." Even though I was obviously accompanied, she still tried to seduce me as "delicious Ada." Eve laughed the incident off.

She had about everything I wanted, even her wayward lifestyle. She was often eccentric in her beliefs, but she was always wired to what was essential and important. We became a cohesive unit, often together when we were not working. During the week, I spent many nights in her apartment. It was a matter of convenience because in the morning, driving against the traffic, it took me only a short while to get to my office. We spent most of our weekends at The Penthouse.

I considered the matter carefully, starting from the conclusion, and I arrived at her apartment one evening with a marriage proposal.

"Are you sure you want to do this?" she asked.

"Very certain. And you?"

"These days, I feel like a shadow without you."

"That's me, exactly. So, will you marry me?"

"Of course. But let me show you something first."

It was a notebook with an undated entry: *Baneta proposes to me. We get married.*

"When did you write this?"

"Last week. I was listening to Vivaldi's 'Spring: Allegro,' and I suddenly saw it all."

Was she beginning to divine through sound, like another version of Mama Zi? But I considered that it would have been more surprising if someone like Eve had not come up with something as unusual as that. I still wanted her.

"It's sealed then. We'll arrange to meet your uncle."

"You think that's the pure form of marriage? We'll let him know eventually, of course. If you want us to get married, and I want that too, then let's get married."

"We'll go to the marriage registry then?"

"All those are afters. First, it's between the two of us."

"A blood bond?"

"Love is freedom and faith. Do you believe in God?"

"I do."

We made our vows to each other in the silence of that apartment, except for the strains of Verdi's "Triumphant March."

"As God is my witness, I, Baneta Baneta, hereby take you, Eve Alexander, to be my wife, for better for worse, until death do us part."

"As God is my witness, I, Eve Alexander, hereby take you, Baneta Baneta, to be my husband, for better for worse, until death do us part."

She moved into The Penthouse that week. I went down to the marriage registry and posted the required notice for the "court marriage." I was convinced my maternal uncle would not approve of Eve, so I decided to let him find out for himself what I was up to – that is, if he could before we traveled. Meanwhile, I took Eve for a honeymoon weekend, and I thanked God for bringing us together. Everything was going very well. In less than a month, we would be legally married. In less than two months, we would be gone. And now that I had my Eve, I considered the book balanced. I might not return. Both of us had no families drawing us back home. Orphans yesterday, twins forever. I no longer needed to run with the night that much.

We soon learned that we had timed our affirmation with a prescience of the workings of Eve's body. She woke up one morning with a strong feeling of nausea. She was pregnant. I marveled at how much had gone into the few months of our relationship. Eve was overjoyed. I had not known that motherhood was that important to her. The way she danced joyously began to put me in the mood for fatherhood.

"You're the miracle of creation," she hailed me. "I was almost giving up on ever having a child, with the doctors speaking forward and backward. And then you came along, and now we're going to have a baby. Our baby."

I was happy principally because she was. When I had contemplated marriage, I had only applied my thoughts to our rich companionship. Now, with a child on the way, I began to contemplate questions. What if this child grew up to become troublesome about his roots, with ancestry hunting becoming more and more fashionable? How would this affect our life abroad, with the delicate arrangements that pregnancy and motherhood involved? How would this affect the quality time we shared together? And...what explanation would I give to Eve or to this unborn child if one red-eyed fellow turned up on my doorstep one day claiming to be my first child?

"My miracle, now I'm going to play you something really special."

That was just like Eve. She celebrated special moments with special selections from her vast library, the way some people mark special occasions with choice wine. I lay back on the settee, according to her instruction, and closed my eyes. And the world changed forever.

The composition was a flute rendition, with a medley of instruments in the background. With its plaintive tone, it was like a lost soul questioning and answering, seeking and finding a way home, which was only homeward because it was a metaphor for the larger story of humankind. It went right into me, deep into me, and I felt myself gliding through the windows of my own history, recontextualizing its pains and joys and reconnecting it to other histories. I was me. I also became everyone. I believe I heard then both the testimonial mantras of those asking never to be forgotten and the unsayable truths of those crying never to be born. There were questions answering the unquestionable, and answers questioning the unanswerable.

I understood then what had probably happened to Bantu out there in the desert. That flute song was my alpha song. I had never heard anything like it before then, and I never did after then. The highest form of genius, I guess, does not replicate itself. I felt richly blessed to have lived long enough, and on the road to Eve, to be able to experience that enriching moment.

"What do you think?" she asked. "What does it make you feel?"

"This is the most fantastic composition I've ever heard. It's my alpha song."

"How did you know? That's the title of the composition: 'Alpha Song.'"

"Who's the composer?"

"This was done by a Nigerian – Elias Brass, from Kaiama. He's dead now."

Memory is the death of death.

My heart gave such a violent kick that I feared cardiac arrest was about to claim me. I had to put my head out of the window and take great gulps of air. Eve must have thought I unaccountably wanted to throw myself out of the window because she grabbed me and drew me back into the room.

"What is the matter?"

"This must be a very bad joke. Elias Brass was my father."

I heard her catch her breath sharply.

"And he never amounted to anything more than annoying everyone with his whistling."

"How could he have been your father? You told me..."

"I disowned him, after he let his second wife drive me away. My mother was his first wife, but she died when I was fifteen. I had to move in with my maternal uncle."

With belief, her expression changed to bewilderment. "Why did you lie to me?"

"I did not lie to you. I am an orphan. My father died five years after my mother. I have no family because my father's people rejected me, and I rejected them too, and I do not particularly care for my maternal uncle. I have lived for nineteen years as an orphan. I spit on my father. I spit on his genius."

She broke into tears, which was unusual. "He was my husband, almost."

"What?!"

"I was sixteen, and I would have been his fourth wife. He died the week we would have been married. It was something he and my uncle had arranged. I was determined to thwart it, but he stole my heart with his flute. He was the one who introduced me to the world of deep art, deep music."

"My father was not a musician."

"But he was, toward the end. There are some people who grow up working on their art, honing their skill. Some others go through life working at something else, then they discover or apply their talent later. That was what happened to your father. In those years, he also ran with the night hoping to catch it. That composition was first called 'Night Song.' They used to call him The Owl when I met him. He made this recording the year he died."

"I spit on him still."

"I think toward the end he wished he could make amends."

"That's nonsense. He knew where I was."

"He kept procrastinating."

"Look, did you love him?" I was not unduly worried that I had been sleeping with my late father's fiancée. I was more worried by the possibility that my dear Eve could have been in love with the creep who was my father.

"Not initially. He was a great man, terrible in the way of all flesh but still great."

I fled The Penthouse, ignoring her entreaties. So, what all my life had amounted to – after almost two decades of rejecting and forgetting – was the completion of my father's marriage program? What sort of terrible ghost had that horrible man become that he would not let me be? Whether it was the futility of my flight or the perceived corruption of the only woman I had ever truly been in love with, I do not know, but I do know that once out on the street I broke down and started crying. I had not shed tears since the day I ran away from my father's house and refused to return. Midway through my tears, I became vocal in my rejection. "I spit on my father," I reiterated over and over, matching the words with the corresponding action, as I wandered aimlessly like a lesser ghost pursued by a more ominous one.

I was gone for three days, in an unmapped world where

my father's ghost dogged my every step. Sometimes, I tried to make sudden turns and grab this ghost and fight it down. Instead, I grabbed some innocent passerby, who excoriated me. It was worse when I tried to knock this ghost down with a once-for-all roundhouse. It landed on someone else, who promptly knocked me down in retaliation. "Why are there too many people on the streets anyway?" I demanded, as I got up. People pondered me with growing alarm. Sometimes, I tried to play hide-and-seek with this ghost. This had the effect of drawing curious passersby, who shook their heads slowly and wondered what "new" madness had seized this "gentleman." In a determined attempt to perish this ghost, I calculated with cunning that if I dashed across the road in such a manner that whoever or whatever was fast on my heels would be crushed, that would be it. It did not work out that way. The startled driver tried to make a sudden swerve and knocked me down. I regained my clarity after that close call, and I decided to return home – to the final battleground.

Eve had obviously been very distraught about my disappearance and had looked for me everywhere she could. My return infused a glow in her, as if that meant I had come home to stay. She tried to help me clean up. I insisted on immediate dialogue.

"Look, Eve," I said to her in my calmest voice, "I wish I could find it in my heart to forgive my father. I wish I could, because that would practically save my life as it is – something I very much want to do. But I can't. I lack that sort of greatness or whatever it is."

"Your father didn't exactly drive you away, did he?"

"How could I have stayed when his wife was pounding me like yam?"

"It was your decision, and he did come for you initially."

"I refused to go back, yes, but then I was barely sixteen. Even my uncle was alarmed by the bruises all over my body."

"Sometimes we need to transcend the past so we can live in the present."

"But this is a past that refuses to be transcended, and now it lives with me."

"We all make mistakes. You must have made yours too."

That picture from Mairo loomed so large then it was as if I could touch it. Would one red-eyed fellow one day stand in judgment over my ghost, like this?

"Everyone has to live with his reality. There will be those who will judge me just as severely. That will be their own reality."

"Your father had his good sides. He was good to me, although..."

"That's your own reality, not mine."

"Even more important, he made his mistakes but he still went on to become a great composer. In time to come, people will gather wherever that flute song is played, and it will make significant meaning to them. Your father's private history will not be an important consideration, only the greatness of his art."

"That will be their own reality, not mine. He was not their father, so why should they judge him like his son? My father realized he had failed as a human being, so he tried to hide behind art."

"Doubtless, many people try. How many ever succeed? Many people live and die, and it is just as if they never lived. From flesh into flesh, garbage into garbage. But there are those who create moments or motions in time that are deathless, priceless. Those are spirits, and they are beyond death. They are the spirits of our civilization. Let it go, Taneba, and find something in your father to be proud of. If we insist on absolute judgment, no one will be sane or saved."

"You can afford to theorize. Everyone's life is significant. Your geniuses need other people to survive, to become, to be appreciated. Every genius is a collective and includes both the man who empties the garbage and the woman who rubs the back. Anyway, I spit on my father still. He was a creep masquerading as a genius."

"Let it go, please. We have our life ahead of us."

The Eve of my eve, the final and forever painful sacrifice of myself at the altar of the night. "Nothing is worth the loss of a true love," Bantu had told me after he reconciled with his former wife. But I was incapable of being the man, or fool, that he was. With Eve kneeling to beg me, I almost decided to try. Then, and forever after, that scene nagged me.

"I love you, Eve, more than I can say. But I can't go on living with you. It's almost like living with my father's ghost. My mind rebels against it."

"But you're my husband now."

"I don't know what else to do."

"And this is our baby."

"Always, regardless."

She stood up and brought out her notebook. The entry said: *Baneta runs away. I eventually have our son.*

"I played Debussy's 'Claire de lune.' I have been praying ever since that I would be wrong."

I left her in tears, wondering what happens to a man's life after it is over but he still has to live it.

Baneta

I left for New York a few weeks after that separation. In the intervening period, I neither returned to The Penthouse nor contacted Eve. My office became my living room, and the nightclubs my bedroom. Everything was different, however, because I carried in me an intimate sense of loss. Many were the times I wanted to return home in the hope of finding a solution that would let me live again. But I lacked the will.

Eve herself must have decided against running after me. "Love is freedom and faith," she had told me. Nevertheless, I sometimes believe she could have rewritten the story of our lives if she had kept after me. All my life, it seems, I have been like a shadow trying to achieve significant reality and perhaps finally failing to do so. That reality of not being able to affect many of the things that have affected me still burdens my thoughts. But there is a point where we must draw a creative line in the sand between what was and what is.

It took me a few months to make sense of the grand cosmopolitan riot that is New York, months in which I was like an orphan plucked from an inclusive foster family and cast into a sea of exclusion. But I did begin to set up the international office of Stephens Holdings and to settle down somewhat. Now truly an alien, I needed excitement, fantasized about it, plotted it. And it was my plot that got me into trouble and taught me all about America in one night.

My new interest was the strip clubs. There was one called Aquarius in my neighborhood. I would spend my after hours watching a parade of pretty girls model their artfully oiled bodies for a few dollars and more. Soon, I got tired of merely watching.

One night, I complimented the girl that to me best represented the spirit of Aquarius. "You're a great dancer," I told her.

"Thanks."

"And beautiful, enough for any man to dream about."

"Excuse me?"

Those same two words. Have they followed me all this way?

"You and I, we could get together..."

"I'm not a prostitute, okay? I'm a dancer."

I did not understand the difference there and then. "I know, but..."

"You want a private dance?"

"Perfect." I understood "a private dance" then as a euphemism.

My comprehension became a bit uncertain when we got into a screened cubicle with a divan and she gave me the option of either having her dance on my body with her clothes on or of watching her dance in the nude – at least six inches away from me. I chose the latter, wondering why she was being rather formal. My doubts cleared when her dance included pointedly seductive gestures, or what I interpreted to be so. Desire became response, vigorously. The last sane thing I remember was her scream.

I lost my temper when the bouncer barged in on our "private dance," and I let him know I would not be unfairly muscled like an alien. The threat of calling the police made no impression on me, except as blackmail. My impression changed when the police arrived and I was accused of attempted rape. First, it was an accusation. Then, it became a charge. And a trial. And a prison term. I was puzzled.

Chief Stephens came to see me. He was sympathetic but businesslike. He did not terminate my employment, but both of us understood that we would re-discuss the matter upon my release. Things happened differently, as they often do. Chief Stephens, who had always seemed strong enough to outlive eternity, died suddenly some months later from medical complications. Stephens Holdings was broken up by his quarrelling wives. I was both in prison and out of a job.

I wrote to Faith, detailing my fate and asking if she would

harbor me in Australia. I was pleasantly surprised when she came visiting. It was a truly uplifting moment; her presence virtually broke down the confining walls. The nomad in her was becoming tired of Australia, and she had come to America to see me and "to look around." She came to see me regularly during that month-long trip. We talked about our nights in Lagos as if we were reliving a feast of glories. We also talked about her fascination with a new religious sect that was principally a chanting fraternity. And finally we admitted the truth to ourselves. We desired and needed each other. I cannot tell exactly the point at which our simple affection took on an amorous undertone. Was it the bonding between two shipwrecked survivors or two souls feasting on the memory of a glamorized past?

She returned to Australia to tidy up her affairs. She was waiting when I came out of prison. We were married. She had secured a transfer to New York, so she kept us going – and led me to a religion of sound in our new-age church. It took me some time to get a job, this time as a desk clerk in a courier company. I never forgot Eve and I sometimes worried that I had not done better than take over other people's women, but I always cherished my union with Faith, my fate. Both of us made sense of America in a splendid way. She filled me with the joy of living, and the years we spent together were among the best years of my life. That was why we named you Viva. She had wanted Tamuno's name. I had wanted Eve's. Viva was our compromise.

After she died, of complications associated with fibroids, I felt I needed a break from living in America. So, I visited Nigeria. But our life follows us everywhere we go, because we carry it in us. The Lagos I came back to could as well have been in a different country. Tamuno's Heaven had become a monstrous department store; Nightingale had become an embassy; Sundown!, a restaurant; 24, a brothel. Only The Red Hat had remained a club, although the name had changed to Lingo! The most amazing of the transformations was Music Temple. It had become a church – the Cathedral of St Toshiba. As I learned, there had once lived a laundry woman called Toshiba who had recently been canonized, and the church had been named after her – with its altar almost at the precise spot where the Toshiba I used to know crooned her love songs to me. How everything changes.

I could find no trace of Eve. She had left the art gallery the same year I fled to America, and no one knew where she was. I traveled to Kaduna to look for Mairo. I finally found someone who told me she had moved with her husband and son to Sokoto. Another person insisted the movement had been to Yaounde in Cameroon. Everything I had been or done – all the hurrah and thunder of a whole decade and more – suddenly seemed of no consequence in the motion of time. Except perhaps the manual I had dispatched to my maternal uncle. Although I made no effort to contact him, I learned that he had made that manual compulsory reading for all postal workers, and it had become known as "Ebenebe's bible."

Tired of seeking and not finding, I suddenly came to a decision – or maybe I finally recognized it. I made the journey to Kaiama Creek to conduct a symbolic burial for my father. I alone perhaps will ever understand the urgency of that longing then and how very hard it was to translate. But I did it. In the embrace of nightfall, I put an owl in a coffin, said a prayer for the dead, and I heaved my sacrifice into the creek. I reclaimed my name after that, and I accepted my father's genius. Still, I have not entirely risen above almost spitting on his memory.

———

Akademie Schloss Solitude
Stuttgart, Germany
February 21-May 19, 2001